THE GAME

ALEX ROSE

BLOODHOUND
BOOKS

First published in 2026 by Bloodhound Books.

www.bloodhoundbooks.com

Print ISBN: 9781917705677

CHAPTER 1

1

'I need you to kill my wife.'

Sean hadn't even sat down. The café was empty, so the man already at a table spoke the words aloud across the room. The only other person present was the café's owner, and he was dependable for silence.

Sean grabbed a chair and sat facing Neil. 'One more time? I think I just heard something funny.'

'You're going with Alan,' Neil said. 'He should–'

'Why Alan? I can do this myself.'

Neil ignored him. 'Alan should be waiting round the back soon. Holly's at home right now.'

In a cartoon, Sean's jaw would have hit the table. 'You want it done there? You want Holly killed at home? And why?'

'Just take Alan and go, and don't ask questions.'

'That's a line for your men, not your blood.'

The brothers couldn't be more different. Neil was thirty-two, four years the elder, but he looked much older. He had a thick, muscled frame, a stress-lined face and thinning brown hair. Sean was taller, slimmer, baby-faced and wore his hair in an undercut with a small ponytail. Neil liked trousers and shirts, while Sean preferred jeans and T-shirts. At school Sean had been known as the playful one, while Neil was noted for a severe demeanour. These traits hadn't abandoned them come adulthood.

'I'll explain later,' Neil said. 'For now, this is your boss talking, not your brother. Go do as I order. And call your Pests. I want them there at exactly 10.30. So you don't have much time. Call me when the job is done.'

'The *job*? Your own wife's a *job*?'

Neil ignored him, got up, and left the café. Stunned, Sean just sat there. As Neil passed the large glass window, he rapped on it with his knuckles and jerked a thumb, indicating that his subordinate needed to get a move on.

Sean phoned one of his 'Pests', as Neil liked to call them, while he walked to the rear car park of the café. That man's shock was as deep as Sean's, but he was also up for the action.

Alan's Ford turned into the car park just as Sean ended the call. The vehicle screeched to a halt and Alan barked out the lowered driver's window. 'This is fucked up. What's going on?'

Sean got in the passenger side and the car tore away. In his fifties, Alan had been in the crime trade his whole life and had the faded tattoos to show it. 'What do you know?' he asked as he turned the car into the main road. 'I only got told the boss wants his missus whacked.'

'Then we both know the same. Neil didn't tell you why?'

'I've heard fuck-all. Hoped you would have more, being his damn brother and all. This is fucked up. Are we actually doing this? It's not some kind of test, is it?'

Sean looked at him. 'Test of what?'

'I don't know. Loyalty. Or maybe it's an excuse to whack me. You know, cos I would have killed his wife. Maybe there's guys with guns waiting for us.'

'I doubt it. I have no clue why, but it would seem this is real.'

'At his house, though. This is fucked up.'

'Yes it is. But that's the game we signed up for.'

2

Alan parked his Ford in a multi-storey car park two miles away, where he and Sean transferred into a cloned car. This was a stolen vehicle with a fake registration plate that matched a legitimate car of the same make, model, colour – to thwart automatic number plate recognition cameras. Alan ran an auto theft crew, so clones, ringers and standard nicked rides were obtainable at a moment's notice. This new one would be on fire within half an hour.

Untraceable car obtained, it was time to go do this madness.

The Chubby Grub was an old public house in Burngreave. With a cemetery to the right and behind, a closed school on its left flank and a country park entrance across the road, the pub sat pretty much alone on the street. Aside from a few pedestrians aiming for the country park or the cemetery, the area was desolate this morning. This urban remoteness was half the reason Neil had bought the pub two years ago.

For a high-level criminal like Neil, a legitimate business to filter dirty money through was a necessity. However, he managed this via numerous other endeavours. His reason for running a pub was social. He loved it, and he didn't taint it with dodgy money. If it brought in ten times the income, he would have dumped his role as head of an organised crime group in favour of being a landlord. Or so he claimed.

Nobody paid attention to the cloned Vauxhall as Alan drove it past the front beer garden, alongside the pub, and into the rear car park.

'Are we really doing this?' he said as he shut off the engine. He had his phone in his hand and stared at it, as if willing his boss to ring and cancel the hit. He'd been moaning throughout the whole journey.

Sean checked his smartwatch. 'My men will be here in sixteen minutes. So let's just get in there and do it. What did you bring?'

Alan cursed and hauled two balaclavas from the glove box. Each man dragged one on. 'Tell me this is a nightmare,' he said.

'It will be if we mess it up. Weapons?'

The glove box now produced those goodies. Sean saw a Taser, a small pistol, a knuckle-duster and a five-inch hunting knife. Alan grabbed the pistol for himself and slapped the Taser into Sean's chest. Sean put the weapon in his pocket and grabbed the hunting knife, and away they went.

High fences and trees created a border between the school and cemetery grounds on all three sides, so they ran unseen towards the pub. The cellar fire door was solid iron, no handle on the outside, but Neil had installed a feature that would allow his most-trusted people to get to him in emergencies. Sean pressed the door hard against its frame for five seconds, which resulted in a clicking noise. When Sean released his pressure, the door pushed itself open an inch.

'How did you do that?' Alan said.

'Forget you saw it. Now listen up. Cameras. Lots. Inside and out. We have to move fast.'

'What if she sees us coming?'

'As long as we go quick, she'll have no time to do anything.'

Alan seemed to suddenly lose his inhibitions. He almost barged Sean aside to enter first. Sean followed him through the dim refrigerated cellar, in whose far wall was the door to the washroom. Despite his insistence on urgency, Sean paused to open the door a crack, just in case Holly was cleaning glasses in the washroom.

She wasn't.

The washroom had a curtained doorway into the area behind the bar and a door to the kitchen. Sean peeked through both in case Holly was preparing food or cleaning the lounge or bar.

She wasn't.

The large lounge was split into three sections by floor styles. A carpeted quarter designated the seating area, with sofas arranged before a large wall-mounted TV and stools encircling poseur tables. Tiles marked the restaurant quarter, which had booths and round tables with floral cloths, and a stone arched doorway into the kitchen.

The remaining half of the lounge was wood-floored and given to gaming. Here you could play darts, mini-skittles, or dump cash in a bank of fruit machines. It also boasted Neil's pride and joy: an eight-foot pool table with red woollen cloth. The bar ran the length of this section.

The two men ran along the bar aisle, towards a door in the back wall at the far end. It led to the ambient goods stockroom. Alan stopped by the optics and shoved a glass under an expensive whisky brand.

'Don't be a dick,' Sean said, pulling him away. Alan had only got a fifth of a shot in his glass, but he threw it down his throat. For the last time, Sean paused to open a door slowly and see what was beyond. Maybe Holly was doing a stock count.

She wasn't.

In the back of this room was a plain iron door. This was the entrance to the sole set of stairs that led to the upper floors. To Neil's private residence. There was nowhere else Holly could be. She was up there, at home, living her life as normal and unaware of the lethal threat bearing down on her.

Sean pressed on the door, and five seconds later the lock disengaged. Sean opened it wide. They faced carpeted stairs and could hear rock music playing from above. In case they needed more proof Holly was present, she was singing along.

But there, at the eleventh hour, both men froze. Alan's newfound resolve had disintegrated. 'Last chance,' he said, his voice quivering. 'We could say we didn't find her. We can pretend the car broke down. This is fucked up.'

'That your motto? Look, it's 10.26. Our boys will be here in four minutes.'

'Phone Neil and see if he's changed his mind.'

'Don't you think he would have called if he had?'

Alan cursed. Sean snatched the gun from him and slapped the Taser into his chest. 'I'll do it because you're shaking like a cold turkey meth head and might blow me away instead.'

Alan loved this. 'You're right. If Neil regrets this shit come tomorrow, he'll be pissed at the guy who killed her. Best that that's you. He's not going to chop his brother's head off, is he?'

'I'm not so sure.'

3

Neil Webb cut short his third set of bench presses and checked his pulse. These days his heart palpitations didn't worry him so much, for he'd suffered with them his whole life and long ago had realised they weren't indicative of a heart attack. The habit of keeping track of his ticker's movements was impossible to shake, though.

His doctor thought the problem was reflux, which was a diagnosis he'd come to accept years ago. Something to do with the vagus nerve. He didn't care to learn any more than that in case it somehow sent him down a whole new path of assumption and paranoia. Reflux he didn't care about and hadn't changed his diet beyond avoiding acidic drinks.

However, exercise usually helped calm the palpitations, so it was a shock to find that flopping fish feeling back in his chest now. He rushed into the bathroom because there was too much noise in the gym, and he didn't want anyone to watch what he was about to do. He checked his pulse again and felt the familiar pauses. He used a stethoscope from his bag to listen to his heart. The ectopic beats were back, and with a vengeance.

He knew why, of course. There was a physiological reason

for his body acting the way it did; but psychology played its part. And this was the mother of all stressful days, right?

His wife was about to get whacked. Sean's men would get rid of the body and sterilise the murder scene, but Holly knew people and they'd soon realise she was missing. Given his lifestyle, the cops would immediately suspect foul play and he'd be the first guy on their radar. They'd find nothing on him, but he was guaranteed a spot in an interview room and a mouthy grilling. That would stress out any–

A knock on the door interrupted him. A voice called through: 'Mr Webb?'

It was Noah, his fixer, or right-hand man – or secretary, according to some of Neil's employees. Middle-aged and well-built, Noah was dedicated to his work, in part because he had no partner or children or family or dreams for the future. He was always close to Neil's side or at the end of a phone. He was also a buffer between Neil and those directly below him in the organised crime group.

Noah must have been worried about why Neil had abruptly fled the gym, that was all. When Neil opened the changing room door, it was to tell Noah he was fine, and that perhaps Noah could give Dr Hassin a quick call to–

But no. When the door opened, Noah stood there with Neil's burner phone for the day and a worried look on his face. 'It's Sean, and there's a problem.'

That dickhead. Sean had either backed out of the kill or fucked it up in some way. He'd half-expected this. He snatched the phone, kicked shut the door in Noah's face, and barked down the line. 'Have you messed this up? Is she dead? What's the damn problem?'

'Holly's not dead,' Sean said. 'But Alan is.'

The palpitations got worse. 'What?'

'She slit his damn throat. His blood is all over your kitchen.'

'Where is she?'

'Ran. Out the door and gone. I couldn't stop her.'

'Alan had a fucking gun!'

'I had it. Dropped it when she threw a damn knife at my face. She was gone before I could stop her.'

Holy fucking shit. Neil clutched the phone to his chest and took deep breaths. His heart got its rhythm back. His cognitive behavioural therapist had told him he needed to find a silver lining in all bad news, and this was a prime chance. A body in his house was annoying, but not a problem. Sean's Pests were coming for a corpse anyway. Maybe it was a good thing that Holly wasn't splattered yet. Maybe he'd angrily rushed into killing her. He knew he could be impetuous. At least this would give him time to think.

But his people had still fucked up, and no amount of therapy would solve that problem. He got back on the phone. 'Stay there, Sean. Your cleaners will be there in five minutes. I'll be down in ten. And you better hope I've calmed down by then.'

4

The 'cleaners' Neil spoke of earlier weren't actually in that trade. The van that was laid up in the rear car park when he arrived at his pub bore the name of a pest control service, Pest B Gone. It fit well given what the employees did. His wife's car wasn't here.

One of them, in coveralls with the firm's name on the chest, was on the front porch, smoking. Neil walked towards him, trailed by Noah at a distance that allowed privacy but put him within earshot should he be needed.

'Don't let smoke get into my damn pub,' Neil said to the Pest. 'Body removed yet?'

The Pest extinguished his roll-up with his fingers. 'No, we haven't been here long. Ongoing.'

Neil headed in and found Sean sitting on a stool at a poseur table, holding a bloody beer towel to the side of his head. His green T-shirt was bloodied. He was the only one here. The rest of the Pest guys were probably up in his private residence.

Sean sat up straight upon seeing Neil approach him. He nodded at Noah and then opened his mouth to speak, but Neil held up a finger: *wait.* Then Neil headed upstairs.

Four men in coveralls and gloves and masks were moving about in his large kitchen, trying to get plastic sheeting underneath Alan's body. Scattered around were the power tools they'd use to chop up his body. There was blood splatter on the cupboards and the fridge and in the sink, and all over a white cake Holly must have been baking at the time. Alan's neck had a massive gash in it.

A fifth Pest was making tea. He'd set out five cups and was pouring milk. Neil took the carton out of his hands. 'You damn morons. Get to work and hurry the hell up and get out of here. Make sure this place looks like a showroom model when I get back.'

Orders given, Neil headed downstairs and took a seat at Sean's table. Noah was at the same table, but the two men seemed to be ignoring each other. The fixer moved away to give the brothers some space.

Neil looked at his brother but said nothing, as was his way when his people needed to do some serious explaining. Why ask for what they were damn well obliged to give?

'Holly just about sliced his head off,' Sean said.

Neil snatched away the beer towel Sean had been using to stem the flow of blood from his head. Against the shaved skin, the inch-long laceration was bright and nasty. Sean said, 'She lobbed the knife at me afterwards–'

'After what?' Neil cut in.

'After she killed Alan. I–'

'You had a gun.'

Sean snatched back his towel. 'You want to hear this or not? I had the gun. But I didn't think we'd need it till we got her out of the house, so I wasn't aiming it. She knew something was wrong because Alan went in first, screaming that she was dead. She was making food and she had the knife. Turned, swiped at him, and lobbed the thing at me. I thought it had gone in my skull because it hurt so much. I dropped the gun. Couldn't see because of all the blood. She legged it and the gun was gone, so I wasn't about to haul ass after her. There. That's what happened.'

'Why didn't she kill you?'

'My gorgeous face, probably.'

Neil sighed. 'This is a mess I'll need to fix. At least you're alive. Alan I can live without, although I'll need a new guy for getting us cars. My wife see your face? Or Alan's?'

'No. Balaclavas. But if you're thinking she won't know who came for her... well, she would have called you if she thought it was one of your enemies.'

Neil had thought the same thing. If Holly ran out of eggs or the microwave broke, she was always on his case. But he'd had no panicked call from her about murderous intruders. 'I know. So she probably suspects me, which I'd say is more proof against her. Why worry about me if she's done nothing wrong?'

The guy who'd been smoking outside must have hung around to finish his cigarette, because he only now returned to the lounge. Neil ordered him to bring a pint of lager and a tonic water. The two men sat in silence until the drinks arrived. The lager was for Sean and he necked half of it in one go.

'So, you want to tell me what's going on?' Sean said when he put down his glass.

Neil sipped his tonic before answering. 'Holly's been letting another man stick her.'

'Cheating? No way. How do you know that? One of your guys?'

'You mean did one of my guys see her? Yeah. Saw her with a bloke.'

'Who is he?'

'Just some guy. He might be next for whacking. I don't know yet.'

'So what happens now?'

Neil sipped again, thinking. 'Well, we find her, don't we? And quick. I already sent people to check on her friends the moment I heard you'd messed this up. On the quiet, so they don't get spooked. It's a long shot, though. I know who all her friends are and I don't think she'd risk it. Or risk endangering them.'

Sean prodded at his wound with dry parts of the towel, to see if the bleeding had stopped. It had. 'She's got no family here. Any chance she'd go back to the USA?'

Neil's wife had moved from Wisconsin, USA, to England ten years ago. It was on a study visa. Holly had grown up watching British TV and wanted some of that life, and just like that she'd dropped everything and fled her home when she left school at eighteen.

She'd attended university for four years and acquired a two-year work visa following that. By the time that visa expired, she'd been dating Neil for three years. She had had to return home, but he had employed solicitors to help her get a visa so she could marry him. She subsequently got a settlement visa and England was now her home.

'She'd never manage it,' Neil replied. 'I doubt she took her passport. Go tell your people to look around up there, as if they haven't had a good nosey already. It should be in a file box on the shelf above the fireplace. And go in the drawer under the microwave for superglue. And get a new top.'

Sean was back in three minutes, carrying the requested items. Neil pocketed the passport. 'Good. So she's stuck here. I'll find her.'

'No,' Sean said, holding up the bottle of superglue. 'You gave me the job.'

'Which you messed up.'

'It's not over yet. Don't cut me out because of one setback. I want to find her. She nearly killed me. I'm pissed. Look at my bloody head.'

Neil snatched the superglue. Sean tilted his head to one side so Neil could apply the liquid to the wound. No instructions were needed because it was the third time they'd been in this very same position.

When the job was done, Neil yanked the elastic band from Sean's hair, allowing the long locks on top to fall like a curtain over the closed wound. 'Okay. I want you and your people to go check our safe houses, in case she's holed up in one.'

As Sean stripped off his bloodied T-shirt, he said, 'That likely? Does Holly even know about those places?'

'I never mentioned any to her, but wives pick things up. If she knows there's one or two sitting empty, that might be somewhere she thinks I'll never look. Go and help your people up there and then get on it.'

Neil believed the conversation was over and got up. He went to his pride and joy, the pool table, and slotted in a £1 coin to release the balls. That was when he noticed that his brother had put on the new T-shirt but hadn't left the scene. He was standing nearby, watching.

'What now?' Neil said.

'If I find her, what do I do? It might be a bit rash to kill her without getting her side of the story. Maybe you have it wrong. Maybe you'll have second thoughts when it's too late. Maybe it's best to just capture her, especially if you want the guy she was banging.'

Neil gave this some consideration as he arranged the pool balls in a triangle. He had acted rashly by giving the kill order and didn't feel the same rage now. Sean was right. She could be killed anytime if they had her imprisoned. 'Okay, we grab her. We bring her back here. But don't fuck up this time, Sean, or you'll be meeting Alan again.'

5

Alan's body was chopped into six pieces. Off came the arms, legs and head. Neil permitted the use of three empty beer kegs, whose tops were cut off to accept their grisly contents. The torso got one to itself, the legs shared one, and the head went with the arms. Hopefully no witnesses would wonder why pest control guys were removing pub products.

Once in the van, Sean got in the front with the driver and the other five guys sat in the back with the kegs. They drove east, to Cowbell Farm, situated between Whiston and a portion of the M1 motorway just past junction 33. It was owned and operated by a man who went by no name except 'the farmer'. He was not part of the crew as such and refused to engage in any criminal activity outside of disposing of fleshy evidence. Maybe he didn't see much of a difference between people and livestock. Local residents had him pegged as odd, and that was without being aware of his history of chronic indecent exposure.

He and Neil had met because the farmer had a large box trailer for an articulated lorry on his land, which he rented out for advertising. It sat on raised grassland at the edge of his property, thirty metres from the motorway and visible from it.

Neil had paid for a week's use to promote the grand opening of The Chubby Grub.

Somehow, while finessing the deal, the two men had turned their talk to illegal activity, and the farmer had agreed a price for his gruesome services. He had a Volkan 1600 cattle incinerator, which had dispatched nine corpses over the last two years. He got a fee of £1,000 for each one and any dead man's clothing he desired. That included an astronaut's suit worn by the Volkan's first victim, although the interior lining had needed a serious clean. Tonight the farmer also got to keep the kegs, pronouncing them perfect plant pots.

Sean was the Pest B Gone boss, but to keep his men sweet he always mucked in. He carried all three kegs to the Volkan and tossed in every body part except the left arm. The farmer took that from the keg so he could remove and pocket Alan's watch.

Job done.

As the Pest B Gone van was leaving the farm, Neil's fixer, Noah, called Sean with an update. It was blunt and rapid, as if the guy wanted to be off the phone as soon as possible.

'There's no evidence that Holly is holed up with friends. We've also checked her local haunts and come up short. She must have gone to ground. You're a go for checking the safe houses. You know where our two empty properties are?'

'Hackenthorpe and Ranmoor. My team will check both.'

'Be quick,' Noah said, and hung up without another word.

Sean told his men the plan. He wanted to check both properties at the same time, so the van headed to the home of one of the men to collect a car. The owner and two others were given the Hackenthorpe safe house, while he and a man called Josh would take the place in Ranmoor.

It was an end of terrace, with the middle three properties converted to shops, and had street parking. The part commercial area was quite busy. Josh pulled up the van at the kerb and both men approached the front door.

'Get the key from under the brick,' Sean said.

While Josh lifted a house brick from a border by the fence, Sean peered through the front window. Josh approached the door with the key, but Sean snatched it from him.

They were inside fifteen seconds later. Downstairs were the kitchen and living room, both furnished and clean, but empty. Josh headed for the stairs.

'I'll go up,' Sean said. 'Go check the kettle to see if it's warm. If she's staying here, she might have popped out.'

'Let me ask something,' Josh said. 'Is Neil really going to kill his missus?'

'What do you know? I heard she's got another man.'

'That's what I heard. Seems extreme. I don't mean any offence to your brother.'

'Just don't say that to his face.'

The two men parted. Sean headed upstairs and into the main bedroom, which again was furnished and pristine. Some of the safe houses were shitholes in vile areas, occupied by unsavoury characters. This one was reserved for high-level and well-paying fugitives. It had last been used by a plastic surgeon. He'd put a woman under for labiaplasty, but had decided to take advantage of her in the worst way. If he hadn't given a running commentary while she was out, her phone's secret audio recording – out of fear of the unknown – wouldn't have picked up the entire story.

Sean was just closing the main bedroom's wardrobe when his partner entered the room. 'Nothing doing down there,' Josh said. 'Kettle's cold.'

'This is a bust. Let's get out of here. It was silly to think she'd come to a safe house.'

Sean called his team as they left. Those chaps had already

been to the Hackenthorpe safe house and obtained the same negative result. Josh got in the van but Sean remained on the pavement to make a call to Neil.

His brother answered with, 'You're alive, so I guess that means she's not there.'

'Very funny. And I didn't expect her to be. You want my opinion? I think she's fled to a city where you don't have eyes and ears. Best to give it a day or so and see what's what.'

'At least we eliminated the possibility. Send your team home, but keep them on standby in case I hear something. I want you to come to The Chubby tonight.'

Neil hung up. Sean told Josh that his brother had ordered him to wait at the safe house. Josh drove off in the van and Sean entered the house.

He rushed up the stairs and into the main bedroom, where he threw open the wardrobe doors.

'Get out,' he said.

6

Almost three hours earlier, back at The Chubby, Sean had allowed Alan to take the lead. He followed his partner up the stairs, to Neil's private residence. At the top was a hallway that ran almost the full length of the rear of the property, with six windows on the exterior wall and framed pictures hanging between them.

At one end was the main living room, and at the other was Neil's games room. All the other rooms were on the side of the hallway with the stairs. The kitchen was the last before the living room. This was where the music and Holly's singing came from.

Now warmed to this lethal task, Alan rushed down the hallway, Taser aimed ahead like a gun. He paused at the kitchen doorway to peek around the frame, threw a thumbs-up back at Sean, then darted inside. Sean was right behind him. Holly was at a counter, her back to the men, still singing while she stirred something in a pan. The music made their approach inaudible.

Alan grabbed her hair and yanked her away from the counter. She moaned in shock and dropped a ladle covered in white chocolate.

The next noise was from Alan: a yelp as Sean slammed the butt of hunting knife hard into the back of his head. Alan fell to his knees, dazed. He might have face-planted the floor if Sean hadn't grabbed his hair, yanked back his head, and opened his throat wide with the sharp blade.

Holly staggered back, moaning, as Alan's blood coated her legs and the floor. The body fell face-down, but she wasn't looking at it: her eyes were fixed on Sean. He dropped the knife and grabbed her blood-speckled face in both hands. 'Listen to me. Are you okay?'

He had to ask again, louder, to bypass her shock. She managed a nod, but it might have been just an exaggeration of the terror vibrations running through her body.

'What's... what's...'

He dragged her by the arm, out of the kitchen and into the living room. He tried to get her to the sofa, but she fell to her knees halfway. He squatted in front of her and hugged her hard.

'You need to get out of here,' he said into her ear. 'Neil sent us. I'm sorry. We were supposed to kill you.'

This news was an atomic blast on top of a dynamite explosion. Her shivering and moaning increased. He held her hard and waited for it to subside. Thirty seconds later, when he felt her rock-hard muscles soften, he pulled away so he could look at her eyes. They were clearer.

'Why?' she said.

'No time for that,' Sean said. 'People are coming in three minutes, and they won't be late. Get your keys, get your car, and go. Go left from here and down Scott Road. Take the first left and drive through the cemetery. Stop when you get there and remove your number plates, okay? Head straight until you reach the church and take the exit on its left side. After that, load up your satnav.'

He got her to repeat these orders as he led her to the stairs.

She had them memorised. He then gave her a house number and a postcode.

'Park a few streets away from the house,' he said. 'Don't show your face at the windows, and don't do anything in the house that might look like someone's there. Don't touch the fridge, the kettle, the TV, anything. Stay in the main bedroom and hide in the wardrobe if anyone comes. I'll come to you later, after I've sorted this shit out. Go now, please. There's a key under a brick by the fence to the left of the door. Leave the door unlocked and put the key back.'

Holly was much calmer now, yet still fully accepting of the danger she was in. Of her own volition, she repeated all of his instructions to the letter, then kissed his cheek, said thank you, and got moving, fast.

When she was gone, Sean grabbed a steak knife from a drawer and dug the point of the blade into the shaved side of his head. This hurt, but he needed a wound to give his story some clout. He'd considered the forehead, which typically bled more, but he didn't want a visible scar. This way he could wear his hair down and hide the wound.

Later, when he got the order to check safe houses, it had been fully expected. He chose the Ranmoor property, of course, because that was where he'd sent Holly. When he snatched the key from Josh, it was because he had to pretend to unlock an already unlocked door. Thankfully, she had hidden in the wardrobe after seeing the van arrive. Sean had held open those wardrobe doors until Josh walked in the room. Closing them with his partner watching had given the impression that Sean had just finished a search.

Now, upon his return to the wardrobe alone, Holly leaped out and threw her arms around him, planting a hard kiss on his lips.

7

'Why is this happening?' she asked.

Sean pulled out of her hug. He noticed the bedroom curtains were open, so he pulled them. 'I don't know.'

'Neil didn't say? I mean, he must have. He would have told you, surely. This makes no sense.'

'Well... there's a story. About another man. Have you been banging some other guy?'

She didn't like that accusation. They faced each other across the length of the room. 'No. How can you ask me that? And that's what Neil thinks? Why?'

'You were seen, Holly. Someone saw you with another man.'

She shook her head. 'What man? Where? Doing what? Having sex? I don't bloody think so. Did I get seen just talking to someone?'

'So there's no one?' He regretted the question immediately.

She sneered at him. 'Apart from you? No one I remember. I mean, how can I know which man if I've been seen just talking to someone out and about for five seconds? I can tell you I haven't slept with anyone else. I didn't meet someone at a hotel. I wasn't alone in a car with a man. This is stupid.'

Sean shrugged. 'It's what Neil believes. I don't know why.'

She sat on the bed. 'And that's why I have to die, is it? "Shitty freak luck", as you said. Because I was in the same room as some other man?'

He remembered a conversation they'd had when their affair started. She had said, *If we're careful, we'll never be found out,* and he'd replied with, *It's not always that easy. Sometimes shitty freak luck picks you for a bad day.*

He sat by her. She reached out to sweep aside the hair hanging over his head wound, and winced at it. 'I got us some breathing space,' he said. 'I convinced Neil not to do something rash. The plan now is to capture you so he can get your side of the story.'

She gave a nervous laugh. 'Oh, lucky me. I'm sure he'll believe me, just like you do.'

He should have said he did believe her. That was right and just and probably the only thing that would comfort her. But he didn't say that because he wasn't sure how he felt. It was hard to fully trust her when she was cheating on her husband with him.

She got his vibe. 'Oh, thanks. So you're getting all high and mighty now? Remember you're the one sleeping with your brother's wife.'

She stood and walked to the window. He had to warn her not to open the curtains. She faced them, as if able to see right through and to the street beyond. 'Why did you kill that other man? I've seen you with him before. He was your friend.'

Was she trying to bite at him, or sincerely confused? 'Don't assume I'm friends with Neil's people just because I go out and about with them. That guy was called Alan–'

'I don't want to know his name.'

'–and he was a lunatic. He's Neil's man for getting cars, but he also liked the vile jobs. He's raped women in the past, just because he was told to.'

'Please stop.'

'No. If Neil needed someone to kill his wife, or even his own brother, Alan was the man. A piece of shit. I didn't know if he'd kill you then me. This was a one-man job, so it didn't make sense to send both of us. I couldn't take the risk.'

She turned to him, mood no longer dark. 'You thought Neil might know about us? That you were the other man? That this might have been a set-up?'

Oh yes. For the entirety of the year they'd been having an affair, he'd worried that Neil would learn the truth. Every time his brother wanted a meet, Sean feared he'd be attacked, captured, tortured, murdered. It was easier now than it had been in the beginning. Holly and he had honed their secrecy skills to a fine art. Their meeting places were always in other cities, to which they'd travel alone and at staggered times.

Still, he always feared the wrong person might see them together. He still didn't know if, as she'd suggested, he was the man Neil had mentioned. He wasn't yet sure he wasn't in the crosshairs. In this game, success was all about trickery and subterfuge, and Neil was a master at both.

His answer to her question was, 'Yes, I worried that this was a set-up. I still don't know it wasn't. Alan's dead, so I don't know what he knew. Maybe nothing. Maybe he wasn't there to kill me as well. But that doesn't mean shit, Holly. He sent me after you without my knowing a damn thing about why. I could talk to fifty people and not one of them would know a thing. But it doesn't mean Neil's not planning a very unpleasant surprise for me.'

She shook her head. 'You're his brother.'

'That's the way of it in this lifestyle, Holly. This is the biggest betrayal. It won't matter to Neil that we share blood. Just like it didn't matter that you're his wife. I'm supposed to meet him at the pub tonight. He might be planning a visit for me to

Room X. In this game, you don't learn you're destined for the meat grinder until it's eating your legs.'

Holly shivered. 'Surely you don't think he's bringing you to the pub so he can kill you in that godawful room? And stop calling it a game, please. This is real.'

'I don't know what he'll do. He had the chance earlier when we were disposing of Alan's body. But that was my team there, so maybe he didn't trust them to side with him... I don't know. I don't have an answer.'

She wiped tears from her eyes. 'It sounds to me like you're in the clear. But I'm not. Neil thinks I've cheated on him and for that I have to be murdered. It's so messed up. Neil won't stop until he kills me. What do we do? How do we fix this problem?'

He didn't have an answer for that, either.

8

At least a dozen people were out hunting Holly, and their updates would go to Noah, who would call Neil if there was something he needed to know. So there was nothing else for Neil to do right now to find his wife. With some free time, he headed upstairs to his home.

He was angry, but wasn't sure why. Was it what he'd found out about his wife's betrayal? Or was it because she'd escaped him? One was a natural emotion, human, standard fare. The other was a mighty blast to the ego.

The honest part of him figured it was the latter: pride. It drove him to achieve greatness in life, to outdo the healthy, happy-go-lucky fools who surrounded him. He wanted to be superhuman, immortal, safe in a forcefield. Those, of course, were impossible, but he wanted to get as close as he could.

He hadn't been blessed with a desire to do good in the world, or a family that promoted stability and opened doors to accomplishment, but there were other ways to earn success and happiness. He was there now, wasn't he? Yet his chronic reflux and heart palpitations were an hourly reminder that he wasn't perfect. Losing control, getting bested by someone else or even his own body, hurt like nothing else.

What his wife had done pierced his very core. He wasn't sure why it stung so badly, but he wanted to hurt her in return. That she'd given him the slip had increased the pain a hundredfold. He wanted to do the equivalent of punching a door in frustration, but to a man like him, leader of an empire, that meant relaying pain and terror to someone else. He wanted to send out his men to hunt down and punish people who'd pissed him off recently.

A bad idea, especially now while he was running on emotion and his brain was clouded. Such revenge missions needed careful planning. If he acted recklessly, it might backfire on him.

Neil headed into his attic man cave with another idea. The slanted roof window gave him a good view of the cemetery behind his pub. Many times previously, he'd stood at this window and watched the police run around fruitlessly. Every time some place got robbed or someone went missing, he blipped on cop radar and they'd spread out around the cemetery with shovels and drones, metal detectors and dogs.

It was fun to stand here and watch them trying to work out if this or that spot was where the guns or the money or the bodies were buried. Hide goodies on his own doorstep? He was happy to let law enforcement believe he was so foolish.

But it was more enjoyable to watch people who also suffered. Like now. A couple walked hand in hand along a footpath running between rows of graves. He watched them turn into the grass, pass a few headstones, and stop at a white one. The grave wasn't old and nor was the couple. He figured they might have lost a child, maybe recently, which pleased him. People like that should be pitied, right?

They could get enough of that from friends and family. Neil

pulled the trigger of his air rifle. It was a modified Umarex Gauntlet, shipped in from America, good for precision up to 300 yards. The couple was about half that away but big and clear in the weapon's scope. He aimed for the male's elbow and got him sweetly. The man grabbed his injured arm and began dancing around in pain. Neil laughed. He swung the barrel a fraction to the right and centred the crosshairs on the woman's plump arse.

Then paused. No. As is, the couple might remain puzzled as to what had hit the male – maybe a bee sting? Another shot and they'd probably cotton on that someone was firing at them, and there was only one high place in view. Talking to the cops now, with so much going on, would ruin his new good mood. He put the gun away. He was content.

For now.

CHAPTER 2

1

People say the apple never falls far from the tree. Thus, the young Webb brothers were almost destined to enter a life of crime because of their father. Donald Webb was a low-level gangster who ran three dope dealers in the Woodston area of Peterborough and offered protection for a local mini-mart, although he'd never been arrested for a crime. The protection scam was a popular one: send in some goons to turn a store upside down, then waltz in the next day and offer to protect the place for a weekly fee.

His kids, Neil and Sean, didn't fathom that Dad was a small fish in a big pond. They knew he controlled people and had a scary reputation, and to them that made him king of the world. Kids want to impress the old man, and what better way than to succeed with a criminal enterprise of their own?

Their mother, Sally, provided a barrier between the boys and their father's planned future for them. Every time Dad expounded upon the benefits of taking what you wanted and bedamned the laws, Mum was there to muddy the waters with praise for a life lived in harmony with morals and your peers.

The battle between parents kept the boys balanced on a fence. Periodically they'd fall one way or the other.

Their first foray into the shady side of the fence involved hounding local paperboys. The brothers would intercept these kids as they made their rounds and beat them and steal their stock – unless half their wages were handed over. It worked for a while and they collected funds from four kids for three straight weeks, before an attempt to recruit a fifth sent that boy wailing to his parents.

The police soon came knocking at the Webb front door. Unfortunately, they chose a time when the mother was out. Dad put on his acting hat to appear angry and promised that he'd rain hell on his boys. Neither the police nor local residents believed it. Donald Webb had crime in his blood despite no convictions and all and sundry expected him to drag his boys into the depths with him. They doubted the mother could prevent it. Apples and trees.

Dad did berate them for the paperboy scam, but only for getting caught. As for the crime itself? He had a motto that he shared with them: 'Adverse Possession'. He told his boys that if you adversely occupied and maintained another person's land for at least twelve years, you could apply to make it legally yours. He didn't know that The Land Registration Act 2002 had changed the rule; and it hadn't applied to stolen goods anyway.

Dad had his own parameters, though. If you nicked something, he said, it instantly became yours. Neil, then ten, tested this by stealing a comic from his younger brother. When Sean complained, he got nowhere. 'The comic is Neil's now,' Dad said. That comic bounced between the siblings umpteen times on that day.

Mum did her best to keep the boys out of deep water, but she was fighting a rising tide. Neil's vicious soul and illicit intent slotted together like jigsaw pieces. He liked to use his fists and to intimidate, which Dad promised would carry him far. Sean wasn't quite as murky a personality, but he revered his father and his big brother and was easily swayed. He had diplomacy and cunning that his father marked as useful to a criminal future. It was hard to doubt Dad when he was the one bringing all the money in and their mother couldn't find a job.

Both boys got to showcase their skills when Neil started dating a local bad boy's girl. To decide who got her, the boys arranged to throw-down in a local park. The bad boy was older, more likely to win, so Sean mediated and got the combatants to instead settle their differences on his own four-foot snooker table. It backfired when Neil lost the game, threw a punch, and the boys fought after all. He got the girl, who dumped him the next day.

When Neil was thirteen and Sean had just turned nine, their mother died after getting hit by a driver on their own street. That left their father to bring them up, and he did it the only way he knew. 'The world isn't kind,' he told them. 'It will do you no favours. There are too many smart kids out there and they'll get all the top jobs. Your mother told you that good intent and clean living will see you right, but she was wrong. You'll end up breaking your back in a factory. Unless...'

With the buffer of their mother gone, Dad held all the cards and knew exactly what he wanted to deal. Homework wasn't on the menu. He put Neil in his now four-man stable of drug dealers and tasked him with mugging other kids in dark spots. Sean was coached on how to pickpocket and trick and threaten classmates at school for cash and goodies. Often they worked together by breaking into houses and businesses and ferrying stolen gear around the city on their pushbikes.

Meanwhile, the brothers had been carefully plotting the downfall of the man who killed their mother, and they didn't need their father's blessing or guidance. The killer had been sentenced to five years, but he served three-and-a-half before being released and promptly returning to his former residence – a house just five doors down from the Webb home. Three days after the killer's return, they made their brutish move.

They broke into his house, broke his elbows, and fled. The killer didn't tell tales and it was forgotten. It wasn't much of a revenge, said their father, but he admired their loyalty to their mother.

Something changed in their father a few months later. One day he announced to his boys that he was done with the immoral lifestyle. No more crime for him. Even stranger, he also wanted his boys also on the straight and narrow. No more missing school. No more robberies, muggings, drug dealings, or theft.

Dad got a legitimate job and made the boys swear to do the same when they left school. He was quite determined and threatened to disown his boys if they ever disobeyed him. His about-face was shocking to all and often neighbourhood gossip.

Neil thought Dad had found God, although religion was a subject never broached in the house. Sean knew something else was at play, for Dad had lost his jolly demeanour. But as to what had come over their father, he couldn't diagnose it. Nonetheless, he was a new man.

Sean, at least, was happy to follow him on this changed path. He wanted to find a career in computers. Neil, not so eager to give up what had been, hoped to run a pub. For the next few years, casa Webb was a law-abiding household.

When Neil turned sixteen, he suddenly wanted a moped. For a reason he wouldn't explain, Dad bluntly said no. He then went a step further by ordering his boys never to drive. He even made them swear.

But this only stoked their intrigue, so Neil got himself

licensed and insured behind their father's back and bought a moped. With his world opened up and no more school, Neil got new friends, girlfriends, stayed out more, and slowly the time the brothers spent together decreased. Sean got on with studying computers and concentrating on his schoolfriends.

Half a year later, everything fell apart. Neil got drunk at a pub and tried to ride his moped home. He crashed it into a car and got arrested, and bang went his licence. Since Sean loved his brother, it seemed as if the world had crashed down for both of them.

Far, far worse was on the near horizon.

2

Despite being quite a common event, Neil mucking in at The Chubby Grub always intrigued Sean. Usually he'd serve behind the bar, but often he'd doorman. Sometimes troublemakers unaware of its owner's reputation wandered in, which gave the bodybuilder a chance to use his muscles.

Outwardly Neil was known as a successful businessman who liked to help the local area. It was standard fare for high-level crime barons to inject cash into their community to enhance a favourable reputation. Alongside the pub, he operated a youth centre, a handful of shops, and he donated funds for the upkeep of amenities.

This was the face most locals saw, so what about all that criminal activity stuff people talked about? Just rumours. Unless Joe and Jane Public saw it with their own eyes, it didn't happen. And his criminal empire had no name, which made it harder to report on or gossip about. Neil was simply a guy who had a lot of tough-looking friends who sometimes got into their own bubbles of trouble, that was all.

Some people knew the rumours had more flesh, of course, and The Chubby was a prime drinking spot for the police.

Sometimes uniforms would wander in because a complaint or an investigation had led them there. Mostly, though, part plainclothes officers or those off duty came to drink and hopefully pick up some juicy details about crimes unsolved or planned. Sometimes they tried to blend in, and sometimes they made no secret of who they were, as if to say *We're always watching*. Neil entertained them all as if he had nothing to worry about.

Another niche group came for Neil's help. As Sean entered the pub, which was busy as usual by seven, he saw one such man. Neil, the pool king, was playing against him. Neil saw Sean and waved. It seemed genuine, which was good news.

Sean spotted one of Neil's crew by the bar, a guy known as Bunny because he kept such animals. They fist-bumped. Sean noted that the London gin bottle on an optic was empty. 'So who's the pool guy this time?'

Bunny looked round at the guy in question. 'Some twonk who's got a teacher who's giving his kid grief. He wants the teacher off school for a bit.'

Small talk over. 'How did Neil find out his wife was banging another man? Were they seen? Did he see something on her phone? What was it?'

'Don't know,' Bunny said. 'Wouldn't say. Not surprised. Bit embarrassing, yeah? Having your wife shag some other guy?'

For sure. Sean was that other guy, but was there a third player? Holly had denied it, but then again she'd been having an affair with Sean behind Neil's back. He could hardly determine her to be loyal. 'So there's no photo of this guy? No address?'

'If the boss knows, he ain't saying. Bit extreme to kill the guy, no?'

If he found out that guy was Sean, then, yes. 'Maybe.'

Bunny finished his pint and said he needed a piss. When he was gone, Sean turned to face the lounge.

As stated to Holly, he wasn't convinced there wasn't a trap awaiting him here. He scanned the lounge for familiar faces, primarily those Neil used for spilling blood or extracting answers from prisoners. He didn't see any of the Room X usuals, which was a good sign. But not definitive. He needed more.

Although the barmaid was busy, she came straight to Sean Webb when he raised a hand. She was a pretty girl of twenty-five who'd worked here since the pub opened. Her dedication ran to working six nights a week, with only Thursdays off, and she managed seven staff. She knew Sean well and they engaged in small talk for a few seconds before he asked for London gin.

She turned to the optics. 'Oh, we're out. Hang on a sec.'

'I'll get it since you're busy,' Sean said. He slipped behind the bar and headed for the chilled cellar. In the far wall, between shelving containing bottles, was an iron door. Room X.

This door had the same secret mechanism of a long push to disengage the lock. Sean pushed it open and went down concrete stairs, to another door at the bottom. This one had a handle. The room beyond was small, had bare bricks walls and a concrete floor. The only piece of furniture was a wooden chair. Originally part of the main cellar, there was a grate in the centre of the floor for draining spilled alcohol. Now it was used for the removal of blood.

Seven people had been murdered here in Neil's torture room over the two years the pub had been in operation. The last, just a few weeks ago, had been a man running one of Neil's drug lines. He'd been loyal, a good earner and a good laugh. But he'd also recruited two thirteen-year-old boys to deal for him, and that was a big no-no. This room was the only part of the pub not covered by cameras, in case the police mounted a raid.

There were no killing tools present tonight, or the men who'd wield them. Another good sign.

Sean returned to the cellar, grabbed a bottle of London gin, and re-entered the lounge. He was far more relaxed now, almost certain that his affair with Holly remained their dirty secret. However, it only heightened the likelihood of a third man.

Maybe, if Neil whacked that guy, his anger might be sated and he'd forgive his wife, or at least cancel the hit on her. Sean wouldn't be sorry to see him go, but would he trust Holly thereafter? Was he even right to judge her like this, given that he'd knowingly stolen a married woman?

Sean didn't know what to believe or what to think. If there was a third man, he would wait for that guy to leave the picture then think about his relationship with Holly. Until then, he had to keep her safe and hidden, at least for a few days.

He took a poseur table near the pool table to watch the game. Neil looked at ease, unworried, totally unlike a guy who had murder planned for his brother. A few tables away, Noah was also watching the game. If Noah suspected that Sean was the enemy here, it was impossible to tell. The guy was a cyborg with just one expression and one directive: be at Neil's beck and call 24/7.

The challenge was eradicated sharply. Neil took one visit to clear the table, and his opponent, £100 down, skulked away. Neil came over to Sean.

'Don't you ever think about just losing a game to help out?' Sean said.

Neil gave him a look like he'd said something silly. 'No. Have you found anything out about my missus?'

'What? No. I had the afternoon off. You didn't tell me to.'

'I know. Thought maybe you would have helped your big bro out off your own back. My people still can't find her. She's not been seen with any friends and she's not hiding out at any of the places we've checked. She hasn't been to any banks. No sightings of her car, either.'

Sean knew that Neil had dodgy cops on his payroll and had

access to NDAC, the ANPR data centre. He originally wanted access to the system to keep his cloned vehicles safe. One of his men was once arrested because ANPR spotted the same number plate in Leeds (clone) and Shropshire (real deal), but only ten minutes apart. A guy in the right place could unflag that anomaly.

But the software could and had been used to trace people by their car journeys. A number of people who thought they'd given Neil the slip had been shocked to find the Pest B Gone van on their doorstep. Knowing this, Sean had instructed Holly to remove her number plates before driving to the safe house. When Sean left that house after seeing her, he took her car and hid it miles away. Thankfully, he'd come across no police cars during that trip.

Now that he knew Holly was safe for the moment, he changed tack slightly. 'Heard anything about this guy she's supposed to be banging?'

'No. I want you to go looking again tomorrow morning. Your first port of call is her doctor. She didn't take her pills when she scarpered. Maybe he's heard from her if she's tried to get more.'

'That's just a phone call.'

'That is, but CCTV ain't. I want you to go round the houses and businesses near here and see who's got cameras, and watch them to trace her route. We don't even know which way she went. And after that, me and you are going to check out Allerby House.'

Sean shook his head. He noticed a man wanting Neil's attention, but he got Noah's instead. As the fixer got between them. 'Every Thursday, Neil. My computer class. Every Thursday. You should know this by now. Every Thursday. But you quite often give me jobs on a Thursday.'

'I do know, and normally I don't care. This is different. Cancel it. Go knock the doors. Don't treat me like your brother right now. I'm your boss as well. We have to get a move on. It won't be long before her mates get worried that she's out of contact, and then the cops will get wind that she's missing. And then they'll be all over me.'

Sean jerked his eyes. 'Guy back there, on my seven o'clock. He looks like one.'

Neil glanced that way. A young man sat with his girlfriend, and he'd been watching Neil a little too heavily.

'Yeah, noticed him already,' Neil said. 'Noah showed his photo to some people. He's just a lowly uniformed constable, probably here off his own back and hoping to catch a jackpot and get promoted. He's drinking my expensive Desperadoes, so ignore him.'

The aforementioned Noah interrupted here, to whisper in Neil's ear. 'Twice in one night?' Neil said with a smile. 'Set the balls up and grab his cash.'

On illegal paper Neil was worth about five million, and he probably had a million in cash hidden around the city. Like many rich people, he soothed his soul by doing charity work. Not the standard kind, though. He would do favours for people if they were having trouble. The work was free, but he only took a job on if you could beat him at pool. To guarantee that hordes didn't invade the pub seeking aid, the cost of playing a game was £100. Very few beat him on his own table. Sean hadn't yet seen someone earn his help.

But this new challenger did. Sean watched in humour as Neil potted a red, thus nominating that colour, and then smacked a second ball, which thudded into the black and knocked it into a pocket. Game over.

Neil laughed, which was a surprise. He'd probably lost three of his last hundred games and Sean expected him to be enraged. But Neil shook his opponent's hand like a sportsman and returned to Sean's table.

'Not going to renege, are you?' Sean asked.

'Piss off. I only did that once before, and that guy lied to me. Anyway, why renege when I know you'd love this job? It's yours. Tonight.'

Sean had planned to go see Holly in her new place. But he had to admit he also liked a bit of spontaneous action. Plus, Neil needed to be kept sweet. 'Who or what's the target?'

'That chap bought a car from a lot. It was a dangerous piece of shit that nearly killed his kids. I want you to vandalise some of the cars.'

'And that takes a team?'

'No, just you. I need this one kept on the quiet. I don't want it spread round that I lost a game. Noah will have the address.'

'Will it get me out of the CCTV thing tomorrow?'

'Hell no.'

'But there is one way.'

Neil laughed. 'Oh, is there now? Let's hear it.'

Sean dumped some cash on the table. £100. 'Please, Mr Webb, sir, master, your greatness, can you help me attend my college course tomorrow?'

Neil might have laughed if his pride hadn't been challenged. 'Rack 'em up.'

3

No high-level criminal could survive by using his registered mobile phone, so Neil's crew employed prepaid devices, known as burners. Usually these were destroyed after a crime or at the end of the day, to make sure the police didn't trace the numbers. If someone used a number the callee didn't recognise, the rule was to stay silent upon answering. Sean did that now.

'It's me,' a voice said. Neil. He had a new burner. 'Slight change of plan.'

'What change?'

'Car lot guy. It's not his cars that need burning–'

'You didn't say burning,' Sean cut in. 'You said vandalism. Popped tyres and shit. What the hell do you think I'm going to burn?'

'Think? Remember who you work for.'

'I quit.'

'You have to die to quit. Burn the guy's office to the ground. Lob Molotovs.'

'Ah. Luckily I've got a crate full of those in the boot.'

'Don't be cheeky. Just burn that guy's office to the ground. There's a Kia Venga waiting for you at...'

Neil's firm could acquire cars almost as easily as phones, and every job required a new one. Thanks to now-dead Alan, there were probably two dozen clones waiting in multi-storey car parks across South Yorkshire. Neil gave the name of one such location then hung up.

Sean looked into his passenger footwell, where he did indeed have empty glass Harrogate water bottles amongst other crap.

Sean drove to collect the Kia. He laid up his own car in the neighbouring bay and opened the unlocked bonnet of the clone. The key, as always, was hidden in the engine compartment. He then checked the boot and found it empty apart from a couple of expected items: gloves and a hoody, which would go well with a fake black beard he always kept in his glove box.

There was another item present, which he hadn't expected. A loaded jerrycan. Neil must have sent a guy out here to place this item. That meant he'd made his change to the plan much earlier than advertised. Obviously he'd held back this information until Sean was on the road.

Sean called his brother's new burner and said, 'I'm offended. Did you think a burn job was too scary for me?'

'Maybe you're losing your nerve a bit. Now don't call me again, not until the morning. And don't fuck this up.'

His standard sign-off delivered, Neil hung up. Sean got in the Kia and aimed it for his destination.

The car lot was on a road that ran through the arch of a bridge in an industrial estate. Given the bridge and the low dip in the road, the lot was pretty much hidden from view. Perfect.

The lot had about thirty cars in a forecourt set out before a one-storey brick office. The property was secured only by a thin chain strung between short posts. All was dark and empty around him.

Sean now wore the hoody and gloves and a surgical mask

from his own collection. It was to avoid cameras, but he saw only one, on a high corner of the office, and it was aimed in such a way that he was able to walk in a crouch down an aisle between cars without being immortalised. He had a Molotov in his hand.

He crouched at the end of the aisle, just ten feet from the dark office. It had a large front window covered by interior blinds, which wouldn't stop his flaming projectile.

As he lit the firebomb, he heard a noise from within the office. A toilet flushing. He yanked the burning fabric from the bottle of petrol and dropped it on the ground to stamp it out. What the hell? Someone was in the office? The owner must have stayed late for some reason, although that didn't explain why all the lights were off. He scuttled back to his car and got on his burner to call Neil with the news.

'That's good, actually,' his brother said. 'He's got a safe with a document that my client needs. Get it.'

'How do you know that? And why would he want some document? This is supposed to be revenge.'

'I know things, bro, and you don't. You just carry out the orders, so here's one. Burst in there and grab the guy. Get into that safe. Don't let him bullshit you and say he doesn't know the safe code. That's a lie. If he does that, or gives you a code that doesn't work, kill him stone dead and torch the place.'

Sean felt his anger rising. 'This is bullshit, Neil. We don't kill Joe or Jane Public.'

'Like I said, I know things and you don't. You know nothing about this guy, who he is, or what he might have done to little girls. Trust me. Or just obey me. Get it done. And don't call me again until morning. If he doesn't give you that code or it doesn't work, kill him.'

Neil ended the call. Sean paused in that car lot and wondered what the hell he should do. This was uncharted territory. He wasn't always given full information on a job, but here he'd heard two different stories. Neil had wanted the office burned up, but now, all of a sudden, there were important papers that he required? Bullshit.

Neil had lied at least once, but it could be twice. His brother always had a good reason for killing... but they were reasons that were good to him. The reason for this hit might not sit well with Sean. He scuttled back to his car, intending to sit and think a while. But as he pulled open the driver's door, he made his decision.

If there were papers in that safe, maybe they would give him a clue as to what the hell was going on. He couldn't shake a funny feeling that this all had something to do with Holly. And he'd promised to protect her.

He dumped the bottle of petrol in the car, grabbed the torch he always carried, and again slipped down an aisle created by cheap cars. He rushed across a blank space between vehicles and office, and used a single kick to burst open the simple wooden door.

He rushed inside, splashing light around the room. He saw a dirty carpet, a desk on one side, shelving containing car parts and documents, and against another wall a sofa. On which, under a blanket, lay a man, who sat up in abject fear.

'Keep quiet,' Sean said. He shut the door behind him and found a light switch. The man on the sofa, who was about forty and balding, just watched and clutched his blanket for safety. Sean didn't have a weapon so he grabbed a pen off the desk. He noticed the safe, low down and set in the wall behind the desk chair. He also noted that no cameras covered the interior of the office.

The man pressed himself back against the sofa, arms up, as Sean brandished the pen at him. 'I'm sure you've worried about hearing the next three words,' Sean said. 'Open… the… Can you guess the third?'

'Safe?' the man croaked.

'That's right. What's the code?'

The man just stared, numbed.

Sean had to repeat his order, slowly. The man needed no additional prompt. '0424.'

'Don't move. Run for that door or go for a weapon, I'll paint this carpet with blood. I would have said *ruin*, but that carpet is knackered already. Understand?'

The man nodded. Keeping an eye on his prisoner, Sean moved to the safe and jabbed in the code. It didn't work and the safe made a shrill beep, like a complaint.

Before Sean could react, the man said, 'That's the code, I promise. My wife must have changed it. I swear.'

Sean approached him again, pen held front and centre. 'I have to go back with the stuff in that safe, or I have to kill you. You get one final chance.'

'Please, 0424, that was the code. She's changed it. She's been having an affair and she kicked me out today. She's done this on purpose.'

An affair? The man seemed too scared to be lying. He was sleeping here tonight, so his story sounded plausible. It gave Sean a moment's thought. 'What colour is your wife's hair?'

'It's red. I mean, it's greying but she dyes it. Why?'

Sean sat on the desk to think. The man blasted him with pleas for pity and mercy until Sean told him to shut up. When he had silence, Sean weighed up his options. He wasn't going to kill this man, but nor could he return to Neil without whatever was in that safe…

'Listen to me carefully, okay?' Sean said after a whole minute's consideration. The man nodded. 'If you tell the police I was here, you're dead.'

'I won't, I promise.'

'Be quiet. I've heard that shit before from a lot of liars. You've had your warning and that's the end of it. The man who sent me is very powerful. He wants what's in that safe–'

'It's just car keys and some car documents.'

'He wants it, whatever it is. If I don't get it, he'll have you killed, and he'll burn this place to the ground. If he gets what he wants, he'll forget about you and you get to be an old man. So this is what I'm going to do. I'm going to go to your house and get the code from your wife. I'm going to leave you here and I won't tie you up. But I'll be back. If you call the cops while I'm gone, it'll be the biggest mistake of your life. And you won't be around to knock it off the top spot in the future. Understand?'

A nod.

Sean got to his feet. 'What's your address?'

4

Dreams do come true.

Or, rather, nightmares. Neil knew full-well that faceless numbers out there wanted him dead. They wanted to take his empire, avenge a slight, or reap respect. Normally he was surrounded by men, protected, but not always. Certainly not here, now. His greatest fear was waking up in a strange room, having been drugged in the night and whisked away. A close second was the scene he faced right now: stirring from sleep with an enemy in his bedroom.

'Don't move a muscle,' the silhouette bending over him said, the voice a whisper. There was a weapon pressed against his throat. But it didn't feel like a knife or a gun. Beside him, Lana slept on.

'Who are you?' Neil said, also in whisper.

'Someone very close to you.'

'And what do you want?'

'The answer to one very important question.' The figure reached out his free hand, and turned on the bedside light. Now illuminated, he pulled back the weapon, which Neil saw was a purple dildo. 'Do you use this on her, or her on you?'

Neil slapped the dildo out of Sean's hand and pushed him away. Naked, he got up, grabbed his brother's arm, and dragged him from the room. Without a word exchanged, the two men went downstairs, into the living room. Neil turned the light on and pushed Sean into an armchair. Neil took the sofa and dragged a fluffy cushion over his private parts.

'You're a damn dickhead. I should make an example out of you by stringing you up from a lamp post.'

'And tell all your men that I got the drop on you with a dildo? Go for it.'

Neil wasn't in the mood to laugh, but he also wasn't quite as angry as he'd been ten seconds ago. He knew he, like Sean, had some explaining to do.

Sean pointed at the ceiling, meaning the bedroom above. Neil said, 'My new girl.'

'That was quick.'

Neil wasn't the one who had to justify his presence here, but he felt he needed to give an answer. 'The house felt too weird. Seeing Holly's side of the bed empty. Never slept there without her.'

'Fair enough. But you didn't meet that woman up there tonight.'

'Although it did feel good to not have to worry about Holly. You know, the house being attacked. I guess I'm jealous of that part of your life. It's just you to worry about yourself.'

Something came over his brother's face. Humility? Guilt? Regret? Did Sean feel lonely without a partner?

'Sounds like she meant a lot to you,' Sean said. 'Which makes this sudden change all the more surprising. Who knows about her? Noah?'

'Not even. My secret. I can't have Noah lurking out there all night. It would start people gossiping, and Lana doesn't want that.'

'She looks about sixty. That your thing?'

'Piss off, she's forty-five. You saw her in the dark.'

'I had a close look before I woke you. Bit of grey showing at the roots.'

A strange question. 'You want me to buy you a pair. Done. Anything else you'd like to know about my private life?'

'Yeah. She know you're a bad boy gangster?'

A good question. Just like he had with Holly, Neil had been careful to downplay the breadth of his criminal universe. 'Speaking of Noah, does he know after all? That how you found me? And who else knows?'

'Noah wouldn't tell me that without running it through you first. He's your man and wouldn't give me the time of day unless you authorised it.'

'Man's my loyal dog. Doesn't trust anyone else. So if not him, how did you find me?'

Sean told him about events at the car lot, culminating in his arrival at this house and seeing Neil's motorbike outside. It was a vehicle registered to him but used very infrequently. 'My guess is you couldn't use a clone vehicle because your guys might have followed it.'

'Well done, Sherlock.'

'Risky to go out on your personal vehicle, though.'

'I was careful not to rob a bank on the way here. Get me some water.'

Sean did as instructed. When he retook his seat, he said, 'So you're banging car lot guy's wife. She booted him out for you. That why you wanted him dead? So you could move in here.'

Neil smiled. He couldn't wait to see Sean's face after this next bombshell. 'I didn't want him dead. His wife did.'

Sean barely batted an eyelid at the big twist. 'You knew he was sleeping at work, so I was supposed to burn him up in that office all along.'

'Which you fucked up.'

'And you knew she'd changed the safe combination. You knew he couldn't open it, which means you tried to trick me into killing him.'

'Which you fucked up.'

Sean sighed. 'Nothing but lies from the get-go. This whole thing had nothing to do with a pool game. You faked that. You threw that game so I'd think that player had set this job up.'

'Of course. You think I could lose a game for real?'

'So he won, but he doesn't get what he wants. He's out a hundred quid and will still have whatever problem he came to you with.'

'His kid's having boyfriend troubles. So I'll have someone give him a warning. Happy now? Now it's my turn to show brother knows brother well. You came here to get the safe combination. Which means you went above and beyond to avoid killing someone. When will you grow out of that?'

'Out of guilt and morals? Hopefully never. I won't be killing him and I don't think you should.'

A fair assertion. 'It was a bit rash, I guess. He's out of the house now and that'll be good enough, after a warning to keep his mouth shut. Don't look so glum. You saved a man's life.'

'Good. How is Holly involved in this?'

'Holly? She isn't. That's a leap.'

Sean had a steely glare. 'Is it? I'm wondering if the story about Holly seeing other men was bullshit. If I was a gambling man, I might drop cash on you planning to kill your wife so you can clear a path to Helen of Troy upstairs.'

Neil sipped his water, but the eye contact between both brothers never faltered. If there was one man alive he could rely on, it was the one sitting across from him. But how much should Sean be told? How much did he deserve the truth? Neil contemplated this for almost thirty seconds, and Sean waited patiently, perhaps knowing what was going on in his brother's head.

He even somehow knew when Neil had made a decision, for he said, 'Okay, let's hear it.'

Sharp brat, his little brother. 'Remember the Nasty Boyz?'

Sean nodded. 'The guys from Barnsley. New kids. Trying to be like us. We ruined them.'

The cheesy-named gang thought it was the bee's knees. The Boyz had adopted a strategy that Neil's crew had used to gain a fast, scary reputation way back: shock and awe. It didn't quite work for them, and one of the leaders had paid a visit to the farmer's Volkan incinerator. The next guy in line went into hiding and the gang soon disintegrated. Like many before them.

Neil explained that he'd been hearing rumours that the remaining Nasty Boy wanted revenge by taking out Holly, so he'd given her a bodyguard. 'But you know Holly. She would have hated having a man trail her around. So I did it on the sly. He was to remain out of sight, but always watch her.'

Neil saw Sean stiffen, probably in anticipation of the remainder of the story. 'How long was he following her?' Sean asked.

'Two days. And last–'

'Who was following her?'

'A guy called Zippy. Don't think you know him. Last night she was at Tesco, and he was watching. She spoke to a cop. He handed her a card of some kind.'

The cop in question, he said, was a known face, a detective who'd investigated some of Neil's men for a vape store robbery a few months back. Carrying a basket of goods, the officer had approached Holly in an aisle and they'd spoken for a minute before he scuttled off.

Sean paused to let this sink in. Neil could see he didn't like what he'd just heard, but he came down on the other side of the fence. 'He might have just been out shopping. You ever think of that?'

'Sure did. I thought about this all last night, while she lay beside me in bed. No way. It reeks of a set-up, a planned meet. I didn't really panic until I was at the gym this morning.'

'Which is when you made your rash decision. Any copper you control know anything that backs this claim up?'

'No. But that means nothing. And it wasn't rash. She's talking to the cops, Sean.'

'And have you talked to her about it?'

'No point. She'd just say what you said about shopping. You really think she'd just come clean? I don't do coincidences. She's selling us down the river. So she's going to vanish.'

He could see this didn't sit well with Sean. Neil said, 'I know. My own wife. Shock of shocks. But we've been drifting apart, Sean. For the last year or so. She's distant, not the same. Not a woman I'd get with if I met her today.'

'I hate to speak out of turn, Neil, but maybe you pushed her away a little. This job you do, it's something you had to keep from her. And the job is your life. Yet you had to keep her in the dark. That can't be good for any relationship.'

'Same reason why you don't have a woman, eh? Look, I don't love her anymore and I don't think she loves me. It is what it is. Don't ask me about it. Decision made, and not out of rashness. I think she ran to the cops and got help.'

'So all of a sudden you're certain she's in with the cops despite your own bent officers telling you they know nothing about it?'

'Sure. She's a big secret exactly because I have coppers on my side. Use your brain.'

'A CI? That's what you're saying?'

Powerful confidential informants had to be kept on the quiet, just in case the people they told tales on had what Neil did: cops on the payroll. Often they were known to just a select few high-ranking officers and dealt with those people via a single conduit – a handler. Sometimes even the Crown Prosecution Service, who would act on their information and cut a deal, didn't know a grass's identity until the last moment.

'Wife of a big-time crime overlord,' Neil said. 'The CPS would snap up a witness like that.'

Sean nodded. 'For sure. But they'd have nothing unless she gave it to them. Do you really think she's turned against you? I mean, really? Anyway, what could she tell them?'

Neil looked at him as if he was stupid. 'She knows what I do, Sean. It's what first attracted her to me. Are you serious?'

'What I meant is that mostly you keep her out of that world. You don't talk to her about the things you do. You told me that. You said she had some analogy about dripping.'

Neil remembered. Holly had wanted to try a traditional bit of British grub and had taken a fancy to dripping – until she learned it was melted animal fat. She wished she'd never found out. Sean thought the same applied here: that Holly wouldn't want to know where he got his money. Spending a £20 note would be harder if she knew a post office teller had handed it over at gunpoint.

But Sean was missing the point. 'She found out about the dripping, though. Just like she'll have found out things about my lifestyle. She couldn't avoid it, especially with the cops turning up at my door all the time. So she knows more than we'd like to think, and definitely enough to do some real damage. The cops obviously think so, too, which is why they recruited her.'

'Does she know about the Allerby Job?'

'No. I haven't even told you the whole deal with that one, so why would I tell her?'

'Because she's someone you stick your dick into.'

'Well, I didn't tell her anything about it. I doubt she can ruin it. But she can mess with other things, so it's important we work fast before the cops start picking us apart. We've got a little time because they're not going to raid places or make arrests until they have everything she can tell them. That could take a few days.'

'Time to do what?'

'Find her, Sean. What the fuck did you think I meant?'

'Kill her, you mean. I think this is overreacting, Neil.'

'Piss off, Sean. You want to find out the hard way that we should have been more careful? We'll keep looking for her just in case she's in a safe house or she's still on her own. But only for the next day. I'm not going to sit around and wait to get fucked over. If I've heard nothing by later on tomorrow, I'll up gears.'

'Meaning?'

'Meaning I don't care if I have to send someone into a damn police station to kill her in front of ten cops.'

5

Noah had the ears of all the bent police officers in Neil's employ, and he knew to let people in the crew know if he got wind that someone was under surveillance. No call had been made, but you didn't last long in this game without a healthy dose of paranoia. Still using the Kia because it hadn't been involved in a crime, Sean drove a winding route, sometimes doubling back on himself, to lose any tail, police or enemies.

It gave him time to think. He'd had the fright of his life upon learning that Neil had put a tail on Holly. He didn't think the man called Zippy had spied him and Holly together, but he knew nothing for certain. It was possible that this Zippy had caught them meeting up but had kept it quiet. Maybe he thought nothing of it, or he was worried about creating friction and pissing Neil off. Sometimes messengers got blamed. Sean had to hope the guy's silence so far meant he'd continue to keep sacred whatever, if anything at all, he knew.

Back in the centre of Sheffield, he drove to a red-light district and pulled up by the first girl he saw loitering on the road. Skinny, scraggy, perfect. She was by an alleyway between three-storey houses and he saw a shape lurking in the darkness. Her pimp.

She came to his window when he buzzed it down. 'Looking for fun?' she said.

'I've got a room at the Harvest B&B.'

'Too far, baby.'

He showed her a hundred quid in twenties. She turned to look back at the pimp, who Sean saw nod. She asked Sean if he could drop her back here, and he said he'd add another twenty for a taxi. The deal was done.

Six miles away, the Harvest was a shabby B&B in an area of the city that usually topped a crime hotspot list. The place had rooms for rent by the hour, ideal for whores and their clients. The desk clerk didn't bat an eyelid as Sean approached the desk with the scraggy woman by his side and a rucksack on his shoulders.

He paid for one hour, which would have dispelled any remaining doubt that he'd bought a fuck. He got a key and an order not to trash the room, and they hit the stairs. On the first floor, Sean stopped at a door and he gave the girl the key and the promised £120.

'Stay in this room for exactly one hour. Have a shower or something. I don't need you now. Thanks anyway. Just make sure you stay for the full hour.'

He left her and, after waiting for the puzzled woman to enter the room, made his way to another dirty door. He gave a coded knock. Holly opened the door moments later.

'This damn shithole,' she said as he followed her inside. The single room was a little grimy but neat. The window faced a brick wall just ten feet away.

'Best I could do,' Sean said. 'I got you some clothing.' He dumped his rucksack. 'Tracksuits of mine and T-shirts and stuff. I'll buy some women's clothing tomorrow.'

'I want a phone. I wanted to call you. I wasn't sure you'd come back.'

'Of course I'd come back. I'll see if I can get you a phone for next time.'

'How long do I have to stay here. What have you found out? Is my husband still looking for me?'

She sat on the bed. Sean remained standing. He watched her face carefully as he said, 'He doesn't think you have another man. He thinks you've been talking to the police.'

'*What?* So that's what this is about? Does Neil think I went to the police about him?'

Her surprise seemed genuine, but it wasn't proof of innocence. 'Someone saw you at a supermarket yesterday, talking to a detective.'

Her shoulders slumped. 'And he thinks I arranged to meet that officer? Is that right?'

'Did you? You need to explain things, Holly. Because this is real bad. I'm not judging you–' was that a lie? '–but I need to know exactly what happened.'

She told him the story, but it wasn't what he expected. She had been shopping, alone, when a man approached her from behind. In casual clothing and carrying a shopping bag, he had said, 'How's things? Good, right?'

It was the ready meals aisle, which made her think he was a single man who'd assumed she was an available woman. She flashed her wedding ring at him. 'Sorry, married.'

'I know, to a piece of shit.'

Her jaw dropped. And now she was a little scared. Neil had enemies. Many of them followed a code that families didn't get touched. Others wouldn't risk harming his wife because he ran one of South Yorkshire's most vicious organised crime groups. But there were myriad smaller gangs with lunatics amongst their ranks, any one of which might think he could gain respect by whacking a top dog's missus. It was a common story.

'Who are you?' she said, looking around for possible heroes.

'I'm the guy who'll be laughing in court when your husband goes down for life.'

The truth dawned. A police officer. She lost her fear. 'Is that right? So why bother me with it?'

'Just wondering what the attraction is. The money? The fear? Do you get off knowing people are scared of you? I mean, Neil's the big man, but you're his wife, and wives rule the roost. Is that what gets you wet?'

'Go away. Talk to my husband if you're angry with him.'

'After we drop him in a cage for the rest of his life, there will be a party to celebrate. You're invited to come, if you don't go down right alongside him.'

'Go away.'

The detective handed her a business card, which she took only to appease him. When he was gone, she dumped it behind some beans on a shelf.

And that was that. 'He was just a police officer on a day off, out shopping,' Holly said. 'He saw me, recognised me, and wanted to have a dig. That's all that happened. I can't believe this. It was nothing. I didn't tell Neil because... it was nothing.'

Sean tried to read her eyes. He wanted to believe her, but he'd spent his adult life around people who lied and cheated and stole for a living. It had an effect on the mind. 'Okay.'

'So I can just tell Neil the story and all should be okay? Will that work?' she said.

He doubted it. If there was a man more mistrustful of the human race than him, it was his big bro. He sat on the bed next to her. 'Not without proof.'

She gave a wry laugh. 'So what can you do?'

How could he answer that when he didn't even know how

to deal with the story she'd just told? There was no way to prove that she hadn't talked to the cops, that she hadn't been giving them secrets for weeks or months. They raided Neil's places all the time, arrested low-level dealers and thieves constantly, and it was impossible to diagnose if Holly had arranged any of it.

Just three days ago a laundromat had been busted and the cops had found cannabis with a street value of £120,000. Neil was only peripherally attached to it, but still it made Sean wonder if she had had a hand in landing armed officers at that address.

'I don't know what to do,' he said.

She took his hand. 'You said we'd wait a few days and see if Neil changed his mind. But that's not going to happen, is it?'

Now that Holly's possible transgression had been elevated from cheat to betrayer? No chance. The cardinal rule had been snapped in two. It didn't matter that Holly was his wife. Snitches get stitches and ditches. Neil was almost compelled to make Holly pay – if she'd sold him out.

'No, it's not going to happen, Holly. I don't think there's any way to prove that you didn't talk to the cops.'

'Because you don't believe me, either, is that right?'

'I do,' he said, although he wasn't sure of his sincerity. 'But it doesn't matter what I think. Neil won't believe or forgive you, no matter what I say to him. We can't wait this out.'

'So what can you do?'

It was the second time she'd asked that question. He gave the same answer as before: 'I don't know. We've got no help.' His next words were inspired by his brother, who spoke the very same long, long ago.

'It's just us, all alone.'

CHAPTER 3

1

A few months after Neil got arrested for driving illegally as a teenager, the police kicked in the front door. But not for him. Their father was nicked. For murder.

Years earlier, a prostitute was killed and her body dumped in undergrowth. The police had the killer's DNA but no match to it on the databases. Until a familial – similar – match was made to Neil's DNA, which went into the system following his drunk driving arrest.

Later, Dad would admit that he'd been worried about capture via familial DNA after reading a newspaper story about the process being employed to catch the killer of a pensioner in Mansfield. He had turned his sons away from crime to ensure that they didn't give their double helixes up to the system. Nor did he want them to join the army or give blood. And he worried about them getting swabbed after a road traffic crash.

It seemed like overkill to the boys, but soon they came to understand that familial DNA was a powerful new law enforcement tool. How scary was it that it no longer mattered how careful you were at a crime scene because some other schmuck a thousand miles away could unwittingly torpedo you?

Dad claimed the prostitute's death was an accident, but the Crown Prosecution Service was having none of it and charged him with murder. He was remanded in custody until trial. Sean was thirteen, Neil seventeen, both at risk of going into care, so their father got hold of the only remaining family member in the country: a grandmother on their mother's side, who lived a hundred miles up north in Sheffield.

She agreed to become their guardian, but shut down any notion that her decision was altruistic. She was old, infirm, lonely, and the brothers would work for her. They'd fetch and carry, be at her beck and call. Deal. It was made official through the courts.

The brothers left their home with just one suitcase each – and Neil's three-foot snooker table. On the train journey, Sean was glum, which Neil assumed was the product of fear.

'Don't worry, little guy,' he said. 'Gran's your protector on paper. In real life it's me. I'll keep you safe. It's just us, all alone.'

Simple words couldn't lift Sean's spirits. He was going to lose his dad forever. Neil again read this wrong. 'You doubt me, bro? Don't. Knuckle promise. I promise to make sure you're safe and sound till you die an old man. Knuckles, mate.'

They fist-bumped. The knuckle promise was something their dad had invented. It only made Sean feel worse.

Gran was waiting at the door – in a wheelchair. Neil knew then that her fetch-and-carry condition was going to be worse than envisioned. She was a little cold with them and got straight down to business. The back garden needed mowing. The bath panel had come loose and desired a spot of glue. And she wanted someone to rub foam cream onto her diabetic foot.

Ever since he'd played on Sean's snooker table to win the heart of a girl, Neil had developed an infatuation with the game. The brothers played to see who'd do the old gal's feet. Afterwards, Sean asked where the foam cream was.

One thing Gran loved to do herself was cook, even though it was tough from the seat of a wheelchair. After an evening of having orders barked at them, the Webb boys settled down for a fine meal. It kind of made everything okay.

That first night with Neil in a small bedroom used for storage, was a bad one for Sean. He couldn't sleep and he couldn't stop thinking about his father. He lay there in the dark, looking at a sliver of moonlight on the wall.

The very next day, Sean finally plucked up the courage to ask Gran for something that wouldn't leave his mind. 'Will you take me to see my dad?'

'Hell no,' she said. 'That monster deserves nothing. I'm going nowhere near no prison. Do you know what he did to that girl?'

He sure did because Dad had been honest. 'He asked her for directions and she attacked him for no reason. He killed her by accident.'

Gran shook her head. 'Silly boy. I'm not taking you to see him. Not going to no hellish prison. He can rot in there. Don't ask me again.'

That second night was as sleepless as the first. This time, Neil woke in the dead hours and realised Sean was restless. Yet again he misread his brother's mood.

'I get your pain,' Neil said. 'It's a new city. We don't know the place, and we don't have any friends. But we'll change that. We'll take over this whole damn place.'

Sean knew Neil had big dreams, and the balls to go after what he wanted. But he was being silly. How could they ever achieve anything or have a happy life without a mother or father?

'I miss Dad,' Sean said.

'That's mad. He's a scumbag.' Not the first time Neil had said this. The police had poisoned his mind.

'I want to go see him in the prison.'

Neil grunted. 'So go. I ain't going.'

It wasn't that easy. Sean had been seen by many law enforcement people, most of them eager to grill him for information. But one kindly soul had been open to questions instead. From this man Sean had learned that prison visitors had to be over eighteen. A governor could make exceptions, but not if the convict had committed a violent or sexual offence. Sean wasn't going to be eighteen for five years. His only hope was that the courts would work out that the murder was an accident and perhaps let Dad go free.

It wasn't to be. Nine months later, after a four-week trial, Dad was convicted. The brothers hadn't been to the trial, but they knew everything that had happened. The prosecution had claimed that the murder was very far from an accident. Dad, they said, had hired a prostitute, driven to a remote spot for sex, then raped, strangled, and stabbed her, before dragging the body deep into vegetation and covering it.

Sean was aghast at how they'd say such a thing! And even more shocked that a jury could agree. Dad got a life sentence with a minimum of twenty-four years.

It wrecked Sean. He was angry at the justice system and wanted to rebel against... everything. He'd never committed a crime unless it was at the behest of his father or in the presence of Neil, but that changed within a month of the conviction.

At his new school, Sean accidentally kicked a football that hit a kid in the leg. The kid yelled out that he'd banged Sean's mother and a gay man had banged his dad. Perhaps insulting just the dead parent or the incarcerated one might have been ignored. Not both. Sean beat the senses out of the kid and got expelled.

He wasn't done yet. He'd be ousted from four more schools

before he was old enough to leave for good. Some said he was destined for a life of crime. The rebel in him didn't care.

2

At almost three in the morning, Sean entered the Tesco where Holly was accosted by a detective. Few customers were present and they were far outnumbered by staff stacking shelves and pushing roll cages loaded with stock. Sean almost felt like an intruder as he made his way to the aisle with the beans.

A young kid was here, topping up the shelves, so Sean had to be sly about feeling around behind tins. Thirty seconds of that gave him his answer. No business card. Someone must have moved it.

Or Holly had lied and there was no card to be found.

He now needed help he hadn't wanted to seek.

He called Neil, who could always be woken by the ringing of his phone. 'What do you want?' his brother croaked, sleepy.

'I've got an idea.'

'A three in the morning idea? This better make me a million. You've got one minute, then I'm going to shag my girl again.'

'Do that first. I'll wait one minute.'

'No joke is funny at this time of the morning. Just tell me the damn idea.'

'I think Holly is in protective custody.' He went on to

explain. Nobody had heard from her, and if she was in with the police and had nobody else to turn to, she would have contacted them for help. And they'd want to protect their asset, right?

'This isn't breaking news, Sean. I said earlier that I think she's with the cops. So, yeah, protective custody. Where she wouldn't be if you bozos knew how to tackle a woman pottering about in her own house. I'm not hearing your idea yet.'

'The detective from the supermarket. He must know something. There must be a safe house because she's a big secret and they can't just stick her in a police station. That detective knows she's an asset, so he might know where to find her, and I want your permission to have a chat to him.'

'The cop was on the vape store investigation, so I'll call Jimmy. He was in on that and should know this guy by sight. I'll text the details. You and him can do the job together.'

'It'll be tomorrow, though. All day. I can't do the CCTV thing. Let me off?'

'Don't challenge me if you can't keep a deal. Okay, you're off the CCTV thing for the copper. What about your college course?'

'I'll skip it.'

Neil paused. 'Okay. Now piss off and let me sleep. Oh, and be careful with this, okay? You fuck with the blue line gang and that's when these boys really get their arses in gear.'

After the call, Sean moved to the clothing aisle and bought some items for Holly. He got a text as he was waiting at the till. It named a Jimmy Brown and gave his phone number. He rang it.

Sean didn't know this Jimmy and wondered what type of guy he'd get. Neil had two types surrounding him: those who accepted Sean as a bona fide member of the crew, and those who thought he was here only because he was brother to the boss. Jimmy soon announced himself as the latter, unfortunately.

'What do you want?' Jimmy said. 'It's the dead of fucking night.'

Sean explained that he was after a name. Jimmy almost begrudgingly told Sean that the detective who'd approached Holly in Tesco was a sergeant called Josh Harper, working out of Woodseats station as part of the major investigation team. 'So what do you want to know for?'

'Because we're going to have a chat with him.'

'*We* as in me and you? You ready for this lark?'

Jimmy was just trying to be clever. He surely knew that Sean ran Pest B Gone, which was populated by rugged, vicious men. 'I'm your babysitter, dickhead. Cut the cheek or I'll smash you to bits. Pick me up at 9.30.' He gave a street name that was a ten-minute walk from his house.

'Couldn't smash a fucking egg,' Jimmy said, and hung up.

Sean headed home and got a few hours of sleep. At 9.30 he was at the meeting point, but it was another ten minutes before Jimmy's car, a dirty Honda Jazz, rolled up. Clad in a tracksuit worn thin, Jimmy was fat, about fifty, and had wild hair and a thick beard. And he wasn't happy. 'I didn't even get breakfast or a dump.'

Sean had half-regretted being bullish last night and had vowed to give Jimmy a chance this morning. The twat had just blown it, so fuck him. 'Bullshit, because there's food all in your beard. Stop moaning. Dump in your trousers. I doubt you'd notice.'

Sean got in the vehicle, after swiping trash from the passenger seat and kicking aside more from the floor to find room for his feet. 'I need a man to buy some burner phones. And for a wait-watch job. Know anyone the cops can't tie to you?'

Jimmy lit a smoke. 'Course I do. I'm connected. Seatbelt on. You wanna get me pulled over?'

Sean had called Neil at nine, requesting a new car. A text came through as they drove, so he directed Jimmy to the car park where the clone waited. It was a Saab saloon from 2008, and it had balaclavas and a loaded jerrycan in the boot. Once aboard something much cleaner than Jimmy's jalopy, they drove. Jimmy decided he was suddenly best friends with Sean.

'Check this. You think this is a man's world or a woman's?'

'What?'

'You think men rule the world? You think we make things for ourselves, like Alton Towers and cinemas and stuff, and God gave us women as another creature comfort? And we make stuff for women so they stay happy and give us sex?'

'I don't know. How long till we get there?'

'Or is it a woman's world? And God gave them men to make things for them. Cars and TV and stuff, all to make women happy?'

'Just drive, man.'

'Open your mind a bit, tosspot,' Jimmy said, but he didn't press for an answer to his questions. In silence, they drove to the dankest part of a dingy estate, where they pulled up outside a decrepit house that had been turned into flats.

'Keep close to me or you'll get eaten alive,' Jimmy said as he got out.

'Thank you,' Sean replied sarcastically.

Jimmy led the way through the communal door and up one flight of stairs, where he hammered on a door. On the floor around it was trash, mostly fast-food wrappers. Amongst the debris was an eviction notice, dated eighteen days ago, that gave the tenants thirty days to leave.

The door was unlocked. Sean followed Jimmy inside. No prizes for guessing that the interior also looked like a shitheap.

Jimmy pulled a machete from inside his trousers, where it must have been laid against his thigh, and checked the vile living room first, then laughed to himself when it was empty. 'Silly me. Ain't two in the afternoon yet.'

He opened a door to a bedroom, where three guys slept in their clothing on the rotten carpet. There was no bed. Jimmy kicked them all awake. They sat up with eyes glossy from too little sleep or too many drugs.

He waved the machete at the trio. 'I need a guy for a day's work. Ten quid to the lucky bastard. Who wants it?'

All three jabbed a hand in the air, as if a teacher had asked a maths question. Jimmy picked up an empty lager can from the floor and placed it on a dresser that was surprisingly clean. 'First one to hand me the can wins it.'

Jimmy found what happened next hilarious, but he laughed alone. The three drug-addled idiots pulled and pushed and clawed each other. The scene was a fraction short of an all-out brawl. Slow progress was made across the room, until one guy finally slipped another's grasp and got the can.

The winning scumbag was taken to the car, which ferried the trio to a town on the edge of Sheffield. Here the scumbag was handed some cash. Jimmy told him to 'go in that phone shop and buy three cheap-ass burners. Skip out the back with the dough and you're dead.'

Phones bought, Jimmy got the scumbag to put credit on all three devices. Sean and Jimmy took one each and swapped numbers. The scumbag used the third for his next task: calling Woodseats police station.

To the operator who answered, he said, 'This is a message for Sergeant Harper of the MIT. I have information about a suspect in the vape shop robbery half a year ago. Tell him that I'll be waiting to meet. One hour from now, at...'

The location was a library on the edge of Sheffield, with

good street parking. Nobody was going to be there to meet the detective.

'What if he's not in?' the scumbag said after hanging up.

'Doesn't matter,' Sean said, taking the device the scumbag had used and destroying it. The pieces would be dumped somewhere. 'He's going to want to solve that case. The message will be passed on. His people have sweated over this for half a year. He'll come.'

And come he did. Parked across the road from the library, after dropping off the scumbag, Sean and Jimmy watched the detective arrive. Jimmy recognised him. The detective went inside the library, came out twenty minutes later, and got into his car. He didn't look happy. They followed his car all the way back to Woodseats station. So, Harper was on a shift.

'You wait and watch,' Sean told Jimmy.

Who didn't look happy. 'All day? I got things to do, dude. You wanted that other guy to do it. Why'd we get rid of him?'

'Well, now I want you to do it.'

'Fuck that,' Jimmy said. 'Neil didn't say shit about waiting around all day. I work for him, not you.'

'I'm not giving the order as your boss. But as the guy who'll rip that stinking beard off your face one hair at a time if you give me any more shit.'

Jimmy seemed to search for something to say. All he came up with was, 'Does it piss you off that your brother's the boss and you're just a nobody he dragged along?'

And that, right there, was why Sean got no respect from half of Neil's men. If Jimmy's opinion had meant had anything to him, Sean might have explained that he liked it that way. Safer. More conducive to a long, free life.

Instead, he said, 'Yeah, burns my soul every minute. We're after the cop's address, remember. So someone's got to follow him when he drives home, and he might leave early. I'll be back around four, which should be way before he clocks off.'

'So where the fuck are you going?' Jimmy said.

'Not that it's your business, but I've got a... physio appointment. Every Thursday afternoon. Neil knows about it.'

'Snap your dick on whores?' Jimmy said, laughing at his own joke.

'I blew out my shoulder ripping beards off insolent fuckers. Call me if he leaves early.'

Sean exited the vehicle, walked a couple of streets away, and called a taxi to take him home for his car.

3

Visitors' room, HMP Wakefield. A place Sean knew very well.

Sean's father, Donald, looked upset as he crossed the room and took a seat at Sean's table. He would have known Sean was the only visitor on the list, but perhaps he had held out hope that Neil would be by his youngest son's side. It never had happened, perhaps never would.

Neil was a touchy subject, and Dad knew it. By unspoken agreement, he and Sean never brought him up. Sean wasn't sure if that was a good idea or not.

'Doing good, son?'

'Always. How's your job?'

Another question that always got asked, and each time it burned worse than before when Sean lied. 'Good. We're busy.'

Dad knew all about Neil's organised crime group, of course, but Sean had convinced him that he played no part in it. He used his role as head of Pest B Gone for believability, but with a slant that removed any hint of a connection to Neil or criminal activity.

After a few minutes of asking questions about Sean's work,

Donald abruptly sighed. 'Jesus, Sean. You know the kinds of people that are in here?'

'The prisoners? Sure. All innocent.'

That joke got no smile. 'Liars and bullshitters. People in the know. This is a locked box, but information gets in and out. Criminals know criminals. I might have heard more than you know.'

Sean didn't like where this was going. 'Like what?'

'Liars and bullshitters, Sean. I miss having people give me things straight. Thank God you come to see me and don't tell me lies.'

Wrapped up in those words was a plea. For the truth. And Dad had hinted that he might know at least some of it. He owed him the rest. 'I work for Neil. My crew does. We do some of his bad stuff. But funds are channelled through the pest company so that it looks legitimate. I'm sorry, Dad. But it's a good cover story that avoids my getting on police radar.'

Dad shook his head in dismay. 'You think you have all the answers. You think you can skate through this way of life and fool everybody. You can't. One day you'll be walking to the shop for eggs and twenty coppers will jump on you. Then you'll find out that nobody got fooled and you've been under investigation for ages and they've got enough evidence to drop you into a hellhole like this for twenty years.'

He knew it, of course. Investigations into major organised crime groups could take years as the police gathered evidence. Sean was good at covering his tracks, but deep down he knew there would have been mis-steps. He hadn't been seen killing anyone, for that couldn't be ignored, but that didn't mean the cops didn't have a growing file on him. A list of his transgressions, his biological evidence collected from scenes, a tree chart showing his criminal connections.

All of it waiting for a big reveal one day. He'd gotten too used to thinking that he had a charmed life just because he'd never had his collar felt. 'I'm careful,' he said, but it was such a weak defence that he tapered off and the last word was inaudible.

'You don't know what the police have on you, what mistakes you made, what people you trust might have told them, or what mistakes they might have made. That's how OCGs are taken down: connections between components. And you won't realise you're in the shitcan until it's too late.'

'Neil knows what he's doing.'

'Your brother thinks he's safe, and maybe he is for now. I hear the police only suspect he runs an OCG. He's got forcefields between himself and what he does. Everything leads to low-level people and stops right there. But you're one of them. Low-level. You don't have the security measures in place that he does. You'll go down long before he does, and they'll want to use you to get to him. Besides, he's got that pub of his.'

'That's legitimate. It doesn't launder money.'

'But how did he get the money to buy it? Can he show a court that he had the legitimate means to make such a big purchase? I doubt it. Somewhere deep down in a financial file in some foreign bank there's the evidence to condemn him, and it'll all float to the surface one day. They get him, they get everything and everyone. It's only a matter of time, son.'

Sean couldn't think of a response. He could hardly doubt Dad's claim, since Neil himself believed his Achilles' heel was not murder or robbery or prostitution or drugs, but money. *Money,* he said, *is the only way to bring down the biggest guys.*

Dad leaned back, perhaps to make sure no watching prison guard suspected that criminal information was being exchanged. 'I also know Neil's wife is missing and that he wants her taken out. And I know my youngest son's face and it's telling me he's under stress. I think the two are connected. Are you in trouble, boy?'

Boy? The last time Dad had used that term, so many years ago, it was for a scolding. Was that what this was? 'How do you know about Holly? She's not been reported missing yet. What have people said? What do they know?'

'Liars and bullshitter, Sean. Sick of them. Tell me everything. Please.'

Please? Sean didn't even pause for thought. It all came out. The affair with Holly, the killing of Alan, and that he had her in hiding while Neil scoured the city for her trail. He said it all with a smile, and his dad nodded approvingly. All faked, of course, but necessary to convince the guards watching the room that nothing was amiss.

'I don't know what to do,' Sean finished. 'But I want to be with her, and I want to keep her safe. I promised to.'

'Have you got money for it?'

'For what?'

'Running. That's what you're getting at. It sounds like that's your only chance. To run with her.'

He'd considered it, of course, but dismissed the idea as fruitless. Now that his Dad had reminded him that the police might sweep him up any day soon, the image of he and Holly living in another city, away from all this, didn't sound so wild. Achieving it, though, was another matter. 'We don't have money. We can't get money. Neil knows when his people get money and when they take it out.'

He explained that Neil had access to the bank accounts of all the men under him. He kept tabs in case people spent beyond their means, which was a big red flag for the police. That was what he told his employees, but there was a bigger worry driving him. He also watched accounts for big deposits that might hint at payoffs by enemies or the cops, or windfalls from jobs on the side. Nobody was exempt from this scrutiny. Not even Sean.

'And I don't have cash,' Sean said. 'Not enough. He doesn't want anyone holding more than a grand because of POCA.'

Dad nodded his understanding. While investigating a crime, the police could seize cash under the Proceeds of Crime Act, but the minimum was £1,000. If they couldn't prove 'beyond reasonable doubt' that the money was acquired – or to be used – illegally, they could force someone to forfeit it to a court on a 'more likely than not' basis. To get it back, the owner would have to prove that they'd gained the money legitimately.

Sean's cash had no paper trail and had never been through his bank. If he was lucky and no charges were filed, he could get it back, but the odds were better that he'd go down for money laundering. Neil had a very good point.

Dad didn't look happy. 'So you work as a pest control man, but you do Neil's bidding. And you earn little more than you would if you did that job for real?'

Sean gave a pitiful nod. 'But I don't need much. I'm happy.'

'While Neil earns much, much more than you. Millions.'

'He's the boss. I don't want to be. I'm happy doing what I do.'

'And you do that job with the threat of a long jail term hanging over you. Doesn't sound like much of a life, son.'

They sat in silence for a few moments. 'What do I do?' Sean said. 'No money, Neil's always watching, and I can't run anyway because of you. I'd never be able to visit you again. But I want to be with Holly.'

'I'm not going to tell you what to do,' his father said, standing up. The visit was over, even though there was ample time remaining. 'I can't do that and watch it end up getting you in deep shit. My only advice is to follow your heart, your brain, and your instincts. You're the smarter brother, perhaps the sharpest man I know. I will say one thing, though. Don't worry about me if you can't visit again. There's more to life, son, and it's about time you started living yours. Before someone takes it away.'

That said, his father walked away.

4

Sean's home was a semi-detached new build in Athersley North. It sat in the middle of a housing estate, on the crossbar of a T-junction. His front window had a view straight down the minor road. He'd rented the property for the nearby shops but hadn't given much thought as to why the place was so cheap. He learned that on night one, when every car approaching along the minor road lit up his living room with its headlights.

It was 2.47pm when he got home, so he had almost an hour before he had to leave to go meet Jimmy. The idiot hadn't called yet, so the detective, Harper, was probably still on shift at his station. Sean checked one of his other burners and found three missed calls from an unknown number. He knew it was Neil and called him back. But first he changed into a fresh T-shirt and clean jeans.

'Where the hell are you?' his brother said upon answering the phone.

'Back home. I had my college class. You still need me to go round looking for CCTV?'

'I sent people already, since you dropped off the radar. Was the class all right? Did you get caught up in that gas leak I read about?'

Sean always checked the social media pages for the college, just in case Neil asked questions about his studies. There had been no damn gas leak, which meant Neil was testing him. He knew Sean hadn't been to college. But did he know everything?

It was risky to be secretive right now, with Holly the focus of attention and he being the guy who let her escape. He couldn't act suspicious during these tense times. 'I didn't go to college, Neil. I went to see Dad.'

He expected anger, but Neil laughed. 'Finally you stop with the bullshit.'

Sean recalled Dad's words: *This is a locked box, but information gets in and out.* 'You already knew?'

'I'm not an idiot, Sean. Who does a college course every Thursday for years? You think I don't check up on my people?'

Sean knew he'd been silly to think he could get away with visiting Dad once a week for so long. Neil must have had a guy follow him one day. 'So how long have you known and why didn't you say anything?'

'About a year, pal. And it's your little pet project, so I let you have it. It's quite sad, Sean.'

Sad that a son wanted to visit his father? 'Sad is a good word to describe Dad. Because his eldest boy has disowned him.'

'Fuck that. Not important. You have all the fun you want with that sex fiend. Just keep it as your secret and don't mention him again around me. Now what's going on with the copper?'

Sean explained. Jimmy was watching the police station. Sean would meet him soon. When the detective clocked off work, they'd follow him home. Either there, or somewhere en route if a suitable location presented itself, they'd accost him and seek answers.

'If it turns out this guy knows nothing about Holly, what then?' Sean asked.

'Then we find out what safe house she's at another way. Just don't do something stupid and hurt the guy, or you'll be part of the biggest manhunt in history.'

'No, I meant what if he's not involved? What if he just approached her in the shop because he knew who she was? What if he tells us that Holly isn't an informant?'

'He wouldn't know if he wasn't in the loop. But we're guessing at the minute. Just keep me informed, okay? Call me when it's done. And keep your morning free tomorrow. Me and you are going to Allerby House.'

'I've got a better idea, Neil. How about I call you so you can listen in when I ask him questions?'

Neil thought. 'You mean call me while you've got the guy?'

'A live interrogation for you.'

He thought some more. 'Okay. Just don't fuck this up.'

He hung up. Sean really wanted to talk to Holly, but she didn't have a phone. Nor could she have one.

Fifty minutes to wait. The house suddenly felt too quiet, too big and empty. It was a common feeling, especially when he was in the midst of a job. If he was on a stakeout, he could be the most patient man on earth, but here he could never relax unless it was the end of a day. And the itchiness was worse when he had time to burn between tasks. He wasn't used to the serene and never had been. He needed to be on the go all the time. Maybe he should get a lodger.

He decided to keep his hands busy by making lunch. But before he could take a bite, someone knocked on the door. He peeked through the front window and saw two cars at the kerb, one plain and one a marked police car. The latter had two uniformed occupants. The former was empty and its driver, a tall middle-aged man in jeans and a leather jacket, was on

Sean's step. A detective, no doubt. The uniforms were probably here only for show, so Sean's neighbours would see them.

He opened the front door with a fake smile on his face and a thudding heart. He'd grabbed his keys beforehand, so he'd have something to nervously fiddle with.

The detective showed him a warrant card and introduced himself. Sergeant Jackson, South Yorkshire Police.

'This about the fireworks going off round here the other night?' Sean asked, knowing full-well it wasn't.

'No, it's about your brother's wife, Holly Webb. You're Sean Webb, of course.'

'What's she done? She skipped out on my brother.'

The detective smiled, giving the impression that he was humoured by Sean's play at innocence. 'Skipped out, eh? One of her friends reported her missing this morning. People have heard hide nor hair from her since yesterday. That worries us, given who your brother is. What do you know about it?'

'Why are you asking me? She's not my wife.'

'No, but you know her very well. We thought you might be able to help us.'

'I can't. I don't see my brother that often. I just go to his pub sometimes. He doesn't talk about marital problems.'

'Given his line of work, it's not unreasonable to assume some harm might have come to his wife. That a fair statement?'

'You mean rival pub owners? Is it a vicious industry?'

'Harm from inside or out, if you know what I mean.'

'Slips on beer spillages in the lounge or in the car park?'

The detective gave a meaty grin that Sean wanted to slap off his face. 'Okay. Sure, Mr Webb. You don't know a thing. Nobody ever does. Let me give you a business card so you can call me if you hear anything.' He fished in a pocket and brought out a card. He held it up, then pulled it back. 'Oops, sorry, wrong one. Here.' A different pocket produced another card, this time the correct one. Sean took it and shut the door.

Shit. This was a problem. That business card the detective had 'mistakenly' pulled out first? It was one Sean had made up for Pest B Gone, just to give the firm that authentic feel. The cards had been put in shop windows and left in a handful of libraries. Callers were always told they couldn't be squeezed in due to busy times.

The detective was passing a message that he knew things. That line he'd spoken, *you know her very well:* what did that mean? Were the police aware of Sean's affair with Holly? If so, what if they told Neil?

He wasn't sure of anything except one vital fact: things were going downhill quick.

5

The back gardens of the homes on his street and those of the neighbouring road were separated by a thin alleyway. He used this lane to reach the end of his street unseen, then carefully made his way to the nearest shop.

By then he'd made a call to one of his Pest B Gone boys, who found him in the aisles ten minutes later. Sean was given keys to a car parked a few streets away. In case his watchers somehow knew about the new car, he tripled his journey time with tricks designed to throw off a tail.

When he reached Holly's B&B, he found a man outside the door, leaning his head on it and speaking loudly to the occupant. The man was virtually begging Holly to open up, promising to give her a good time. He was tatty and seemed drunk. Day and night seemed interchangeable in these parts.

Sean didn't say a word. He slapped the man hard on the back of the head and glared him down when fists were clenched and profanity voiced. Soon the guy skulked away. Sean did his coded knock on the door.

Holly answered with an angry face. 'I need to get out of this shithole. There was a man here. Did you get me a phone? He could have done anything?'

'That's him, there, walking away. He changed his mind. Did he think you were a whore?'

She turned and walked into the bedsit. Sean closed the door behind him and stood by it. 'I'm sorry for doubting you about the cop in the supermarket. I'm sorry you had to go through all this. I forgot to get you a phone.'

That was bullshit. He'd refused to supply one in case she tried to call a friend, or do something else that gave away her location. Given the threat by the scumbag outside, maybe he should reassess things.

She sat on the bed. 'But I'm still going through it, Sean. Please tell me you have a plan to save us.'

'I might have. I'm in the middle of it and I need to go in ten minutes.'

She didn't like that. 'And what is it you're doing?'

He paused. He didn't want to say. Sometimes, just like parents during the first trimester, he didn't like to make announcements in case things went wrong. 'You'll see, babe. Hopefully, within the next few hours, I should have good news for you. And some proper clothes. I bought some, but they're in the boot of my car. I had to leave it behind.'

'Like you left me behind.'

He hugged her. 'Don't say that. I'm trying to keep you safe. Both of us. That's why I'm doing what I'm doing.'

She hugged him back warmly, but the words she spoke were cold. 'Just make sure this thing you're doing isn't something stupid, Sean.'

6

'Are we taking him at his house?'

That question from Jimmy had an obvious answer. No. That would involve a long wait until the skies were black, and a home invasion. Detective Harper might have kids. He might have grannies and aunties and all sorts staying over. 'We'll take him at the first good spot we come across.'

The cloned Saab continued to follow the detective's. That good spot appeared just a minute later, a mile east of the police station, on Hemsworth Road, on the southern edge of Lees Hall Golf Club. A hundred metre portion of the road passed through high, leafy trees, and there was nobody about. Perfect.

Jimmy figured the same thing. Without query or announcement, both men dragged on balaclavas at the same time. Jimmy stamped his accelerator onto the floor and cut into the oncoming lane. Once alongside the detective's car, he yanked his steering wheel to the left, to ram the vehicle. Right before it happened, the middle-aged detective looked out of the driver's window and Sean looked out of his own. Their faces were just inches apart when the cars kissed, and their eyes met.

The detective's car was thudded to its left, off the tarmac

and into long grass, where it bounced and skidded and came quickly to a stop. By that point Jimmy's car had halted in the middle of the road and both men were running.

The detective knew he was under attack and locked his door and pulled his phone. Jimmy crashed his machete into the window. Sean, by his side, reached into the vehicle and snatched the phone, and lobbed it away. Jimmy then put the blade against the detective's throat.

'Go on, tell us you've got a newborn baby and you're your mother's primary carer,' Sean said. Wise cracks while in the heat of action were something he couldn't help, although he always regretted them in the calm of long afterwards.

The detective didn't get chance to respond. Sean reached inside the car to disengage the central locking. He opened the door and both men dragged the detective out. They marched him, blade against neck, into the trees, where he was tripped to his knees and told to lie flat on his stomach, hands locked behind his back. He obeyed without word.

'Not wondering why?' Jimmy said.

Now that he was where they wanted him and the blitz of activity was over, Harper wasn't so awestruck. He was far from relaxed, but he spoke without stutter or ragged breath. 'Maybe revenge for something. I'm sure you'll tell me.'

'In a moment,' Sean said. He pulled his phone and dialled Neil's number. Noah answered instead. When Sean got his brother on the line, he said, 'Got him. Live. You ready?'

Neil laughed. 'You're a madman, bro. But go for it. Put me on speaker so he can hear me.'

Sean did so then squatted by the detective. 'Neil Webb's wife. Tesco. A few days ago. You came up to her. What did you say to her?'

'Nothing,' Harper moaned. 'I mean, nothing bad. I didn't

insult her or anything. I didn't make any threats. What did she say? That I threatened her?'

Jimmy tapped the detective's temple hard with the side of his machete. 'No more lies.'

'Okay, okay. Look, fellas, I was just winding her up. Is that him on the phone? Mr Webb, I didn't insult your wife, and I'm sorry if I upset her. That's the truth.'

'Where is she?' Neil yelled through the phone.

'I don't know. I thought... I don't know, I swear.'

'Thought what?'

'There's rumours that you... did her in.'

'You're horse-shitting me, and you're going to pay. Break his damn fingers.'

Jimmy immediately used his free hand to reach for one of Harper's. Sean slapped it away. 'Just fucking wait.' He stood and walked a few metres away, and he killed the speakerphone setting. To Neil he said, 'Hang on a minute, he just said he doesn't know.'

'Where's my wife?'

Sean realised his brother was trying to speak to the detective. 'I took it off speaker. Neil, you heard him. He doesn't know. She's not with the cops.'

'Are you for real? Of course he'd say that.'

'I believe him. You heard how he acted when we mentioned Holly. He's worried that we're here for revenge.'

'Are you fucking stupid, Sean? He's playing you. It's a trick. He knows. Now break that bastard's bones until he tells you where they're hiding that bitch.'

'I saw his eyes and you didn't, Neil. He doesn't know anything about a safe house. You heard it as clear as I did. He thinks we're here to slap him to defend her honour. Use your logic.'

'Watch who you're talking to. Put me back on speaker and

let me talk to that knobhead. I'll find out the truth. Don't make me come down there.'

At this moment Jimmy stood up and turned to Sean – away from the detective. 'What's going on? Are we chopping this guy up or what?'

In that moment, Harper saw his chance and snatched it. He was on his feet in a second, giving the men his back and firing his legs. Jimmy heard it, turned, and swung back the arm holding the machete.

'No, don't–' Sean said, but an atomic second too late to change anything. The blade came down, cutting deep into the detective's shoulder where it met the neck. Harper uttered a terrible squeal but continued running. His flesh and bones had a tighter grip on the blade than Jimmy's hand did, and his forward momentum yanked the weapon right out of his enemy's fingers.

Two steps later, he stumbled and fell. Jimmy rushed for him and Sean, yelling for a cease of action, bolted for Jimmy. He was too late again. Jimmy bent down, grabbed the machete, yanked it free from the writhing man's shoulder, and gave him another whack.

Sean shoulder-barged Jimmy away before the third blow, but it didn't transform a damn thing. Harper's head was cleaved open, and if he wasn't dead he would be very soon.

7

Both brothers were highly pissed, but they displayed it in different ways. Neil barked orders down the phone. He wanted Harper's car and the body taken to Cowbell Farm for disposal. He wanted a wide swathe of the woods set alight to destroy evidence. The cloned Saab would also have to be destroyed. Nobody had driven past to see the scene, which was lucky, because in his current mood, Neil might have ordered another death. As for the fallout once Harper was reported missing, Neil would try to shift blame elsewhere.

After that, he turned to future of his men. He dealt with Jimmy first. 'Go down south or something, and lie low, you piece of shit. Give it six months or so. Don't contact anyone from up here. But I'll take care of you down there, although I should goddamn bury you for this. Open your big mouth to someone about this and I'll do just that, with your fucking sister's corpse on top of you. Call Noah and he'll help you arrange how to get down there. Now fuck off before I change my mind.'

His orders to Sean, while equally vehement, were of a different variety. He didn't want to send his brother away. 'You stick to that pest control shit, you dumb fuck, since it's all you're good for. But I'm dialling you down, okay? Restricted duty due to stupidity. Maybe you'll only be fetching pizzas from now on, although you'll probably fuck that up. If your boys moan that they're out in the cold, tell them it's because their leader is a brainless squid. Now, sack of shit one, help sack of shit two clean that mess up.'

Jimmy was quite peeved that Sean hadn't fielded a hefty punishment like his own. After Neil's call was done, Jimmy said, 'I see how the boss decided to come down easy on his bro. You've got a fucking charmed life, haven't you? He carries you and protects you from all the scary, bad shit. Can't put a foot wrong, eh?'

Sean ignored him. The two men got to work quickly. Sean took the detective's wallet and they loaded the body into the boot of his own car, which Jimmy would drive to the farm. Sean would follow in Jimmy's vehicle. A new ride would be waiting for them at the farm. Still no other drivers had been past, and no CCTV covered this remote section of road.

Sean displayed his own anger in silence. Jimmy read it in the dagger eyes Sean harpooned into the side of his head as they loaded the dead detective into the boot of the car.

'What?' Jimmy said. 'Had to be done. Ain't the first. Too much for you? Squeamish?'

Once the detective's car was on the road again, Sean doused a large section of grass in petrol and Jimmy set it alight. It seemed to please him. They got out of there, still unseen.

He followed Jimmy's vehicle to the farm. As always, they avoided the CCTV-covered A-road that led to the main entrance and accessed the property by turning off a rural lane running north along its western flank. This put them in an unused grass field by the M1. There was a packed-dirt track encircling the field, but it didn't offer a direct path north to the farm buildings because of a stream with a busted bridge.

They had to drive anti-clockwise around the whole field, which took them past the blank side of the box trailer positioned near the motorway. On the side facing the motorway, it laughably advertised a burglar alarm company. Even worse, the farmer once claimed a family had wanted to advertise their missing family member there – someone Neil had had whacked and burned just a few hundred metres away. No one believed that tale.

The farmer was waiting at the end of the track, to guide them through his land to the incinerator. He always insisted on this to make sure nobody deviated from the route and tore up his fields, even though they had already been churned to mush by his own machinery.

Jimmy again noticed Sean's demeanour as they unloaded the body from the car. After they heaved it into the Volkan, he said, 'Would you have preferred the bastard to escape and tell his cronies all about us? We'd be hiding in a sewer or in cuffs if not for me. Calm down.'

Sean hadn't said a word to Jimmy since they left the kill site, and didn't change that now. The farmer fired up the flames, then led both cars to the barn where they'd be turned to fragments of metal. Again he walked ahead like a director leading a funeral procession.

When the drivers exited the vehicles after guiding them into the barn, which already played host to a run-down Seat Ibiza, Jimmy decided to voice his distaste at Sean's attitude for a third time. 'Are you sad, is that it? Sad about some damn copper? Grow some guts, you pussy.'

Sean opened the bloodstained boot of the Saab. 'Toss that machete in. You can't keep it. DNA.'

Jimmy didn't want to lose his weapon, but in it went. As soon as his fingers let go, Sean arced a kick into the man's stomach. It doubled him over. Sean grabbed his straggly beard and hauled him forward so his head entered the mouth of the open boot. Down came the lid, hard into the back of his neck. Sean added the weight of his torso, with one foot hooked under the rear bumper to keep himself locked in place. Jimmy panicked and started thrashing.

'Why are you killing him?' the farmer said, standing in the doorway. He sounded no more concerned than if he'd asked why Sean was suddenly taking his shoes off.

'Odd number of friends. Superstitious. Just give me a couple of minutes here.'

Sean held Jimmy's neck trapped between the metal jaws until the body lost strength and fell limp. And then for another two minutes just to be sure. Jimmy collapsed to the pitted concrete floor, dead, when Sean released his weight from the boot lid.

'That's another thousand quid if he's going in the fire,' the farmer said.

'Can you burn half now and the rest when I get more money?'

'Cash up front, pal.'

It was a joke, and the guy was supposed to laugh. But his curtness annoyed Sean. 'No thanks,' he replied, heading for the door.

'Hey, you can't just leave him here.'

'He's not my property. Came here on his own two legs. If you want him burning, go do it. But if you pay me twenty quid, I'll help you carry him.'

The farmer couldn't believe his ears, but Sean stuck with his play just for the fun of it. Eventually, the farmer gave in and the two men delivered another meal to the Volkan.

Sean collected the new vehicle and drove back to the car park where Jimmy's Honda Jazz waited. He parked it in the spot where from which they'd collected the cloned Saab and took a walk. A mile away, he called a taxi to take him home. He paid the fare with the farmer's £20 note.

He got his own car and drove to The Chubby Grub. Thursday evening was dominoes night for the local old folk, and they were allowed to bring their dogs. Neil didn't allow entry to anyone under thirty, including staff, so he worked behind the bar all by himself. He liked the chilled atmosphere.

Neil was playing pool with a man of about sixty. Neil saw Sean but didn't acknowledge him, which was a clear sign big bro was still pissed at him. Sean watched him purposefully cannon into the black and sink it in a pocket, to end the game. His opponent waved his arms triumphantly. Neil headed behind the bar and Sean took a stool before it. Neil poured him a pint and got a bottle of water for himself. They moved to one of three booths near the back of the lounge. Neil still hadn't spoken.

'Jimmy doesn't need a holiday,' Sean said. 'He won't be telling anyone anything, not until he's resurrected. But he'll probably be back as a slug, so you're safe.'

He saw Neil's shoulders relax. 'I won't even ask. That's going to cost me more for the incinerator. Where's the body? Where did you do it?'

'You need a loyalty card. Buy four get the fifth free. Anyway, he's burned up already. I did it at the farm.'

Neil shook his head, but he was smiling. 'Jesus Christ, bro. You're unhinged, and you hide it well.'

Sometimes Sean didn't doubt that. People could piss him off easily, and just as easily he could end their lives. But only scumbags the world wouldn't miss. That didn't make it right, but he never lost sleep and didn't believe in heaven and hell.

'At least that's the problem of Jimmy's mouth sorted,' Neil said. 'Luckily for you he was the only guy who saw you backchat me, and now he's gone. That's two of my men you've put away. Can I keep some?'

'One or two. But you do hire lunatics.'

'My brother seems to be the biggest one of all. And don't think you're forgiven for that cop, even if Jimmy did it. Some serious damage control will be needed to stop the rozzers coming to my door for this one.'

Sean dumped the dead detective's wallet on the table. When someone got killed, Neil liked to have the victim's identification and banks cards, which could be planted somewhere to help 'feed the fuzz' a murder suspect. 'You didn't get where you are today by being no good at that.'

Neil had to serve a customer. Upon return he said, 'Holly's now been reported missing.'

Sean had to admit that he'd been approached by police, in case Neil already knew. He told the story and emphasised that he'd given up nothing. 'So doesn't that prove she's not in league with the police?'

Neil clucked his tongue. 'I don't know. The cops might want us to think that.'

'They'd let the public think a woman's missing when she's not?'

'If she's a CI, only a few of the top brass know. They had no control over one of her mates reporting her missing, or the low-level cops going looking for her.'

'I don't buy that. They'd get in trouble for hiding her and letting the country think she might be dead. I think she's just hiding out on her own. No safe house. No CI status. The cops think you whacked her.'

Neil gave this some thought. 'I know. You might be right. Doesn't decrease the urgency. If she gets captured by the cops or decides to hand herself in, she's going to tell them everything she knows. We can't risk losing the Allerby Job.'

This allowed Sean a nice lead into his burning question: CCTV. His worry was that cameras would eventually show

Holly driving from The Chubby to the safe house – the one Sean had apparently searched.

Neil shook his head. 'My own cameras showed her go left out of the car park. There's a newsagent on Scott Road that showed her head down there. There's another further down, but she wasn't on that. I think she turned into the cemetery. I've not seen anything since. There's too many ways out of there.'

'She knew what she was doing,' Sean said. Thanks to him, of course. Avoiding cameras was exactly why he'd sent her into the cemetery. The footpaths weren't designed for cars, but they were wide and mostly straight. At that time of the morning very few people would have seen her vehicle in the grounds.

There were six exits and unless Neil knew which one she'd taken, he'd have a lot of CCTV in the surrounding streets to get through. The exit Sean had directed her to had a police station nearby, and for sure Neil would not be sending people into that zone to bully householders for their Ring doorbell footage.

'I guess she picked up a few tips from me,' Neil said. 'But we'll get her. Anyway, moving on. Allerby House. Meet me at this postcode tomorrow at noon.' He wrote it on a napkin. 'Now get out of here. No under thirties allowed. Besides, I can't risk you killing one of my customers for looking at you funny.'

8

'I messed up.'

'How? What have you done?'

During the drive to Holly's B&B, Sean had hoped for heavy traffic, or roadworks. He hadn't been looking forward to this conversation. This admission.

He'd also delayed broaching the subject by showing her the clothing he'd bought for her. But he couldn't avoid the sore matter for long, so he now launched into it. He told it all. Every detail of his silly plan.

Neil had believed that Sean wanted to interrogate Detective Harper to find a safe house address for Holly, but that was all a lie. In truth, he had hoped the officer would confirm that Holly wasn't sided with them, wasn't an informant, and hadn't sold out her husband.

The news of the detective's death hurt her badly. She sat on the bed with her head bowed and cried. Sean had to wait. Eventually she gave a vocal response. 'What did you hope to achieve with this damn plan of yours?'

In that ideal world, Neil would forgive Holly, and she would be free of him.

'Free?' she said. 'I'm married to him.'

Ah. About that. 'He's got another woman.'

'What? Already?'

He couldn't tell her Neil had probably been dating this woman for a while. He explained that he'd seen a chance for a beautiful ending. If Neil had a new lover, he would let Holly out of the marriage, and maybe he wouldn't mind if his own brother dated her.

'You idiot,' she said. 'This isn't a soap opera. Neil still wants me dead, and one man already is. A police officer. An innocent man.'

'I know. I'm sorry. I feel bad enough about this, Holly. I was trying to do the right thing. I didn't think it through.'

'Well, you need to think long and hard now. Every law enforcement agency in the UK is going to jump aboard the investigation.'

'I know. I tried to save the guy.'

She gave him a smile. It was weak, but the intent made him feel better. 'Thank you for trying to save me. But what do we do now?'

If there was one shining light in the darkness, he'd found it by interrogating Detective Harper. Until that moment, he'd still held doubts about Holly. He'd wanted to believe she wasn't in league with the police, but total commitment had been out of reach.

Now it wasn't. Neil hadn't believed Harper, but Sean had. That day at the supermarket hadn't been a planned meet between informant and handler. It had been a random encounter instigated by an off-duty copper who saw a chance to lob some abuse at the woman sleeping with the guy he couldn't nail.

She had Sean's trust again, and that meant he could give extra consideration to a wild idea that had been bouncing around his head. By no means was it ideal and might not even be feasible. But it was the only option available.

'We run.'

That paused her. He waited for a laugh, or a slap, or some other method of telling him that his plan was outrageous. It didn't happen.

'For real?'

Now that she hadn't shot him down, yes, for real. 'We take off out of this city, go somewhere new. Me and you.'

'Can you abandon your life just like that? For me? That's what it would take. Neil won't stop coming after me. And if you vanish, too, he's likely to think both things are connected.'

'Abandon my life? What damn life?'

He told her about the visit by the police, and what it meant: he was a target. He'd been living in a dreamworld by thinking he had somehow avoided becoming a blip on law enforcement radar. Now he was clear-headed and knew what the future held. He couldn't hope to live a normal life until the end of his days.

He'd once told Holly that he wanted a house that killers wouldn't break into, a wedding that the cops wouldn't stake out, and kids who wouldn't be murdered by enemies on the way to school. Well, he could quit the crime trade right now, but it would be like giving up a fifty-year, thirty-smokes-a-day habit: the damage was already done.

Vengeful enemies might forgive and forget, but the police never would. The news was full of stories of villains being snapped in handcuffs even decades after a crime. Like his dad had said, *It's only a matter of time, son.* Marriage, mortgage, kosher career? Maybe in the next life, bozo.

'Don't talk like that,' Holly said. She stood so she could look directly into his eyes. 'We'll be okay. We'll deal with whatever comes. We can get through this. So let's start thinking about what we need to do. I need you committed.'

She was right. In the same way that he could instantly lose the plot and do something lethal and wild, he could also snap himself back on track at a moment's notice. He did it now.

'Okay. You need to call some friends and tell them you're okay. That's priority one. We can't have the police thinking you might be dead and then launching a murder inv–'

'Have I been reported missing?' she cut in, surprised.

'Yes, by friends. It was always coming. So, you call them, let them know you're fine but that you won't be coming back. Say you left Neil because he's an inconsiderate husband, something like that. Something that will also get the cops off his back about it. That might ease him down a gear or two.'

'I will. I will.' She took both of his hands. 'Can we really do this? Run somewhere Neil won't ever find us? Start a new life together? Just like that?'

'Not quite just like that.' He explained that going missing wasn't quite as easy as saying 'I'm off and don't come looking for me'. It might work with friends, but not the police, and especially not for her. Given who her husband was, they would want to ask her a thousand questions. 'They're going to think you might tell them juicy things about Neil's criminality. They'll want to ask those questions in their own backyard, meaning at a station and on tape.'

'I won't go in.'

'I wouldn't put it past them to try something cheeky. Section 136 of the Mental Health Act, for instance. They could use that to remove you. The wife of Sheffield's biggest bad boy criminal isn't going to be allowed to just disappear with everything she knows.'

Holly looked horrified, but also nodded her understanding. 'So what do we do?'

'We need money. A lot of it. We can't get normal jobs, certainly not for a while. Not until we can work out a way to get the police to leave us alone, and not with Neil still on the hunt. Have you got any you can access?'

'No. I mean, I could always have money, but Neil has all the bank cards. He always let me have money when I needed it. It wasn't a control thing... it...'

'I get it. A paranoia thing. You know that he watches his employees' transactions.'

'I have a bank account in my name, though. I can visit a bank and–'

'No. Neil mentioned that you hadn't been to a bank, so I think that means he has people watching them. Maybe not all the branches because there's too many, but if you picked the wrong one... Besides, now that you're officially missing, the police will have contacted your bank and everyone's now en garde. Even if you go to a branch a hundred miles away, the staff will grab a phone and the cops will meet you at the door.'

Her shoulder sagged. 'Don't you have a secret stash?'

'No. I live frugally. Never needed cash.'

'The thrill of the lifestyle was enough for you, right?'

He ignored the comment, aware that he didn't really have a defence. 'There's hidden money, but I don't know where. I'll try to think of something, but I'll need time, though.'

The shoulders sagged further. 'So I have to stay here?'

'Hell no. Soon the cops are going to put your face out there in the public. Someone will recognise you. I might know a place you can go, though. But you won't like it.'

'All dream holidays must end, I guess,' she said with sarcasm but a genuine smile. 'So how will you get this money?'

He wished he knew.

9

Allerby House was a grade I listed country house set in 500 acres of natural parkland near Burton-Under-Edge, just off the Stocksbridge Bypass. Entry to the grounds was free, for only parts of it were walled, mostly alongside main roads, and there were a hundred ways in for pedestrians. Accessing the 17th century building cost £2.50. Families and couples and even a busload of schoolkids had chosen this fine morning to visit.

Sean met his brother in the main car park close to the house. Neil looked a little worn out and was quiet. In another setting, like The Chubby during closed hours, Sean might have worried that Neil had come across some information dangerous to their relationship. But not here. If Neil planned to do him harm, it wouldn't happen in such a public place.

But his brother's tired eyes made him feel guilty. He had stolen the man's wife. The marriage had fallen apart and Neil had tried to have her murdered... but no sum of wrongs equalled a right.

Still without a word spoken, Neil jerked his head – let's go – and they walked onto the grass and up an incline towards the large house.

Fifty metres short, they stopped at a path where there was a free bench. The elevated position gave a fine view for miles around, except for in the direction of the giant house.

'I should come here more often,' Neil said. 'It makes you realise how nasty the concrete jungle is.'

Sean wasn't in the mood for idle chat. Neil had been planning what he called the Allerby Job for months, those two words were about as much as he'd told anyone. It wasn't like him to keep details of a score so close to his chest, and it made everyone thirsty for more. Sean was amongst them.

'So what are we doing here? It's not to enjoy the scenic view.'

'Don't spoil the moment. Just sit and look.'

'I've looked. Awesome. Come on, Neil. This job is just days away and I don't know anything.'

'Let's walk some more.'

Neil led him towards the house. The schoolkids had formed a queue at the entrance. When they were close enough to be in its shadow, Sean said, 'This place will be highly alarmed. There will be security guards overnight. Dogs might roam.'

'This way,' Neil said, veering to take a path that ran along the left flank of the building.

'Are we after Victorian sewing machines?'

Neil ignored him. On the other side of the hill it sat upon, they paused again. Neil pointed out the view once more. But much closer to home this time: a picnic area with benches on a flat section of grass carved into the hill, about fifty metres away.

'We're robbing people of their Cokes and sandwiches?'

Neil needed a second to get the joke. 'No, further. Down the bottom.'

The hill flattened out about a hundred metres away, but little changed thereafter. It was just more grass, although there was a square pond with stone animals at the corners.

Neil pulled from his pocket a tri-folded flyer, which he'd also folded in half. He opened it up to show a map of Allerby Park on the back. The building was behind them, so they faced north.

'We're not breaking into the house,' Neil said. He tapped a portion of the map. Sean looked down the hill, at the corresponding part of the landscape. The same flat expanse of lawn with the pond.

'Gotcha,' Sean said. 'Japanese Koi. Four hundred quid a pop.'

'Just listen. I'm not stupid enough to rob from a stately home. Shit's worth nothing. Look here.'

Neil's finger moved along the map, east, towards a line of trees and, just beyond them and running parallel, the perimeter wall. Inside this alleyway created by brick and tree were a small, tarmacked area (CAR PARK C) and a road that ran to a gateway (ENTRANCE C) in the north perimeter wall. None of this was visible to Sean's eyes because of the treeline, although he could make out a small gap in the trees that gave access to and from the car park.

Neil's finger traced down the exit road, as if leaving the park. Sean was puzzled because the map showed no features on the eastern side of the trees. That space contained only the road and car park. 'Am I missing something?' Sean said.

But then he saw something. There was a feature after all. About thirty metres from the end of the road, set on the thin strip of grass between road and perimeter wall, it was a tiny pin with a picture of a knife and fork in it. On the map's key, this was called ENDRO'S RESTAURANT.

'We're robbing a restaurant?'

'You'll see. Let's walk.'

They headed down the hill, aiming at an angle towards the treeline. Sean took the map from Neil and looked again at the restaurant. He understood why Neil thought it would be a prime target. The road was hidden and the building was close to Entrance C, for a quick getaway onto the main road.

'Let me ask you a question,' Neil said. 'Remember I mentioned a guy called Zippy? The guy I put on tailing Holly that day when she met the detective.'

Sean had to calm his roiling guts. Had Neil acquired dangerous new information after all? 'Yeah. What of him?'

'He turned. He's been working with the Robinson crew.'

Sean felt his muscles relax. Threat over... for now.

The Robinson brothers thought they were big-time gangsters and tried to model themselves on the Kray Twins from the 1960s. Their numbers weren't big and they didn't have the clout that Neil wielded, but they were vicious bastards and had a scary reputation because of it. They dealt in drugs and prostitutes and protection, but also liked to steal from other gangs.

One of their more infamous members was a Brazilian hitman called The Rider, who taxed drug dealers and robbed shops. He posed a scary sight, all in black: bike, race suit, helmet. Only he didn't exist as such. The Robinson brothers had invented him and sent different guys out on the bike, perhaps hoping to create an urban legend. Like the artist Banksy.

'Last night The Rider robbed one of our burger vans in Shirecliffe,' Neil said. 'My people saw part of a grey ponytail sticking out from his helmet. It was Zippy.'

Sean understood. 'And you got him?'

Neil told the tale. Just a few hours ago, Zippy had been at home, where he lived with his mother, when three men burst in while he was watching the movie *Fight Club* with her.

'The Brad Pitt character is just imaginary,' one guy said. 'Now you know the ending, so let's go.'

Two guys grabbed Zippy, still in his pyjamas, and dragged

him away. His next ten hours would be spent locked in a car boot. His mother, who had no idea of the lifestyle her boy led, could only watch in shock. The third thug lingered for a few seconds to confirm that she knew the dangers of talking to the cops.

'He denies it all,' Neil said, 'but one of my men saw the dirt bike in his lock-up garage. Right now Zippy is locked up and he'll be at Room X tonight. For trial. I've got The Triad coming in specially.'

Muscles clenched again. This was real bad news. Zippy probably didn't know about Sean's affair with Holly, since that was meaty information the Robinson brothers could use to bargain with Neil. But if he had spied them together and had kept that bombshell quiet for some reason, well, it was coming out when he got worked over in Room X.

'The Triad? Those idiots? Overkill.'

'They get the job done.'

'Anyone could when they've got torture equipment. There's no skill in that. They're just idiots. Kids could do what they do with the right tools. The real challenge is to talk someone into giving information up.'

Neil laughed. 'How would you know?'

'You think I can't? You think I've never had to? Cancel those guys and send me in there. I'll show you how a master works.'

'Shut up. Since when did you ever like that side of things?'

True, he'd never gotten involved in the Room X activities. Not his style. But nor was getting his head lopped off because of a woman. He now had a chance to find out if he and Holly were blown, and he might be able to make sure Zippy never told a soul. There was a problem, though. Neil insisted that two people had to be present with a prisoner in case he tried something naughty. There would be no way to talk to Zippy alone.

'And I won't need stupid tools to do it, either. Hundred quid says I walk in there and just use my gob and I get Zippy to give up where he's hid the money.'

Neil folded his arms. 'Okay, then you've got it. But bring your money.'

'And make sure nobody asks him any questions until then. I want him fresh.'

Neil laughed. 'Okay, bro. He's just rotting alone right now anyway.'

'Good. So tonight I...' Sean paused, surprised at what lay before him.

During this talk, they had walked through the squared gap in the trees, past the car park, which had space for only a dozen vehicles, and down the exit road. Sean's word faltered as he saw the restaurant called Endro's, about a hundred metres away. But it wasn't a restaurant at all.

It was a half-finished construction, with scaffolding and bricks piles and other detritus scattered around, all of it wrapped up in portable plastic mesh fencing. Sean didn't say a word until they were up close.

'Allerby House is owned by English Heritage. It's a charity. Relies on donations. If you steal from them, that's–'

'I do have a soul, Sean. This restaurant is owned by a private company. It's a corporate partnership. That's why it's perfect.'

'For stealing cement or something? There's nothing of worth here.'

'Exactly. You think I'd plan something this major for cement? It's a corporate partnership, which means the people who run the park don't know the ins-and-outs of this construction project. I do know the builders don't work at the weekend. Now stop asking questions and take a photo.

'What? What is going on here? Are you making this shit up as you go along?'

Neil laughed. 'All will be revealed. Follow me.'

Sean took his picture of the restaurant and they walked on, past the building and through the open exit, which had a fixed height barrier at two metres. Neil told Sean to take a picture of it.

'What is going on here?' Sean said.

Outside the perimeter wall, Underway Lane ran parallel, with only a six-foot strip of grass separating them. On the far side of the road was a low stone wall, beyond which were rolling fields. In this remote area, neither side of the road had a pavement.

Neil pointed to their right. Thirty metres away, perimeter wall side of the road, a portion of the grass had been removed for a bus stop lay-by. Neil got Sean to take a photo of that, too.

'Are we coming by bus? What the hell is this job?'

'I'll explain that later, little bro. It's happening Sunday.'

'Two days? Are you kidding? Then I need to know the score.'

'And you will. On Saturday night. Your patience can wait a day.'

Sean laughed. 'It's already worn thin.'

CHAPTER 4

1

On the day he turned eighteen, Neil finally achieved what he'd planned for so long: he got his own place. It was a flat on the middle floor of a three-storey block in a less-than-desirable part of the city, cash rented. He was over the moon. And he wanted a flatmate.

Gran was happy to see the back of the brothers. In the intervening years, she had become irritated by them. For hours every day, Neil cracked balls around on a six-foot snooker table he'd put on top of the dining table, while Sean read books to loud music. They'd made friends with local hoodlums and a steady stream of fools knocked on her door. Even when the brothers went out, they'd join groups of idiots to loiter on the road, which caused Gran's neighbours to constantly complain.

Money was an issue, too. Gran had expected Neil to work upon leaving school, but he was still unemployed two years later. He made income from shoplifting and street muggings, but these activities, and the spoils, had to be shielded from Gran. He'd managed to take driving lessons, buy and insure and tax a car, but somehow without earning a penny.

At fifteen, Sean was still a minor and legally required the care of a guardian. Neil expected to have to apply, but Gran said she'd continue to take that role as long as the brothers were out of her hair. She got Guardian's Allowance.

On leaving day, Gran got the boys up early and shooed them out the door without breakfast. Neil had been driving for six months and had an old banger, which they loaded their suitcases and Neil's snooker table into. En route, Sean tried to take advantage of Neil's happy mood.

'I want to go see Dad,' he said.

'After what he did? Are you for real? This came out of the blue.'

Sean understood why Neil would think that. With nobody to take him to the prison, Sean had ceased talking about Dad. Now it was different. 'I had to wait until you turned eighteen. You can visit him, and you can take me.'

Neil didn't have to think. 'No way. I'm not going there. He's a fucking beast.'

'It was an accident. He got stuffed.'

Neil rubbed Sean's hair. 'You're a smart kid most of the time. But we all have some dead zones in the brain. This is one of yours. Don't ask me again. Wait until you're eighteen.'

Sean was Neil's blood, but there was something off about his big brother. Something perhaps more monstrous than Donald Webb. Sean knew he could get a lot of leeway with Neil, but there would be a limit. And he might regret overstepping that line. He would not push the subject. He would wait the three years until he was legally allowed to visit Dad on his own. Until then, the letters they swapped would have to suffice.

On their first night in their new flat, Neil and Sean were visited by one of the other block residents, a middle-aged lady called Kitty, who lived directly below them. Her first utterance was to state that she was the local gossip and that they could come to her for a chat about other people anytime. As if to prove her worth, she launched into a tirade about their neighbours.

She had some bizarre nicknames for them. The most intriguing three were the 'ninnyhammer', the 'grisette', and the 'vagabonds'. The ninnyhammer was a fat, middle-aged man who liked to play loud music and mouth off to complainants. The grisette always had strange men around, and they probably paid her for sex. The vagabonds were a young couple deep into heroin and street terror.

The Webb brothers met them one after the other over three nights. First up, the ninnyhammer, who had the flat on their left. Close to midnight on that first evening, his music started blasting next door. It shook Neil's bedroom wall. Hell no.

Sean saw Neil leave the flat, but had no clue why. The blanks got filled in when he heard a mighty thud outside and glanced out the window. And the loud music had stopped. Scattered on the grass outside the block were pieces of a big, old hi-fi system. Neil was back seconds later. 'Peace and quiet,' he said.

'He might call the cops.'

Neil shook his head. The ninnyhammer didn't dial 999, and never again played loud music.

The next night, the brothers were playing snooker when they heard shouting from the flat above. And thuds and bangs that sounded like people brawling. When it was over, they heard feet thudding down the communal stairs, fast. The brothers watched out their window as an unknown man ran away down the path to the road and away. Neil decided it was time to meet the grisette.

When the scraggy twenty-something opened the door,

exposing a dark flat, the first thing she said was, 'Can you lend me twenty quid? I need to put my electric on. Or I'll suck your dick for twenty.'

Neil said, 'Not my thing. Skint anyway. Was that guy a punter? Refused to pay?'

'Are you calling me a hooker?'

'No. Maybe a whore. Nicer ring to it. Haven't you got a pimp?'

'Piss off.' She slammed the door. When Neil walked away, Sean got out his wallet. He, too, made cash from lifting goods from stores and selling them on. He slotted a £20 note through the letter box.

On the third night, the vagabond couple headed out to meet friends, who parked their cars on the grass outside the block, even though the street had spaces. Ten youths loitered around, dropping their mess, being loud, and giving abuse to pedestrians. Neil didn't give a flying hoot until he saw the male vagabond, who was about twenty, lean against his car.

Sean followed him out the door, where he watched his brother walk right through the middle of the gang and up to the vagabond. 'You seem to be touching my car, my friend. Can you get off?'

The vagabond slapped the bonnet a bunch of times, each strike sending a gong-like peal into the air. 'This car, my friend? This one here.'

Neil used a similar slap right on the guy's face, which floored him in one. 'Yes, my friend, that car right there.'

The brothers turned to the others, ready for action. 'Who's hard?' Neil said. 'Next guy, up you come. There's ten of you, so odds are someone's got the gonads.'

If they did, none was on show that night.

Sean had long wanted a real job, and a couple of days later he secured an evening shift as a till operative at a mini-mart. His age meant he couldn't legally work after 7pm, but the role was cash-in-hand and doubtless off the books. He didn't care.

After his first shift, which he'd enjoyed, as he walked home he called Neil to tell him there was a second role available at the store. Neil said, 'Nah. I've got something going on work-wise. A good earner. You'll see when you get back.'

Once he got home, he found a visitor. Neil sat in the living room with the grisette, who had a black eye. He said, 'This is Sandra. She wants our help.'

Every night, Sean had heard men entering Sandra's property for sex, and on two occasions things had turned violent. He said nothing, already suspecting what kind of help Neil was offering.

'She's sick of punters bashing her and not paying,' his brother said. 'So now we get involved. Protection. This is how it works.'

Sandra already advertised her sexual services on an escort website. Now, when men called her, she would send them to the Webb address instead of her own. Neil and Sean would meet the punters, take the money, and explain the rules. There was only one: hurt this lady and we'll triple it right back at you.

'You want us to be pimps?' Sean said.

'Protectors. She charges thirty for half an hour, fifty for the hour. We get twenty-five per cent, and fifty if we have to step in and save the day. She can do four, five or more a day.'

'Let me think about it,' Sean said. He was firmly on the side of *no,* but didn't want to say it in front of them both.

Sean had the choice snatched away from him the next night. He answered a knock at the door without thinking, to find a nervous-looking fifty-something man in the hallway. And the penny dropped. A punter. He hadn't expected Neil's new business plan to be up and running already.

The guy stumbled over his words. He hadn't figured on a

male answering the door, and certainly not a kid. Sean helped him out. 'You want her for one hour or a half?'

'One hour,' the man said after a fretful pause.

'Fifty,' Sean said. He took the money and directed the punter to the flat above. 'If you touch her in any way that she doesn't like, you'll get the same, okay? Slap for slap. Penetration for penetration.'

'I won't. I just need... my wife left me and...'

'Sure. I get it. Just don't fuck about, okay? Go have fun.' He shut the door.

Much as he hated to admit it, the fifty felt good in his hands, and he'd enjoyed imparting a threat.

Neil returned at 2am, and he woke Sean up to ask how business had gone. They had made over £100. Neil said, 'Not bad for just saying a few words, right?'

Not bad wasn't the same as *good.* The next day Neil brought Sandra to the flat and told her his new idea. He'd heard her on the phone, talking to friends – might one or more of them also like to make extra cash?

Three weeks later, Sandra no longer lived alone. She had three roommates and the group earned roughly fifteen hundred pounds a week. Neil was happy. Sean felt like a scumbag. He kept his cashier job for some sanity.

But Neil wanted even more. He'd long been dealing small amounts of weed, but one night he saw a chance to expand. His own dealer was a decent chap and Neil didn't want to betray him. That feeling didn't apply to others.

Since their confrontation weeks earlier, Neil had had no interaction with the vagabonds beyond steely stares while passing on the stairs or the street. When Neil saw the male collect a baggie of heroin, or B, from someone in a car parked right outside the block, he had a light-bulb moment. He rushed from the flat and met the vagabond in the foyer.

'No hard feelings, eh?' he said.

The vagabond shrugged and tried to walk past. Neil blocked him with an arm, in the hand of which was a £20 note. 'I want some B. Who's your dealer? I'll give you twenty every time I call him.'

The vagabond liked this, and he imparted a phone number. Neil called it and got a man with a southern accent. He asked for £50 of B. The dealer said he never visited a first-time buyer's address, so they met an hour later outside a closed post office on a corner where teenagers hung out. The kids seemed to infest every corner of the estate and every spot with a light. The guy who turned up was fat and nerdy-looking. Neil bought his bag of B and said, 'I need Krokodil.'

The dealer shook his head. 'Don't do shit I've never heard of.'

'Well, if you get any, I need five hundred quid's worth. I'll pay half now if you can get it.'

The dealer almost licked his chops like Scooby Doo and dialled a number from memory. When he put his phone to his ear, Neil slammed an elbow into the fat bastard's face. After the man collapsed like a house of cards, a trio of hard kicks guaranteed there would be no comeback.

A voice was squawking from the dealer's phone, which lay five feet away. Neil picked it up and said. 'I want weed and B in sweetly big quantities, but I don't trust your middle men, so I'll deal direct with you.'

'Who the fuck are you, pal? Where's Badger?'

'Forget Badger. I'm taking all of his customers. You can deal with me direct.'

The guy hung up and he ignored all further calls from Neil for the rest of that night and most of the next day. Until he answered one with, 'Badger says he's out of the game. Because of you.'

'Maybe he's now going straight. Maybe he'll go to college. Might be the best thing that ever happened to him. Tell him he's welcome.'

The dealer paused before saying, 'You don't get the stuff as and when in dribs and drabs, okay? I give you a grand's worth a week, and you owe me seven-fifty for it. You sell none one week, I still get my three-quarters. Every week. Got it?'

'Sure thing.'

The next day, the dealer, who had cornrows and wore a varsity jacket over ripped jeans, met him at a greasy spoon that would probably get its front door nailed shut the next time the Food Standards Agency rocked up. The dealer said, 'Just call me Zeus,' and slid an Xbox controller box across the table. Neil peeked inside to see it was tightly packed with dope. When Sean saw it, he said, 'I'd like an Xbox.' The two men gave him a funny stare.

Zeus ordered Badger to visit Neil with a map detailing his dope distribution points and customer names, including the vagabonds. A week later, all the dope sold, Neil paid Zeus his £750 on time. He got another Xbox controller box.

For a while the relationship worked well. Neil and Sean drove the streets, handing out dope to Badger's customers and lowlifes they'd recruited on their own. On week four, Neil paid Zeus three days early. It was time to up the game, so Neil requested and was given two Xbox controller boxes. £2,000 of weed.

On the day he collected that package, they got robbed.

Midnight. Five masked men in black kicked in their front door and entered with machetes waving. Two guys hit each bedroom to collect a brother, then dumped them on the living room sofa. Guy five watched it happen and did all the talking when the Webbs were seated together with blades pointed at their faces.

'Don't fuck around, lads. Give us the dope and the money, and walk out of here without issue. If we have to turn this place inside out, your heads are coming off.'

Neil gave the location of the £2,000 package of dope and a biscuit tin bearing roughly the same amount in cash. He didn't mention other hiding spots for money. One of the henchmen grabbed the loot and brought it to his boss, who filled his pockets while the brothers watched. 'Nice doing business with you, fellas. Maybe we'll be back one day.'

'We owe for that dope,' Sean said. 'Now we're going to have to pay our dealer with fake cash.'

It was a strange admission, and the men didn't know what to make of it. Without another word, they left. Neil got up to watch through the window, but Sean remained seated. He said, 'I just had a weird nightmare that five blokes burst into our flat and robbed us.'

'What was that crap about paying with fake money?'

Sean was happy to explain.

A week later, Neil met Zeus again in the greasy spoon. The dealer turned up with two heavies, which was a new detail. Neil paid the balance of £2,000, earned through the hard work of his stable of girls. Zeus held one of the notes up to the light, to check its authenticity. Also a new detail. He then handed over another pair of Xbox controller boxes.

'You got a lot of Xboxes?' Neil asked.

'I buy and sell. Get you one cheap if you want.'

'I'm not a fan. I like pool and darts. Anyway, see you next time.'

Back in the car, Neil said to Sean, 'Good call. That fucking tosser.'

On the night of the robbery, Sean had mentioned counterfeit money to the thieves to test a theory. And Zeus had, for the first time ever, checked Neil's payment to make sure it wasn't fake. The dealer had obviously heard about the plan to pay him with duds. And how? Because the slimy backstabber had sent the thugs to the flat.

'So what do we now?' Sean said.

Neil smiled at him. 'Let's get you a free Xbox.'

2

On a Saturday night six months ago, Sandra, the first prostitute ever recruited by the Webb brothers way back, had paid her first and only visit to The Chubby. A local couple was having their wedding reception and a doorman was turning away strangers. Sandra slipped by him and got into the lounge. She approached Neil after he'd finished a friendly game of pool against an employee.

He didn't recognise her, so needed a reminder. If she thought their history would garner aid, she was in for a surprise. He told her didn't offer his assistance for free. But, aware of his pool-game-for-help scheme, she had come prepared. She and friends had scraped together the required £100 pounds to combat him on the table.

At this point Sean returned from the toilet. He recognised Sandra and moved close so he could overhear her tale. Life hadn't been good in the years since she'd left their employ. Unable to find work or a residence, she had fallen in with a homeless crew in Doncaster, who lived under a railway bridge crossing the River Don, up near an Asda store.

The crew had been having trouble with a local gang of thugs

who sometimes woke them at night. It had happened five times over the last two weeks and on each occasion people had been assaulted, their property either stolen or lobbed into the river. One man, who had lightning bolts tattooed on his neck, seemed to be the violent ringleader, and he'd broken Sandra's nose. Sean could see it was bent out of shape.

Neil didn't care, duly wiped the floor with her, and told her to get lost. As she departed, she saw Sean, gave a little nod, and walked on. They didn't exchange a word.

Two hours later, Sean found the Asda next to the railway lines. He stepped over the metal guardrail at the edge of the car park and walked down the overgrown embankment. There was a riverside path, but he remained in the undergrowth. He was fifty metres from the bridge, under which he saw eight or nine people sitting around, lit by a fire in an oil drum. They had sleeping bags, pillows, even furniture like a chest of drawers and a small fridge powered by a battery. It looked cosy.

He watched for two hours, until almost midnight, at which point he stood up to go home, figuring nothing was going to happen tonight. That was when it happened.

A van parked in front of the guardrail halfway between his position and the bridge. Making no attempt at secrecy, three thugs in dark clothing got out and came down the embankment, to the riverside path, then ran towards the bridge. Pandemonium broke out as the homeless spotted them charging, but only a couple ran away. Caught, the others were pushed and punched and forced to empty their pockets. The thugs threw blankets into the river and cackled like witches.

Nobody saw Sean coming, so he took out the nearest guy without issue. He wore a pair of stun gun gloves, one of which he clamped around the man's neck from behind – a manoeuvre specifically warned against in the manual. The thug instantly shrieked, seized up, and was no problem to thrust into the river. His two comrades were now impossible to surprise.

The next nearest guy had a stick, which he raised, but he didn't make a move because Sean withdrew a Taser 7 from a coat pocket. Now he wasn't restricted to close quarters damage. His enemy considered a fight for all of three seconds, before leaping into the water to join his friend. It left number three all alone. Mr Lightning Bolt.

But he ran, too. Away, out from under the bridge. Or he tried to. Two electric probes got him in the back and agitated his nervous system. Down he went. A series of kicks and punches made sure the man wouldn't pose a near-future threat. Sean emptied the man's pockets, which produced a wallet that divulged a driver's licence and a bank card.

'You don't know me, but now I know where you live. The next time you come here, make sure you kill everyone and move all the bodies and leave behind some clues that suggest these people have relocated to another city. Because if I suspect you've been naughty, I'll come see you. Don't report this bank card lost for a week, okay? If it gets cancelled before then, I'll be at your door at three in the morning one day soon. Nod your understanding and give me the PIN.'

After he'd sent the man limping away, the homeless crowded Sean like a superhero. He gave the bank card and pin to Sandra. 'Take out the maximum from a cash machine every day, for a week, then dump the card.'

The adoration made him feel silly, so he quickly left the scene. And that was that. He expected to never to see Sandra or her friends again.

3

'Hey, pervert, want a photograph?'

When he'd gotten closer, the woman peeing in the undergrowth had recognised him. Sandra had been happy to see Sean, but not as pleased as he was to find her and her crew still occupying the space beneath the bridge. Five minutes later, he'd met the old faces again and they had agreed to a swap in circumstances: now they'd help him.

That was earlier. Now, as dusk settled and he paid his second visit of the day, everybody waved upon seeing Sean walk down the embankment. One of the number ran to meet him. She virtually leaped into his arms.

'Treating you good?' he asked.

'Yes,' Holly said. 'They're good people.'

She looked at ease, which surprised him. Holly had always struck him as a little posh and Neil had lavished gifts and money on her, to create a very comfortable lifestyle. When he'd brought her to this new hideout a few hours earlier, she had seemed like a kid being dropped off for a first day at a new school, sans the crying. That had changed. 'No culture clash?'

'No. I expected to hate being here, but I surprised myself.

It's nice to have genuine people around. People who don't watch their behaviour. People I can swear around. I'm getting used to this.'

He understood. As the wife of a gang lord, Holly had an aura that terrified some people in her local community. Pedestrians, shop staff, whoever – they all treated her with utmost respect because of her husband. Or rather, what he could do. One word from her in response to an insult or a bad manner and vicious goons would exact revenge.

They headed to the space under the bridge, where he fist-pumped some of crew. Sandra approached him.

'To say thanks,' he said, holding up the large shopping bag he'd brought. She took it with glee and some of her comrades crowded round for a look inside. It was full of edible goodies. Some of it immediately went on the stove.

Sean and Holly sat on her blanket. He said, 'This little space of yours is cosy.'

She lost her smile. 'Cosy or not, this is not what I want. I want a life with you. So when do we embark on that? Right now doesn't sound too bad.'

'Not right now. I need time to get prepared. I have to hand back my house, clean out the stuff I need, and I can't just skip without word. I'm going to convince Neil that I need a break. I have to go see him soon, so I'll mention it then. There's a big job he's got on that I need to talk my way out of.'

'What is it?'

He paused. 'I can't say.'

She stood up, and glared down at him. 'Why? Do you think I'll pass the details to the police? Are we back to this again?'

'No. There's no need to tell you, that's all. You'll just worry about me. Besides, I don't even know the plan myself.'

'So tell me what you do know? Is it a bank? Are you going to kidnap someone for ransom? What?'

Again he paused. 'Why are you so interested?'

She flicked a dismissive hand at him and walked a few feet from the bridge. She stood at the edge of the river, staring into it. He joined her. 'So now you're pissed at me, right? I don't know any details, Holly.'

'Fine. You can go now. Go plan crimes with the man who wants me dead. Come get me when you're ready. Maybe I'll still be here and waiting, and maybe I won't.'

4

It was a busy Friday night at The Chubby Grub, with two dozen patrons having fun. Down in Room X, the man known as Zippy wasn't having a good time at all. He was tied to a chair, a ball gag in his mouth to prevent screams. But he knew that later, his captors would seek wails of pain.

A guy entered Room X just to make sure the prisoner was alive, then headed back up the concrete stairs and into the chilled cellar, where he joined his two comrades. They sat around a small table, playing cards, waiting for their big moment. These were the brutish, remorseless boys who called themselves The Triad. Their skill was torturing information out of people, and they were eager to get going. That said, they enjoyed a bit of banter and were currently discussing punishment techniques.

'Salt on the feet is a good one,' #1 said. 'Salt. Goats would lick the feet and–'

'What the hell?' #2 cut in. 'You planning to make Zippy aroused and tell us stuff out of joy?'

'Don't knock it. This tickling things drives you insane. Insane.'

'Not in an hour or two, fuckwit.'

'Ice,' #3 said. 'Ice machine right there, look. Bucket of ice, feet dipped in. We tell him he's going to lose his feet. He'll talk non-stop after that. And that'll hurt like hell. I read about this guy in the Arctic who–'

'Force-feeding,' #1 said. 'We stick a tube down the throat and keep shoving food down it.'

#2 laughed. 'He can't talk round a tube, fuckwit. Can we just stick to simple shit like pulling his teeth...'

The three men fell silent as the head barmaid entered. She gave just a nod and then changed a post-mix gas canister.

The barmaid exited the cellar, and returned to the bar, where she pulled a pint of Coke for a customer and then took his food order into the kitchen. A male and female cook were preparing meals.

'But if she's on holiday, then why haven't we heard where?' the male said.

'But who are we to be told?' the female responded. 'Don't you think we're too low level to be in the loop?'

'I don't buy it. You know what the boss does. People who piss him off go missing. I heard a rumour about her having a bloke on the side. If you think his wife is away in the Bahamas or something, why did the cops turn up here this afternoon to talk to him?'

The barmaid slapped down the food order on a counter. 'Watch your mouths,' she told the cooks. 'People who gossip piss the boss off. Especially those talking about his wife. The police are always coming round here. It means nothing. I heard the holiday thing as well, so let's leave it at that. Talk about sports or something.'

The barmaid collected a fruit salad bowl and took it to a booth in the lounge, where another trio of Neil's goons was playing Ludo on their phones. They'd been discussing a worry filtering through the ranks.

'But she was seen with that copper in the supermarket,' said #4. 'Even the boss thinks she might be in protective custody, singing like a canary.'

#5 nodded. 'True. I heard from some guys that he's cut back on some jobs. He cancelled a recon visit to Meadows Street. He cancelled that bookies thing last night, as well. That says he's worried about what she's telling the cops.' He referred to a marijuana farm in a house on the aforementioned street and a robbery at a betting shop.

#6, who pulled a packet of cigars from a pocket, said, 'I'm not sure Holly knows about any of that. And he hasn't cancelled the Allerby Job, has he? And that's a biggie, whatever the fuck it is. That's the one the cops would want to catch us at. He's not worried about that. He hasn't told us anything about it, so I doubt he told her anything.'

#4 spoke around a mouthful of salad. 'We're grunts, and that's his wife. We don't know what she knows. I tell my wife everything. His wife knows more than we think, for sure. I bet she calls half the shots.'

#5 said, 'My worry is the boss talking to the cops. No, hear me out. We don't know what his wife has given up, so we don't know what they have on him. How do we know he isn't working with them? He might have cut a deal. He's cancelled some jobs because the cops can't allow them to go ahead.'

'But the Allerby Job is still a go.'

'Yeah, maybe only because there's, like, twenty of us involved. Maybe we do that and the cops will be there to hoover us all up. That's his big present to them. Maybe that's why he's told no bastard a thing about it yet. I'm calling in sick that day. Fuck that.'

#6 got up to go outside to smoke. As he stepped out of the

main entrance, he held the door for a straggly-looking guy in a red ball cap to leave, and noticed someone else coming in. 'All right, Sean?' he said.

Sean nodded and moved past, into the lounge. He waved to Neil, who as always was on the pool table. He took a seat close to the table. Neil was playing a man of about sixty in a worn suit, who looked like his world just caved in when Neil blew him out of the water.

'Please, Mr Webb,' the man said barely a second after the black thundered into a pocket. 'It would be so easy for you. Just this one thing. We can play again. I'll pay again. This is unfair.'

'Be on your way, mate. Best if you leave, cos your face doesn't fit happy hour.'

The man continued to protest, and it got the attention of those around. That annoyed Neil, who gave a little nod at Noah. The challenger was about to be escorted out. Sean decided to do the honours and grabbed the guy's arm.

When they got outside, Sean said, 'Just walk away. Don't push it. Try again in a week or so when he's forgotten your face. And next time, watch your mouth around him.'

The old man plucked a business card from his pocket. 'Please just give him this. In case he changes his mind.'

Sean took it just to keep things sweet. The card was for a business called Acorn Proofreading. As well as the home address, the card listed a name – Jacob Jansen.

When the old man was gone, Sean returned to the lounge. Neil was racking the balls up to play against himself. Sean said, 'What was that guy's issue?'

'Oh, something about his kid's ashes. His daughter died of a brain thingy about ten years ago. He had her ashes in a necklace but he got burgled the other week. Cops got the guy, some fool lowlife from the Hounds estate, but had no evidence and had to let him go. The old man wanted me to go strong-arm him to hand it over.'

'Didn't you feel bad about that? Could have let him win.'

'Rules are rules, pal. Besides, Adverse Possession. That necklace belongs to the thief now. I have no cause to go rob a man who hasn't harmed me.'

That old 'Adverse Possession' line from their dad. Sometimes it was more of a convenient excuse than a fast policy. Neil was very competitive and unforgiving sometimes. For sure he was irritated by Jansen's claim that he was being unfair.

'Speaking of necklaces,' Neil said, 'when did you start wearing one?' He grabbed a cord around Sean's neck, to lift out the pendant that hung below his shirt. And his eyes widened. He quickly stuffed it out of sight again. 'Jesus, don't be flashing that thing around.'

A few years ago, Sean had stolen a car from a bad guy and found a Viking-style finger knife in the boot. It had a 5cm steel blade and a looped handle for the index finger, which also had a cord so it could be worn as a necklace. Its grooviness had convinced him to keep it.

And now it might come in handy. If Zippy was aware of Sean's love affair with Holly, he would have to be sworn to silence. There might be only one way to achieve that.

Speaking of Zippy, Sean asked if he was here yet.

'Downstairs, waiting for you. The Triad wanted to start ripping him up, but I said we'd wait for you to go do your magic. You bring the money?'

Oh yes. The bet. 'I did, but I won't need it. You don't trust me, do you? You brought those guys in anyway.'

Neil grinned. 'Backup for when you realise you ain't as clever as you thi–'

'You murdering bastard!' someone yelled.

5

The brothers looked towards the owner of the voice. By the entrance was a woman in a trench coat, with unbrushed hair and eye make-up streaked by tears. She wasn't crying now, Neil saw. Her face displayed the opposite emotion to sadness: rage. He recognised her as Francy, Holly's best friend. Just great.

She strode towards him, watched by a now-silent Friday crowd. Neil put down the pool cue so nobody would think he was wielding a weapon. Noah, though, stepped forward and put his hand in his pocket, where Neil knew he had a knuckle-duster.

'Hang fire,' he told his fixer.

Francy came very close, but she stopped on the other side of the pool table, using it as a barrier. Everybody was watching. 'Where is she?'

'I don't know. She left me. I thought everyone knew that.'

That's what you want people to think.' She snatched up a pool ball and lobbed it at him. There was no intent to harm, though, because the shot was weak and the ball barely hurt his arm. He bit back the urge to tell her that was a foul.

'It's the truth, Francy. I don't know where she is. I thought you might. You remember that I sent someone to ask you if you knew?'

'You killed her,' the woman yelled. Neil heard the murmur of shock pulse around the lounge. 'What have you done with her? Why would she just go missing?'

'I don't know what you're talking about,' he said, nice and innocent as he could. 'Why would you think that I'd hurt my wife?'

Actually, why wouldn't she, or anyone else? He'd heard the rumours, fuelled by crap the cops had spread. They had fed the media lines designed to be read between, like *Holly knows some unsavoury people* and *Her husband is a known criminal and operates in a dangerous world* and *Neil Webb hasn't given us any satisfactory answers about his wife's whereabouts.*

Francy's voice got louder. 'Where is she? Where did you bury her?'

Clearly this woman was about to go into meltdown. He kept his manner calm. 'Listen, Francy, step outside with me and I'll tell you what I know. Will you do that? We've got an audience.'

Which was becoming less so. Already his people were walking around, quietly instructing the customers to focus on their drinks and ignore the show. The barmaid had just kicked in the music system and loud rock cascaded from speakers on the walls.

Francy turned on her heels and stormed for the door. Neil told Noah to fetch a certain something then followed her. She moved onto the front lawn, away from a handful of patrons smoking by the porch. But Neil turned left and walked down the side of the building, where they wouldn't be seen. He casually leaned against the flank wall of his property, to promote a calm demeanour, and stared at Francy. Eventually, with a huff of breath, she approached him.

'So tell me,' she said, still angry but not as loud now. 'Where is she? I've heard stories that you did something to her.'

'Of course not. We've been arguing, yes, but I wouldn't ever hurt my wife. Don't you believe that? Did Holly ever give you that impression?'

'No, but she told me your marriage was falling apart. I heard you think she's been telling the police about you, and that's why you killed her. You're a monster.'

Noah appeared, carrying a handheld device. It was a wireless radio frequency scanner that cost almost ten thousand pounds, although Neil got it for free. He swore by it.

'Francy, I need to check you for a wire,' Neil said. 'If you want the truth, you'll let my man scan you. You okay with that?'

'A wire? The police didn't send me here. You're not searching me.'

'No, we just run this thing over your clothing. If you want the truth, this is what it takes. It's your choice.'

She was angry and alarmed, but also intrigued by his promise of answers. She gave her permission by reluctantly holding out her arms. The scanner found her phone and many others in the possession of his customers, but Noah was skilled with the device and reported that there was nothing delivering a signal to or from Francy that was a cause for worry.

She wasn't wearing a wire for the police. Good. Nobody had sent her here, except herself.

Neil smiled at her. 'I know where your kid goes to school, where your husband works, and where you live.'

'What?' Fear welled in her eyes. 'What do you mean by that?'

He wanted to use a cool threat, something outrageous and memorable, but he remembered that this lady had once baked him a cottage pie when Holly was in hospital overnight. That meant something. 'Look, just keep your nose out of my business. And don't talk to the police. You called me a monster. I hope I don't have to show you how right you are.'

6

While Neil was out threatening his wife's best friend, Sean headed to the chilled cellar, where the three bozos calling themselves The Triad were playing cards. They were probably watching the door to make sure no staff entered Room X, and that Zippy didn't escape. They had a bucket of ice for some reason.

'Has anyone asked Zippy questions yet?'

They didn't look happy to see Sean. One said, 'No, Neil said you were to do all the questioning. If he doesn't talk to you, we'll sort him out. Hey, you see this ice? I had this idea–'

'I'll get him to talk,' Sean said, then walked through the iron door, down the concrete steps, and through the door at the bottom. One of The Triad followed him. Neil's two-man rule for being with a Room X prisoner.

Zippy was hunched over in the wooden chair in the centre of the blank room. He was tired, hungry for sure, but his eyes were alert. Sean removed the ball gag from the man's mouth. 'Know why you're here?'

Zippy nodded. 'Someone said. The burger van robbery. All fingers seem to point to me somehow. But The Rider is all different people. They think I've sold out to the Robinson crew.'

Zippy not only didn't seem scared, but he spoke with a smile. It suggested he knew something that he felt might save him. 'After you got snatched, the guys looked in your lock-up garage. Bike's right there. Point those fingers somewhere else and you might walk again.'

'I could do that. No camera in here?'

'Not wise. Imagine if the police found it. You can talk freely.'

'Good. A man and a woman. A Premier Inn in Derby, about six months ago. Saw them with my own eyes. The guy is the one you should be worried about. Maybe they're up to something nasty against Neil.'

Sean paused, staring hard. He felt The Triad thug right behind him, listening. 'Who have you told about them?' he asked Zippy.

'No one, actually.'

'Why would you keep something like that to yourself?'

'I was somewhere I shouldn't have been. Couldn't admit I was there. Plus, it just struck me as funny. I kept it for a rainy day. It's raining.'

Sean turned to The Triad goon. 'You, go get Neil for me... Shut up, I don't care about the two-man rule right now. He's tied up. Go get Neil.'

The goon reluctantly left Room X. Sean touched his chest, where the finger knife hung below his shirt. 'Just to confirm. Who did you see at the Premier Inn?'

'You, and you know it. You're fucking the boss's wife.'

Now there was no doubt. Sean recalled the day in question, when he met Holly for sex at the hotel. He thought they'd cleverly avoided prying eyes. Ironically, Zippy hadn't been following Holly back then. They had been rumbled purely by chance, by someone who was probably doing something he shouldn't have been, whatever it was. For the second time, a random piece of 'shitty freak luck' had now come back to cause havoc. He hoped these things didn't come as a trio.

He moved behind Zippy, and yanked on his necklace cord to extract the blade from beneath his shirt. Zippy tried to turn his head, but Sean grabbed the man's grey ponytail to hold him steady.

'Neil's boys go to work on me,' Zippy said, 'and I'll try to save myself. I'll blurt out everything I know. That little thing might be one of them. Unless...'

Sean tugged on the ponytail slightly, just to tilt up the chin a fraction. To tighten the throat, make it easier to open up with the blade. He had no choice. 'Unless I get you out of here? Can't do it. The Rider's bike's is sitting in your garage right now. That kind of defines red-handed.'

'Well, you'd better find a way to get me out of here. Or Neil's going to hear a story. You're out of options.'

Sean slipped his index finger into the handle of the knife. Actually, he wasn't out of options at all. He had one available route for sealing away dangerous information in the tomb of this man's mind.

7

Sean entered the cellar just as Neil walked in with The Triad goon. 'I got a clue from Zippy,' Sean said.

'He talked? No pain?'

'No pain. He denies working with the Robinsons and being The Rider, but he says the real guy is someone he met at a Premier Inn in Derby half a year ago. There's a notebook at Zippy's home. It's got an address for this guy. I want to go get him and see what his story is.'

Neil thought a second. 'Okay. Go get James–'

'No, just me. I said I'd get the information you wanted. I don't want you to give me help. You'll reckon I didn't do this alone and renege on the bet.'

Neil laughed. 'Like your big bro, pride runs the show, eh? Fine. If chalking one up on me means that much, go do it.'

'Have no one touch Zippy till I'm back. I might need to question him again. That okay?'

'Sure thing. No one will mess with your little pet project. But don't be daft and get yourself killed.'

'I guess that would be a fail. Just make sure my hundred quid is waiting when I get back.'

Zippy's house was just fifteen minutes away, but it took Sean an hour to get there. He couldn't use his own vehicle so had to collect the clone that he'd driven back from Cowbell Farm after killing Jimmy. He also had to perform his anti-surveillance manoeuvres before obtaining that vehicle.

At Zippy's home street, he cut down a side road that led to the lock-up garages behind the houses. Each had a small, dirty Perspex window in the up-and-over metal door. Despite the gloom inside, he could see the shape of the black dirt bike, as advertised. And a larger window round back.

He had to squeeze between the garage and a brick wall to reach it, but he hit pay dirt. The window had bars, but the entire wooden frame was rotten. Three tugs plucked it out like a plug. He laid it on the trash-littered grass by his feet and clambered into the garage.

Luck was truly on his side. The one-piece race suit was folded across the bike's seat, the helmet hung from the handlebars, and the key was in the ignition. There were also tools he could use to bust the door lock from the inside.

The race suit and helmet fit like a glove. He cut a slice on the outside of one knee and wound tape around his ankle. He slipped a footlong crowbar inside the gash. It rested against the taped part of his ankle and protruded from the slit by an inch, which would allow quick retrieval. He refused the biker gloves and put on his stun gloves. They only activated against flesh, so he could ride the bike and wield the crowbar. Now he was good to go.

He swung a leg over the machine and felt a strange sensation. Neil had always loved and owned motorbikes. Sean hadn't ridden one for many years, but had once been quite adept. He could clearly remember the last time he'd been on one. He sometimes wished he could forget.

CHAPTER 5

1

In the short time since the teenaged Webb brothers had moved to Sheffield, Neil had worked hard to befriend a bunch of lowlifes, primarily so they could be cheaply put to mundane tasks at a moment's notice. These ten-a-penny scumbags were the key to building a powerful stable.

He got a man to watch the café where Zeus met his dealers. His task was to wait for Zeus to show up and follow him to an address. Later that afternoon the lowlife reported back: a flat above a Naughty Pizza shop. In the early evening, Neil and Sean drove there to have a look. It was a dingy shithole in a crime-ridden slice of the city. The pizza place wasn't open for business yet.

Neil said, 'I expected something grander from a high-level dealer.'

'But this place makes sense to me,' Sean replied. 'Zeus wants to surround himself with his target customers.'

'That's not going to be my way of things when I make it big. And it won't be the way for whoever's running Zeus. Distance, that's the key to putting a brick wall between you and the cops.'

The street was commercial and while all the other shops

were shut, a couple of nearby nightclubs still operated and the pavements weren't empty at 1am, when the brothers returned. Dozens of young people walked – or staggered drunkenly – here and there. The pizza shop was busy with trade, having opened at 9pm.

The brothers were on motorbikes so they could hide their faces under helmets, and in case a quick getaway was in order. Neil got off his ride and approached Sean. He put a hand on the back of his little brother's neck, his go-to move when it was time to remind him who ran the show. 'Listen up. You might not have gotten this vibe, but I have. Your dad's a monster, right? Unhinged. Unpredictable.'

He waited for Sean to object. Sean knew better than that by now. 'Yes.'

'It helps us. The apple doesn't fall far from the tree. People think his genes have gone to us. We've got some clout because people think we're dangerous. If we're going to make it big, we use that vibe.'

It was the second time Neil had used the term 'make it big'. Recently the brothers had been running down different paths. Neil had made it clear he had no plans to find a worthwhile, legitimate career. He was building up criminal contacts in preparation for a life as an enemy of the law. Sean, however, knew the risks involved in such an endeavour, and he'd been aiming his sights the opposite way.

He studied computer programming from home, having decided that science was going to shape the future world. He'd started to make money by buying decrepit PCs, then repairing them to sell on. He'd also taught himself some basic vehicle maintenance and had a few regular customers because he was cheap. Combined, these two enterprises brought in little income, but the joy of the legitimate work outweighed this negative.

Sean hoped to use his brain to further himself, while Neil wanted to rely on his vicious streak. As proved by his next words. 'The vibe? Shock and awe, little bro. I read about it. It's a military tactic. Instil fear in the enemy, destroy the will. We don't just rob this guy. We make an example. We make sure people know what happened. We give them a terrifying story. That's how we get respect. We do this right, there will be no comeback. You follow my lead and I'll show you.'

The flat above the pizza shop was accessible via a fire escape round the back. As they slipped down the alley between buildings, the brothers pulled on balaclavas. The old fire door at the top of the metal stairs had been replaced by something thin and wooden, which burst open under a single kick. In they went, fast and hard. Neil had a pair of rounders bats, one in each hand. Sean had one of his own.

Zeus was in bed with his girlfriend, having sex. She was under the covers, blowing him, while he lay back with his hands behind his head, a picture of comfort. It barely altered as the two helmeted men stormed into the room. In fact, his demeanour made them more surprised than he was, and they paused.

'Bad idea, guys. I'll fuck you up. I'll give you a chance to leave.'

The girl threw the covers off her and scuttled to her man's side. But she didn't say a word. The quilt slid to the floor, but only the girl seemed ashamed of her nakedness.

'Take the cash that's in the fruit bowl over there,' Zeus said, still calm, still smiling, as if home invasions were a daily routine. 'Two hundred quid. I'll write that off. Job well done, guys. But fuck off now or I'll come after you.'

The shock and awe hadn't worked, and Neil was visibly pissed. He took off his helmet, to show Zeus his enemy's face. It worked. The dealer sat up, angry – but also a fragment more worried. He knew this wasn't just a simple robbery.

'What the fuck is this? Do you want to die? Is that it?' Zeus looked at Sean. 'And is this your shitty little brother? You dickheads think you're hard? You're just scumbags like your dad. Go find some whores to rape and stab and get the fuck out of–'

There he stopped making words. Noise, though, he continued to spew as Sean leaped forward and brought his rounders bat down hard on the dealer's knee. It jolted Neil into action. The girl ran from the bedroom as the brothers rained down blows on her man.

They battered his body but left the head alone. Despite his anger, Sean had concentrated on the dealer's upper body to make sure Neil didn't get access to the skull. He didn't want this guy dead because even the cops couldn't ignore that. Sean targeted the man's chest and shoulders and arms, while Neil turned the hips and legs the colour of a dawn sky.

'My dad was wrongly convicted,' Sean said when it was over. Zeus was a blubbering, bleeding wreck.

Neil approached the fruit bowl mentioned earlier, which sat on a dressing table. He grabbed the cash, held it up, and said, 'Sure you don't mind? Not fake is it? And yes, that's why we're here.'

He ordered Sean to go find himself an Xbox. There were about ten boxed ones in the living room, by the sofa that the girl cowered on.

He picked one up. That was when he heard more fleshy impacts from the bedroom, even above the noise of drunken customers in the shop beneath them. The girl seemed to jolt with each blow she heard, so Sean spoke to her. He took off his helmet for a more human approach.

'Sorry you had to witness that. But that's the game your boyfriend's brought you into. Get out of it. Or at least tell him to chalk this one down to experience.'

She looked at him with wide eyes, not comprehending. It might have been the shock.

Sean knelt before her. 'He'll probably want revenge, and then it'll be tit for tat day after day. We feel good today, then he'll feel good tomorrow when he fucks us over. Then us when we return the favour, then him again, and so on. But for you it'll just be a constant hell. Dump him before you get hurt.'

When Sean returned to the bedroom, he found Zeus now bruised and bleeding from new areas, and of course it was the face and head. Sean grabbed Neil's arm before a fatal blow could land. 'Don't kill him. We need him alive so he can spread the word that we're bad motherfuckers.'

His bullshit worked. Neil stepped back, panting. He liked the thread Sean had opened up. 'You hear that?' Neil yelled at Zeus. 'Tell people we're the new bad boys in town. In fact, it's now your job to spread that word. The next time someone fucks with me, I'll take it as you not doing your job properly, and we'll be back.'

Word of the attack soon filtered through the streets, and fast. The story quickly got embellished. Apparently Zeus had been attacked by eight members of a new gang in town. When Sean went to his Gran's to check if Dad had sent a new letter from prison, he was surprised to find that even she'd heard the news. Knowing he lived in the same area that this 'new gang' operated in, she warned him to be wary of people, to stay off drugs, and to not follow Neil's advice because 'He's bad news, I just sense it'.

Neil didn't like the story, because he wanted the infamy attached to his name. But he also worried about the police, so he let the rumours run. He was also concerned about revenge and paid some lowlifes – just a few quid an hour – to watch his property and the surrounding streets.

One guy, a skinny, bedraggled, hopeless alcoholic calling himself Buzz, agreed to set up home in the wheelie bin compound round the side of the block of flats. This guy had lost his parents as a child, spent time in the care system, and been homeless for the last twelve years since turning eighteen. He remained in that stinking compound all day and night, with nothing but magazines and his fee of a bottle of whisky every morning.

Weeks passed without incident. Zeus, though, seemed to have bided his time. Sean was working on a neighbour's car one evening when an apparent new customer and his friend drove up. Foolishly, Sean didn't think twice about entering the car to take a look at the man's faulty speedometer.

Neil was in the flat and oblivious and he got a phone call moments later. 'We just nabbed your brother,' a guy said. 'Out you come. We'll send a car. If you ain't on the street when it gets there, we'll post his eyes through your door.'

Neil also didn't think twice. He made a quick phone call, took a big drink of water and ate a banana, just in case he didn't get the chance for sustenance for a while, and left the flat.

He was on the pavement for thirty seconds before a car appeared. Four guys were inside. One of the two in the back got out, which probably meant Neil was supposed to sit between them.

Neil got out his phone and took four pictures, one of each guy's face. Then he turned and lobbed the device towards the bin compound. Like a ghost, Buzz slipped out from behind the bins, grabbed the phone, and retreated. They all watched him scale the back wall and vanish.

Neil got in the car and was sandwiched between the two

backseat passengers. 'Now I've got your faces,' he said. 'So my brother better be okay. Zeus better not have been a silly boy.'

'Zeus is small fry,' said the driver as he pulled the car away from the kerb. 'You messed with a bigger, more dangerous fish.'

2

Ring rust was definitely a thing, but half an hour cruising the streets on The Rider's motorbike got Sean's muscle memory nicely warmed up. He was eager for action. One night, one oft-used and reliable playbook, and five targets. This was going to be fun, unless shitty freak luck stuck its oar in.

Target #1. The Rider drew the bike to the kerb outside a house in Mosborough. It was a middle terrace with no front garden and a door giving right onto the pavement. There were a handful of people around, including a guy two doors down who stood in his open doorway, dressed in shorts and nothing else, and smoked a roll-up.

Sean plucked the crowbar from its hiding place inside the calf of his race suit and jammed it between door and frame, and had the entryway open in two seconds. He rushed inside, fast and loud.

Target #2. Sean bolted down a grimy hallway, past the living room, which was empty, and to the kitchen, from which he'd heard people talking. Two men were present, both sitting at the kitchen table and bagging up drugs. The one who tried to go for a baseball bat on top of the fridge became the main target.

Sean grabbed the guy's wrist and downed him with 15,000 volts.

Target #3. Sean released his electric grip on the man's neck and put the rusted prongs of the crowbar to his throat instead. At that point another man burst into the living room, having been alerted by the noise. He held a wicked machete, which trumped a crowbar, but this guy was short and skinny and The Rider was imposing. Sean didn't even look at him.

'Get the gear and the cash,' he told the newcomer. 'Bring it here or I'll bust you both wide open. Now. And drop that fucking blade.'

'You know who owns the gear?' the man on the floor said when his pal vanished to complete the task. 'Neil Webb, that's who. Big mistake if you take it. He'll kill you.'

'Give me any hassle and when I get to hell, you'll already be there and holding the door open for me. Just lie there and shut your mouth, okay?'

'He'll kill us if we lose that gear.'

'I'll kill you if you try to stop me. You want to die right now or tomorrow?'

The guy picked tomorrow. His partner returned, carrying a canvas satchel.

Target #4. Sean picked up the small suitcase. He paused and stared at the guy asleep on the seat. He could take this guy out with ease, plus the one whose shower he could hear. And he yearned to start rioting. He wanted the rush. But he'd come for drugs and money, and they were already in his hand. It took some serious deliberation, but in the end he slipped out of the caravan as quietly as he'd entered.

The caravan was nestled by trees in a field. Its remote location was probably why the dealers had left its door wide open. It made Sean think.

Target #5. Once at his destination, Sean found a gaggle of

teenagers on a street corner and pulled up next to them. He held up a £10 note, told a story, and asked for a certain someone's name and address. The kids knew the story well.

That address was on the fourth floor of the six-storey block of flats right behind him. Sean parked his bike where he'd stopped and crossed the road. He expected to have to buzz some flats to get in, but the electronic door was busted and opened at a pull. In fact, the whole building was run-down. The hallway floor was stained. The stairwell stank. The door of number 18 had peeling paint. He knocked and stepped aside to avoid the peephole.

It was opened by a skinny woman who might have been pretty once. Now she had grimy skin, lank hair, and the eyes of one friendly with drugs. The night's activities had set his blood humming, and he was eager for violence. He had to restrain himself from pushing past the woman to enter the flat.

'Is Toby here?'

She turned and walked down the hallway. That was easy. He followed her. He found Toby sitting on the sofa in a room that was unnaturally clean for its location. Toby wore just underpants and was rolling a giant joint. The guy didn't seem bothered that a stranger was in his home. It was obvious that drug customers came by a lot.

'You better have serious cash for coming up here this late,' Toby said. 'I don't have no spice. Fuckers keep knocking up here for it, and it ain't my thing. What you after?'

Sean had the crowbar within reach. He wore his stun gloves. He was shaking with adrenaline and eager to start hurting people. So it came as a surprise to him when he reached for his wallet.

Forty minutes later, with The Rider's bike and outfit stashed, Sean knocked at a semi-detached house on a quiet street. Someone opened the door on a chain and presented just half a face, but Sean recognised the old man who'd been at The Chubby earlier.

Sean held his phone up to the crack in the door, to show the man a website page. It was for a second-hand retail store called Cash Spawn. The old man immediately unlocked the chain, opened the door, and grabbed the phone for a better look. 'That's mine,' he said, incredulous.

Sean would have loved to arrive here holding Jacob Jansen's necklace with the pendant containing his daughter's ashes. But the thieving lowlife called Toby had sold it on. Cash Spawn had it listed for £120.

Sean took back his phone. 'That's the Barnsley branch. I'm guessing the police didn't enquire with second-hand stores, which I would have thought was standard operating procedure. Especially for jewellery. You might want to make a complaint.'

'Thank you,' the old man said. 'I owe you, sir. Anything you need, you just ask. Thank you so very much.'

He held out his hand to shake, but Sean was already walking away.

3

It was 11.03pm when Sean got back to The Chubby. He decided to peek in through the lounge window to gauge the scene. He didn't know what tales a certain captive might have told during his absence and didn't want to walk into a trap.

The crowd had thinned and of the eleven people still present, only three weren't part of Neil's crew. That trio were a loved-up young couple in a booth and a middle-aged man, quite drunk, who chatted-up the barmaid as she cleaned the countertop.

Neil was emptying money from the pool table. Sean watched and tried to read his brother's body language from afar. The air didn't have a bad vibe, but he couldn't be certain of anything.

One of Neil's men approached him. He was called Spanner because he'd trained as a mechanic, but that wasn't his role in the firm. He controlled the marijuana side and ran the frontline salesmen. What he said to Neil put a frown on the boss's face. Sean knew he'd timed his return perfectly. He went for the door.

As he entered the lounge, Neil spotted him and waved him

over. 'I went to Zippy's house and–' Sean started, but there stopped as Neil held up a hand.

'House in Canklow,' he said, quietly. Patrons were present. 'The dealers just got robbed. They just called Spanner.'

Sean knew it, of course. He pretended to be surprised. 'Rival gang? Or you think the dealers are full of shit?'

'Check this. They reckon it was The Rider. Bad timing since we've got the bastard in my cellar. I sent someone to question them in more detail.'

That would involve violence. Drug dealers were hardly trustworthy fellows. 'Wow. Well, I don't think you do have The Rider. We've all heard the rumour that he's different people. I was just at Zippy's and I found no evidence that he's our man. I believe him.'

Neil wasn't sure what to think, given his expression. They heard a phone ring and saw Spanner answer it. Then he hung up and came running again. Only one of the brothers knew why at that moment.

'The Rider's hit another house,' Spanner said.

'Are you fucking kidding me? Get a crew and check in with all your people. Make sure this isn't a damn conspiracy to rob me.'

Spanner got down to his task. Fuming, Neil got heavy-handed as he continued to empty cash from the pool table. 'Why are you just standing there, bro?' he said. 'Go with Spanner or something.'

'What about the innocent guy locked in your torture room?'

Neil paused, clearly having forgotten about Zippy for the moment. 'Is it too risky to leave him breathing?'

'I'd say no. He can't tell the Robinson brothers about his little visit here. They'll wonder why he got out unscathed.'

Neil nodded. 'Just make sure of it. Get him out of here. Give him a ton from the till.'

'Where's his phone? Did your boys get it when they snatched him?'

They sure did. Neil liked to collect enemies' electronic devices to see what they'd been up to. They were kept somewhere safe and away from The Chubby in case the cops traced them. Neil sent a man to fetch Zippy's mobile. Sean waited on a stool, watching the TV.

It took just eighteen minutes. When he had the device, for which Zippy had earlier provided the PIN under threat, Sean played around with it then ventured down to Room X. Zippy looked about ready to cry, but he got quite happy upon seeing what he believed was a friendly face. 'Is my problem sorted?' the man said. 'Or are we both fucked?'

A not-so-subtle reminder that Zippy had information dangerous to Sean's health. Sean dampened his anger. As he untied Zippy, he said, 'We're letting you go and we're paying you for your time.'

Zippy was suspicious. 'For real? What did you do? Why am I being let go? Are you lying? Am I going to be killed?'

'It seems The Rider isn't you, so you're in the clear. Here.' Sean held up a hundred pounds from the cash register.

Zippy still looked wary and didn't touch the cash. 'How do I know you trust me? How do I know you won't come blast me in my bed? Because of what I know.'

Sean held up Zippy's phone, which displayed messages between the owner and a number not stored in the phonebook. Messages Sean had written. The more Zippy read, the wider his eyes got.

ZIPPY: Hey Sean I got something that might interest you.

UNKNOWN: Who the hell is this?

ZIPPY: One of the Robinson brothers' crew. A guy who can give you time and locations where they'll be.

UNKNOWN: For what reason?

ZIPPY: So you can fill them with bullets. I want on your bro's team. And that's my gift to you. Two fat brothers on a platter. Deal?

UNKNOWN: Drop by The Chubby Grub for a chat.

'What the fuck is this?' Zippy snarled, all his previous wariness a thing of history.

'This is a very good reason for the Robinsons to circumcise your whole body with a potato peeler. Make sure I have no reason to show them these messages.'

Seeing the bigger picture, Zippy relaxed a little. 'So we're doing a deal, that's what you're saying?'

'I'm leading you out of here. Go home and keep your mouth shut. I got rid of The Rider's bike. Fake a robbery or something if you need to explain why it's missing. Remember, I saved your life tonight.'

Zippy nodded and put out a hand to shake. Sean didn't like this bastard, but the man had sat on explosive information that would have ruined Sean. So he shook that hand.

After bidding Zippy goodbye at the rear fire exit, Sean returned to the lounge, where he found Neil almost bouncing off the walls. The last customers had already left. 'Two more houses got hit,' he moaned. 'Four now. All by The fucking Rider! Money and gear, fucking gone.'

'Someone got a good haul tonight,' Sean said.

4

Three hours later, at 2.30am, Sean parked in the Asda car park in Doncaster. At the bottom of the riverside embankment, a couple of the homeless living under the bridge saw him approach and they waved. When he got to their blanket city, he fist-bumped those still awake. Amongst those out for the count was Holly, who had a clean sleeping bag on cardboard near the abutment.

Instead of waking her, he snuggled up, needing sleep himself. A couple of the guys were still up and chatting by the dying oil drum fire, so he didn't expect to drift off. But suddenly it was seven in the morning and everyone was wide awake and busy. A couple of people were washing in the river, some were tidying up their bed spaces, and others, Holly amongst them, were cooking breakfast on a portable hob.

Bizarrely, he'd dreamed of a post-apocalypse community hiding from radiation and zombies, although not under a bridge. A moment of fear upon waking now made him laugh, which got Holly's attention.

'You like to sneak around,' she said.

'Old habits die hard.'

'And you didn't wake me. That was nice.'

'I'm shocked you didn't wake everyone with your snoring.'

'Funny. No breakfast for you.'

He did get some, though, and he paid £10 for it even though nobody wanted to accept it. After food, he said to Holly, 'I had a new idea.'

'What is it?'

'One of those show-not-tell ideas.'

'That sometimes means a person is too embarrassed to put words together. I'm intrigued.'

They climbed the embankment and entered the car park. They headed towards the Asda. She was very puzzled. Thirty metres into their walk, Sean stopped in the car park beside a vehicle. He waved his hands at it.

'This?' she said, surprised.

It was a Swift Voyager motorhome. 'Battered and old, but it runs. I had the idea after I saw a caravan.'

'You bought it? Isn't that risky?'

'I didn't use money from the bank. I called in some debts. People Neil doesn't know.'

The lie felt bad, but how could he tell her the truth? He had robbed four drug dealers. Clearing Zippy's name had been only part of the reason. They needed money.

'Why did you waste it on this? How much was it?'

He told her he'd found it online and visited the owner very late last night. The man had been happy to do the deal immediately for cash. The price was £11,000, but Sean haggled and got three grand shaved off. He didn't mention that he'd smelled weed in the owner's house and had offered him some as part-payment.

Still she wasn't impressed. 'But we needed that money.'

'We also need a vehicle. I didn't want us to use hotels. Neil's been checking hotels for you. He'll check again and spread the net wider when I vanish as well. He's going to put two and two together.'

She rubbed her forehead. 'I don't know, Sean.'

'Think about this. We can stay where we want, move on at a moment's notice. It's nice and cosy. No paper trail. Come look.'

He opened the habitation door and swept a ladies-first hand. Holly entered and he followed her. There was no bulkhead between the cabin and living area. The driver's seat was busted, but the passenger seat swivelled 180 for easy passage between the two areas. It had a small kitchen worktop and a four-seater table. The bedroom, at the back, had a door.

There were no electrical appliances and for some reason all the plug sockets were missing, but he promised her those were easy fixes. The whole thing needed a clean and a few repairs, but the price was a steal for a vehicle costing eight times that brand new.

To seal the deal, he took her to the bedroom, which was clean but also old and showing it. He opened the wardrobe. 'Look I've moved some of my clothing in and bought you some more.'

She wasn't quite over the moon, but also not quite as annoyed as five minutes earlier. She sat on a seat, looking around. 'I guess it will do for a short time. But we need a real place, Sean. I can't live in this for too long. And we need money, which we don't have.'

'But we will. I'm working on it. So, if I can get cash, we can go whenever we like. Life on the road for a week or two won't be too bad.'

After a pause, she said, 'I guess so.'

'So you're in?'

Her answer took more thought, but she smiled when delivering it. 'I'm in.'

5

The brothers met in the car park of a Tesco on the edge of Sheffield. Both men had taken steps to make sure they weren't being tailed and Neil had a car Sean hadn't seen before. Sean got in beside his brother and away they went. Noah's vehicle was behind them.

'So where are we going?' Sean asked. No details had yet been given.

'Manchester Airport. Something's coming in by truck.'

'The Allerby Job? Is it the thing we're stealing?'

Neil nodded. 'That's right. There's nothing in that stately home worth a thing to us. But what's coming there tomorrow is. And we're having it.'

'But what are we nicking? Cash?'

'You'll find out soon.'

'Bearer bonds?'

'Not that soon. Don't ask anymore until we're there.'

It was close to midday when they reached the gates of the Runway Visitor Park, which was busy late on a Saturday morning. The park provided a nice day out for those who liked planes. Amongst other activities, you could tour the insides of various aircraft, including Concorde, or you could picnic, or shop, or watch your kids in a play area. And there was a raised viewing platform that gave a spectacular close-up of planes landing on a runway, which was the reason for the brothers' visit.

Neil checked his watch. 'Half an hour to go.'

The jet that came in to land half an hour later had Etihad Cargo printed on the sides, but before it had even touched the runway, Neil stood up. 'Time to go.'

'We're not watching?'

'We won't see it unloaded from here. But the plane is here and that's the important bit. Let's go.'

'Jewels?'

'No. But I'll tell you it cost the owner twenty grand to ship it here. Now let's go.'

People cheered and kids whooped as the plane touched down, but Neil and Sean had already left the platform. They exited the park, collected their car, and drove to a road close to the World Freight Terminal. Sean figured that they would see the prize, whatever it was, when it left by truck on the next leg of its journey.

'Twenty grand in shipping costs, eh?' he said. 'Must be heavy. Gold bars.' It was only half a joke.

'Settle down. We might have a bit of a wait.'

Ninety-one minutes, to be exact. Sean got his arm slapped and looked up from his phone. He watched three vehicles exit the freight terminal and drive towards them. At each end of the convoy was a black Range Rover with two serious looking, black-suited men inside. Between them was a white box truck. Unfortunately, it had no windows in the cargo box and no markings to give a clue as to the contents. Whatever it was had to be kept secret.

'Rare, mummified remains?' Sean said.

'That's right,' Neil replied.

What? 'For real? Mummified remains?'

'Well done.'

Neil waited until the convoy had passed, then guided his car away from the kerb in pursuit.

Sean said, 'And nuclear shit. Plutonium smuggled inside mummies.'

'You got it, bro. Nice one.'

Sean shut his mouth, aware that Neil had finally had enough of the barrage of guesses.

On the M67, Neil slipped into the middle lane to overtake the convoy. Sean got a good look at the truck and the Range Rovers as they slowly slipped by. 'These guys armed?'

'Maybe. Not sure. But they know their stuff. Ex COMSUBIN.'

'Oh, those guys,' Sean said sarcastically.

'Italian navy special forces. The guy who owns the thing is from Italy originally. Lives in Florida now. That's where he shipped the thing from and where it's never going back to.'

'I'm just getting more intrigued by the minute.'

'Well, you'll have to wait about sixty more.'

In Sheffield, they visited an industrial estate and parked down a side street. Fifteen minutes later, the Range Rovers and box van cruised by on the main road. Neil and Sean walked to the junction and peered out from behind the corner of a fence. About fifty metres away, the trio of vehicles turn into the grounds of a property wrapped in high, serious fencing. A sign out front named the firm: 7-Star-Car. Sean quickly googled it.

'Luxury car storage. Breathable covers. Dehumidified storage rooms. Twenty-four-hour security. So, a car?'

Neil nodded. 'Now you know.'

'Well, I don't. It could be an old banger with sentimental value.'

'It's not,' Neil said, snatching Sean's phone. 'Let's go back to the car.'

Once they were seated, Sean was handed his phone back. Neil had performed a google search and Sean found himself looking at a WordPress webpage about the Verninac Paix.

The black hypercar looked like a spaceship, like something from the next century or another dimension. It was Superman in a world of Thors and Incredible Hulks. This one-off machine, by French manufacturer Verninac, had cost its American buyer $15,000,000, which was well over £11 million. The owner wasn't named and Verninac refused to release that information.

The website included more photos and even a video, which showed the Paix being driven down a wide, pristine road towards the camera – with a Range Rover following. There was no front number plate (and no practical place to put one because of the horseshoe grill), which seemed to add to the mystique and its alien feel.

There was a glorious beach/sea view in the close background, but every set of eyes on the street watched the supercar glide by. The camera panned to follow the Paix as it slipped past. The man holding it had blurred the rear numberplate, unfortunately. Sean had hoped to gain a clue as to the owner. He had to settle for staring at six – six! – exhaust pipes.

That individual's name wasn't the only thing beyond him. The one-of-a-kind car belonged on a plinth, or in Hollywood, or in space. Not in South Yorkshire. Yet here it was. 'You're telling me this thing will be at Allerby House tomorrow?'

'Yep. It's the pride and glory of the show.'

Show? In answer, Neil took Sean's phone to load another website. It featured Elegant Engines, a single-day event showcasing the finest classic vehicles and supercars. To take place this Sunday, 12-4pm, in Allerby Park. Public tickets were £25.

Sean was puzzled by this. 'You're going to steal the Paix from the car show? That doesn't make sense. There's going to be hundreds of people there. And security. And cars blocking each other.'

'Not from the car show. Have a think.'

He did. 'A deliberate ambush, right?'

This military term was one of many Neil swore by. Some thieves opted to steal goodies *in situ*, which was easier to plan, but Neil preferred to hit a target when it was in transit. Less security. Cash vans were easier than banks. Enemies were more vulnerable between A and B rather than in a lair.

'So you plan to steal the truck while it's taking the car to–'

'No, Neil cut in. 'We don't steal the truck. Just the car, after it's off the truck.'

'Before? But we'd need a truck to transport the car. You can't drive a thing like that away. Everybody will be looking for it and...'

Something came to him, so he accessed his phone's photos. Pictures of the back road into Allerby Park and the half-constructed restaurant sitting there, the height barrier at the gates, and the lay-by on the main road.

'I get it,' he said.

'Do you?' Neil said, grinning. 'Then explain it to me, Einstein. Let's see how smart you are.'

6

The box truck pulls up in the lay-by outside Allerby Park, and the driver opens up the side and back panels. The gleaming black Paix is unveiled like a gift. The wealthy owner of this exclusive and expensive vehicle gets out of a Range Rover and transfers to his pride and joy. The height barrier at the back entrance to the country house won't permit the delivery truck.

'Correct so far?' Sean asked.

'So far, so good,' Neil replied. 'Let's hear the rest, smartarse.'

The Paix's owner starts the eight-litre quad turbo engine. The truck driver unclips the vehicle from its moorings, then helps guide the driver down the ramp, onto pitted tarmac that almost doesn't deserve to touch Michelin tyres that cost over $40,000 a set. Once more a three-vehicle convoy sets in motion, this time with the supercar instead of the truck in the middle. The Paix is wider than its compatriots, but much shorter. The trio moves into the road for a thirty-metre journey before turning left to enter Allerby Park via Entrance C.

Almost immediately, the convoy comes to a halt. Outside the half-built restaurant, and blocking the road, is a flatbed truck. Ten men in work coveralls and high-vis jackets toil on and around the building, two of them on the roof. Workers shouldn't be here on a Sunday, but the Paix owner and his bodyguards don't know that. If staff from English Heritage wander along, they might not know it, either. The country house and the restaurant are owned by separate companies.

One of the men on the ground waves at the convoy. 'I'll shift the truck, mate,' he yells. 'Just a sec. Nice ride, by the way.'

That guy enters the truck and starts to turn it in the road. Meanwhile, the other five guys approach the cars. Nice and casual. Two of them split up to take both sides of the lead Range Rover, two aim for its brother at the rear, and one guy gets the Paix–

'That's me. The boss gets to drive the supercar.'

–Up on the roof, the two men just watching bend down out of sight, and when they reappear one detail is different. Two seconds ago they didn't wield shotguns.

The guy standing by the driver's door of the lead Range Rover pulls out a handgun, smashes the side window, and aims the weapon at the man inside. On the passenger side, his partner does the same. This scene is mirrored at the back end of the convoy.

These are expendable vehicles. The Paix is not. The gunman standing by its driver's door aims his weapon at the window, and the shocked man inside. 'Out you get. Bulletproof glass is an optional extra–'

'Nice. I'll actually use that line.'

The rich owner exits with his hands in the air. Either side of him, his bodyguards do the same. The truck driver has positioned his vehicle in the middle of the road with its rear facing the convoy. He sets about installing ramps on the tailgate. The two guys with shotguns come down to cover the prisoners while comrades zip tie their hands behind their backs.

Five men lead the prisoners into the shell of the restaurant, where they are tied up and their phones taken. One shotgun guy is left behind to stand guard.

Outside, two men hop into the Range Rovers and shift them from the road. Neil climbs into the Paix. He works the seven-speed gearbox and guides the vehicle forward, slowly, carefully, onto the ramps and onto the truck. He gets out and then helps his men haul a tarpaulin over the hypercar. It is at that point that the adrenaline and fear and stress makes him burst into tears and wet his pants–

'You're a funny fucker, aren't you?'

7

Neil clapped his brother. 'Give or take a few details, that's spot on. One thing you missed is a guy at the back gate. He'll be there just to stop people coming in if they don't have a car on show. We'll take care of him. You see how easy this is? It's just a car-jacking, really. I've got the construction outfits, the weapons, everything. They don't need to be told a thing until the last minute. I've planned out the finer details myself, over a couple of months. I couldn't have people talking about that Paix to wives and their mates.'

Sean understood. With a complex framework already in place, the players would need to know only where to be, and when, and who to point a gun at. It was no different to, say, turning up at warehouse job to fill boxes. The Allerby Job was a major score, but when boiled down to basics, it seemed quite straightforward. Neil was also right to worry about gossip.

But he wasn't as optimistic as his brother. 'A car that costs that much will have some serious security. You got a plan for that?'

He saw his big brother clutch at a point just below the left breast. Neil fished a couple of chewable antacids out of his pocket and chomped them. 'I need a snack. Let's go.'

'You need the hospital?'

Neil gave him the finger and started the car. But he then told Sean to drive, so they swapped positions. Sean knew his brother always had that little thought at the back of his mind. The one that worried about a heart attack. He didn't want to suffer one while at the wheel.

Sean drove out of the side road, then turned right, away from 7-Star-Car and towards the exit of the industrial estate. 'So. Security.'

Neil massaged a spot above his temple – but Sean knew his brother was covertly checking his pulse. 'Immobiliser. State of the art. PIN authorisation, so the engine won't start without it. Relay theft protection, so we can't clone the key from a distance. Verninac's own, secret recipe, so it's not something we can research online.'

'Apparently you're not worried about that.'

'The engine will be on when we take the car. Key in the ignition. And we already know where the car will be.'

'But once the company knows the car is stolen, they'll shut the car down remotely. The PIN won't matter, even if you get it from the owner. And there will be a tracker. In a car like that, it's going to work by GPS and VHF. Verninac can no doubt remotely turn it on whenever they want.'

Sean was in a business that sometimes used stolen cars, so he knew a little about trackers. Supreme, modern ones used a mix of VHF and GPS. Very High Frequency signals couldn't be jammed and could penetrate earth and metal and brick, so thieves couldn't thwart it by hiding a vehicle in a shipping container or a building or underground.

The only flaw was that VHF signals had to be activated, usually when a vehicle was stolen. So the best trackers also employed the Global Positioning System because it gave out a constant signal.

Neil smiled at him. 'And I'm not worried about that, either. Think you can work out why?'

Sean had a theory. 'GPS can be jammed, so my guess is you think we could set up a jammer to block the GPS once the car is in range. If we can take the car before the owner can hit the panic button, the VHF signal won't be activated. You think that will give us enough time to hide the car and disable the tracker?'

'And I have ten mechanics ready to go. Two grand each. Reliable for silence. They'll swarm the car when I get it to safety.'

Sean had worried that Neil's plan was too outrageous and too close to impossible, yet in a strange twist he found himself suddenly defending it. 'I know there's a way to bypass the immobiliser using the controller area network bus. It's beyond me, but there are guys who can do it.'

However, Neil also turned devil's advocate. 'But Verninac's own telemetry system kills that plan stone dead.'

He explained. For those customers opting in, newer Verninac models featured a telemetry system – obviously the best that engineers could devise – that was monitored 24/7 from the headquarters in Rennes, France. Technicians kept up to date with over 10,000 data signals, allowing them to inform the owner if something was wrong with his precious machine.

Software problems could be rectified wirelessly. If the car had a physical problem, Verninac would dispatch a specialist, informally known as a flying doctor. They had three covering the whole world, and one would be sent, with parts if necessary, at a moment's notice.

'The telemetry system controls the in-built tracker, and it'll activate it in the event of imminent theft.'

Sean thought he'd misheard. 'Imminent? How does that work? Can it sense bad guys nearby?'

The telemetry system would send out alerts if there was inconsistent behaviour or activity suggestive of attempted theft. If, for instance, a door was opened at an uncommon hour, or the driver's seat registered an unknown weight, or if the car was put on a truck, it would flag on the owner's mobile phone and at the Verninac headquarters. And the tracker would activate. Gone were the days when an owner realised their supercar was missing only when they woke up in the morning.

'We've got a truck,' Sean said. 'We're going to stop the car on the exit road and get the driver out. These will flag, right?'

'It's worse than that. The owner will have geofences in place. Like at his home and work and other places where the car regularly goes. In these zones the computer might ignore certain strange behaviour. He'll have one set up for Allerby Park because during that car show a lot of activity will happen. People will sit in the car, the headlights might go on and off, and the door will remain open for long periods. If the Paix leaves the geofences without warning, or at unscheduled times, that will also flag. As it will if the Paix doesn't even enter Allerby Park.'

'And that'll start the tracker's VHF signal? Right then the police will be able to trace the car.'

'You need a few extras for your eleven-million dollar outlay.'

'And you have a plan to beat this?'

Neil winked. 'More on that at our final meeting later.'

Sean had gotten his own cheekiness from his brother, and he knew how steadfast the guy could be. Neil liked this keep-shit-back game and wouldn't give it up until he was ready. Sean moved on.

'Anyway, it doesn't matter if you get away scot-free with the car if you can't offload it. You've already got a buyer?'

'Of course. You think I planned to keep it? I'll tell you about him, but, again, all in good time.'

'This is a such a wild and risky plan, Neil. Especially because you've kept all the details quiet. Can you promise it will work?'

Neil looked at him. Sean knew Neil never promised a thing unless he was one hundred per cent certain he could deliver. 'I can't do that. The plan is good, but there's a saying about no plan surviving first contact with the enemy. I can't control side issues and all the little things that could go wrong. So, no, I won't promise. As for telling people the plan, not yet.'

'Fair enough. I just hope nothing minor blows it away and we all end up in prison.'

Neil sighed. 'We might end up there, but not because of this. Because of my wife.'

This again. Neil had mentioned her less and less recently, and Sean had started to hope it meant he'd soon forgive and forget. Apparently not. 'She's not with the cops. That I can promise you. I just know it.'

'Then convince my people, Sean. Holly being out there is driving some of them paranoid. I'm getting wind of guys wanting to leave the firm. They're worried about what she's telling the cops. I reckon they're worried that I'll go state's evidence as well.'

Sean laughed. 'You? No way.'

'Way. They think I'll side with her if I get arrested. To save us both. I always told my people I kept Holly out of my business. They knew it and were careful not to talk shop around her. But I feel the vibes. I know they're worried that she's got dirt on all of them. I know they're worried about me.'

'Someone's said that?'

'No, but it's real. I need to restore order, restore faith, and there's only one way to do that.'

'Which is?'

'To kill that damn bitch before she wrecks everything for all of us.'

CHAPTER 6

1

'So where do you fools get off kidnapping schoolkids?'

The four brutes in the car with him stayed silent, so Neil pushed again: 'I see one hair harmed on my brother's head, there will be hell to pay.'

Finally someone couldn't hold his tongue. 'Maybe you won't ever see him again, so how about that?'

It was a bullshit threat, Neil knew. The bozos who'd snatched him were doubtless the same bozos who'd taken Sean, so there would soon be a reunion. It happened at a crack-den on a run-down estate where everybody minded their own business. The bedsit had almost no furniture and a constant, overwhelming shit stink. The kitchen had nothing in it bar a fridge and a single wooden chair, to which Sean was tied. He didn't look injured. Or scared, curiously. So far, so good.

There were two other men here, for a total of six bad guys. One was mean-looking and clearly the bodyguard of the other, who was middle-aged and wore a suit. He had thinning hair and many small, old, badly healed scars on a face Neil recognised.

'Mr Keating,' Neil said.

'You know who I am. Good. Saves time.'

He sure did. Keating was a playbook crime kingpin. He had worked up from the bottom rung, now ran a major empire worth millions, and clouded public perception with legitimate money made through law-abiding businesses – in his case a fast-food chain called Naughty Pizza.

Keating was known to have serious buffers between his public life and from his shady dealings, and the cops, while knowing lots, could never prove a thing. His first and last arrest? Thirty years ago, for placing stones on railway tracks as a wild teenager.

The kingpin got down to business. 'You put one of my dealers out of action.'

'It makes sense now, why he lived above one of your pizza places.'

'You then took over his zone.'

'He was out through injury.'

Keating suppressed a smile. 'I don't care about Zeus, and I don't care who runs that zone. As long as I get paid. You and your brother can walk out of here, but as my people.'

'Work for you?'

'I like your style and your balls. Right now, yes or no?'

'Tell me what you're offering. I'll say no if it's cooking pizzas.'

Keating didn't hide his next smile.

The deal was done in sixty seconds. Zeus was out. Neil would now distribute Keating's drugs to lower-level dealers in that zone. Walking home, Sean asked Neil why he'd given in so easily.

'Given in? Use your brain. I didn't fold. I got us in the door with a big firm. Now the sky is the limit, little bro. You might not be clued up on how this world works, but luckily you've got me watching out for you. We're now in the big-time. Thank your brother, please.'

Neil began by selling marijuana and ketamine, before moving on to cocaine and heroin and more. He earned £2,100 that first week and the numbers only increased. A year after that day in the bedsit, at just nineteen years of age, he was earning £5,000 a week. His name was getting known. The cops showed an interest but Keating kept them at bay and, while there were arrests, Neil never got convicted.

When Neil turned twenty-one, Keating promoted him into the Niche, his name for the firm's inner sanctum. These now four people, one a female, were the voices that gave the orders. Keating was more like a figurehead, although he had to be consulted on all major decisions and had the power of veto. It was another buffer.

As part of the Niche, Neil doubled his income overnight. He got three whorehouses to manage, extra drug routes, and, to give him a legitimate income, was made assistant manager of one of Keating's pizza stores.

There was one more thing, and that was where Sean came in. Until then, he had been on the periphery, avoiding cop interest, and earning most of his own income by fixing computers and cars. On the criminal front, Neil employed him only to collect money from dealers and to dish out some comeuppance to those who annoyed his brother or Keating. It was mostly low-level vandalism against properties and vehicles. That was about to change.

'You understand that you don't have what it takes for this job, right?' Neil said when they met at a snooker hall one afternoon. They tended to meet once a day, provided Neil didn't have pressing business.

'What do you mean?'

'What job do you want in the future?'

'Maybe a computer programmer. I like–'

'And that's my point, Sean. I mean, to succeed in this

business takes commitment. I've got it. I know where I want to go, where I want to be in ten years. Computer programmer? That's words from a man who isn't fully invested.'

In a life of crime? No, that wasn't a lifestyle Sean dreamed of.

'It also takes a special kind of brain,' Neil continued. 'You just don't have it. You're smart, but not in the right way. You're got skills for thumping heads and street-smarts, but that's not enough. You're not as savvy as you need to be. You gotta be able to know how to talk to people. Gotta have a rein on your anger. Remember Zeus? You smashed his knees because he made a crack about your dad. Not good. A leader of men just isn't you.'

Sean shrugged. 'Maybe not.'

'Some of the people in the firm, they think you're a hanger-on. Here because of who your big brother is.'

He knew it, and he really didn't care. 'I guess.'

'But we all have skills, Sean, and I see yours. If you can harness that vicious streak, it can work well for you. So here's what I'm thinking...'

Determined to become important to Keating, Neil had constantly offered advice, and one piece had found a home: his beloved shock and awe tactic. It was the best method for stamping out adversity, he said. His plan: create a hit team that would be used for intimidation and revenge. Give that team sovereignty, albeit answerable to Keating but not directly linked to him.

Keating owned ninety-five pizza shops in the UK, forty-two of them in South Yorkshire alone. Controlling pest infestation cost him many thousands of pounds a year. Neil's plan was to start a pest control business.

'It will be fully registered and insured and all that legal shit,' Neil said to Sean. 'We'll have a van, a name, uniforms, a shitty little office, the lot. A real business. A bunch of fake callouts to his pizza shops will allow Keating to push money through it, including to the employees. And guess who gets to become manager?'

'Me?'

'My gift to you, bro. I always promised to see you right.'

The company would seem legitimate from the outside, but it wouldn't do a single day's pest control. Nobody would be trained to. Instead, the team would deploy to... fix whatever problems Keating faced. If an enemy criminal needed teaching a lesson in his own home, or transporting to a torture room in the back of one of Keating's pizza shops, the Pest B Gone van would draw no suspicion from witnesses.

A month later, just shy of Sean's eighteenth birthday, the new company was up and running. Pest B Gone had a tiny ground-floor office, formerly housing a taxi firm, in a tacky shopping parade. Its six employees were required to wait around in the office all day and leap into action when the phone rang. Keating seemed to think his hit team would be as busy as one employed by a Mexican drug cartel and Sean half-expected him to install a fireman's pole and a bat signal. Handily, nobody would go stir-crazy because the joint was sandwiched between an amusement arcade and a betting shop.

The five men under Sean were just like him: vicious, tough, street-smart, but lacking the fire that could drive them to greatness. That was Neil's narrative. Sean quickly understood that his men were more like the staff who, in a regular business, would spend lengthy periods facing disciplinary issues. He also quickly got the vibe that they didn't respect him. Neil tried to claim it was his young age, for the men were all over thirty, but Sean knew it was all about nepotism. They treated him like someone who didn't deserve to be their boss.

Pest B Gone got its very first job four days later, on the morning of Sean's 18th birthday. When his mobile rang and he saw Neil's name in the screen, he expected to hear the singing of Happy Birthday. Instead he got, 'Sean, I need you to do something, right now.'

He gave an address in Doncaster. Four male students lived there, one of them called Danny. This guy needed to be taught a lesson. Danny should have his fingers broken. 'And tell him to watch where he puts them in future,' Neil added.

Sean asked the nature of this Danny's transgression, but Neil wasn't forthcoming.

'All you need to know is that this isn't a Pest B job.'

That meant they couldn't use the highly traceable company van, for this was a task that might come to the attention of the police. It meant this Danny wasn't part of a criminal gang. That he was a just a regular guy. It added intrigue.

'Give me more, Neil. I'm your brother. Is this to do with Jane Doe?'

Neil's recent jollier mood was what had alerted people to the fact that he might be in love, although he'd never admitted more than to having a 'girl' – who Sean had nicknamed Jane Doe. No one had clapped eyes on her, but Sean knew she lived in Doncaster, just like this Danny guy. There had to be a connection.

Neil, surprisingly, poured it all out. Jane Doe was Holly, she was a student, and he might just be smitten. Danny was a fellow student at her university and last night had goosed her in a nightclub, just for a joke. Holly had told Neil about it, but she'd laughed it off as no big deal.

'Well, I'm not fucking laughing,' Neil said. 'So go do the fingers and see if he likes that punchline. Come see me right after it. There's something important we need to talk about. And remember that you and your boys aren't Pest B today. This fucker will cry to the cops.'

Danny lived close to where he studied, which was

Doncaster University. Keating had a guy called Alan who was expert in supplying cloned cars, which would be stored in multi-storey car parks to await collection when needed. Sean and his team drove to collect one, then visited the student called Danny, who was asleep in bed when his door was booted in.

As boss, Sean called the shots and got one of his men to break a single finger on Danny's hand. He was warned about keeping his digits to himself, notified of the dangers of moaning to the police, and then left alone.

An hour later, Sean met Neil at a snooker club, where Neil soaked up the details of the revenge mission with a smile on his face. He then turned to the reason he wanted to see his brother.

'You're eighteen now, boy. Happy b-day. Now you can place a bet. Drink a beer. Buy fireworks. You can watch porn. Know what else you can do?'

Sean sure did. He'd been waiting for this day. 'I can visit Dad in prison.'

Neil put a hand on the back of Sean's neck, which meant bad news was coming. 'Except you can't.'

'Why?'

Neil's old theory about using their father's infamy as clout had gotten them a strong foothold in the crime world, but it only went so far. And when you pushed it, that clout turned rotten.

'We're bigger now, Sean. We don't need history to move us forward. That thing your dad did now hurts us.'

Neil always referred to their father as Sean's dad. It was always *your,* never *our.* 'Wait. Are you saying what I hope you're not saying?'

'Keating feels the same way. It's not like your dad was a hardened gangster. He raped and killed a prostitute–'

'By accident.'

'No, Sean. No. He's a monster. What he did was pathetic

and degrading, and we're suffering because of it. You understand?'

'No.'

'What he did gets us no respect. It just makes us look like animals. We can't have people thinking we're as low as him. So we need distance from him.'

Sean's anger rose, but he kept it internal. 'You're barring me from seeing him?'

Neil nodded. 'You'll hurt the firm, and hurt us. So you can't see him. No visits ever. I need you to agree that it's for the best. Right now.'

Neil wouldn't be convinced otherwise. Sean had some options here. #1 agree and forget his father. Or #2 baulk and fall out with Neil.

'Okay,' he said, deciding on option #3.

2

At 6pm, a guy called Declan Smith was driving to work when a Ford Mondeo pulled in front of him. It flashed a pair of blue LED lights in the back window. Police. The driver cursed. A matrix display message sign lit up next: FOLLOW. Just great.

He tailed the unmarked police car down the next side road, which was a residential cul-de-sac. Both cars stopped and two similar-looking men got out. Plainclothes, which was a worry for Smith.

He was more suspicious than worried when the two guys got in his car without word, one of them next to him in the passenger seat. And scared when that guy produced a knife.

The guy behind reached across to show Smith a phone. Images scrolled by. His sister. His house. His mother. His wife and daughter. Photos taken without their knowledge. The final image showed some lethal, big knives arranged in a fan on a tiled floor.

'This is what we want,' said the guy in the front. He was half-brother to his partner. They were low-level enforcers, and they were the only two people aside from Sean and Noah who knew what Neil planned to steal on the Allerby Job. 'We need to stick these knives into your family's hearts. So you need to phone the police about us threatening you, and tell your workmates all about us–'

'No, no, no,' his half-brother cut in, laughing. 'We only do the knives thing if he tells people. Remember what we actually want him to do?'

'Oh yeah,' the front passenger said, following the script. 'That thing at his work. You okay with doing something for us at your work, Declan?'

They knew he was headed to his job as a security guard at 7-Star-Car, where he faced a 7pm–7am shift. His role was simple: hang around the inside and exterior of the building, making sure baddies weren't hopping the fence or already secreted inside.

And he had to check in on the cars to make sure they were okay. Eight months ago a lithium battery in an electric supercar caught fire for no discernible reason and since then security guards had a key for the Prime Chamber, which had humidity and temperature control because it held the top rides. Just in case.

Declan, obviously, was worried that these men wanted him to steal a car, and he knew which one. The new Paix was there overnight. The unit often had Ferraris and Zondas and other hypercars, but the Paix was by far the most expensive vehicle they'd ever stored, and it was irreplaceable. The management was worried sick and they'd put an extra two guards on the rota. They'd also added two more cameras to watch the fence and changed the old code for the main gate.

There was no way he could steal it. Nor could he even get the key, for that was safe in a locked box with the general manager, who was at an undisclosed hotel. Besides, the car had a tracker and immobiliser.

But the fake cops didn't want him to steal the car. They wanted something a little different.

'At 7.30 pm exactly,' one said, 'we want you to let a little bit of air out of the front right tyre. Then pump it up again exactly as it was. And call us half an hour later.'

Declan was puzzled, but he agreed. He could easily lift the cover from the car when he inspected the chamber. He could sneak a small pump inside. Ten seconds' work. What the men wanted was strange, but certainly not criminal. He'd do it to save his family. Of course he would.

3

Sean made a stop to see someone then headed back to the Asda by the river. It was 8pm, already dark, but Holly wasn't aboard the motorhome he'd left in the car park. He called her burner phone and she told him she was with her friends under the bridge.

She turned up a few minutes later. He saw that she was wearing his gym tracksuit, which had the name of the establishment on the back. It had been a free gift for joining, although he'd only attended a couple of times with Neil. It looked better on her and he said so.

She brushed it off. 'Where do we stand?'

'Tomorrow morning I'll take you to place I've arranged. You'll wait for me there.'

'Where is it?'

'I can't say yet. But after the Allerby Job–'

'I don't know why you still want to go through with that,' she cut in. He was on a seat at the kitchen table, but she still stood in the open doorway, as if eager to get back to her friends. Or just away from him.

'We need the money.'

'It's risky. You could get arrested. And dangerous. You could get hurt. Why can't we just leave in the morning and find money another way?'

Reason two, that was why. 'Neil will be suspicious if I back out at the last minute.'

She shook her head in exasperation. 'And he's the big man in charge, of course. Big brother. He says jump, you say how high. So he comes first.'

'It's not like that, Holly. We can't both just disappear until we have the money to lay low for at least a few months. On the point of which, after this job, everyone will be forced to lie low for a while. Neil won't be suspicious if I'm out of contact for a week or so. I could even say I'm going on holiday.'

She didn't shut down this theory, but she didn't jump for joy, either. 'You think that will work?'

'Neil will love it. Sometimes guys get holidays after a big job, so it won't be out of the ordinary. That's a week for us to find somewhere and get settled before the alarm goes off.'

She thought about this for a few seconds, then sat at his table, facing him across it. 'I don't like it. But I trust you. But I'll also hate you if you get arrested.'

He reached across the table to take her hand. 'Then I guess we should get one last shag in.'

She agreed with a weak smile. Afterwards, she dressed again in his tracksuit. She wanted to share a meal, but he had bad news. 'Neil's called a final pre-mission meeting for ten o'clock. I have to go.'

'Pre-mission meeting? He likes to pretend everything is fancy, doesn't he? Off you go, then. Maybe I won't be here when you get back.'

He couldn't tell if she was joking or annoyed. He tested it by saying, 'Maybe I won't come back.'

She was deadly serious now, though. 'That's what I'm scared of.'

4

At 8.06pm, the half-brothers who'd played cop got a call from the security guard at 7-Star-Car. Declan had successfully completed his task, that of messing with the Paix's tyre pressure, and now wanted to know if his family would be left alone.

The brother who'd answered the phone said, 'And what's happened?'

The security guard told him that one of the managers had called the firm. Apparently the Paix's telemetry system had alerted the manufacturer about the loss of tyre pressure and subsequent repressuring. In turn the owner had been informed and he'd called the general manager of 7-Star-Car, who had dispatched a mechanic to take a look. That mechanic had asked if anyone had been near the Paix, which had received the answer no. He'd then checked the tyre pressure and found it fine.

The security guard had heard the mechanic report this to the boss on speakerphone from the office. The manager said he'd inform the owner. And that was the end of it. The mechanic had gone home.

'So you will leave my family alone?' Declan asked.

'Not yet. You've got another job. In fact, we've got a few for you.'

Days earlier, one of them had enquired at 7-Star-Car about storage options and knew that all cars were left with their windows cracked open to aid air circulation. Next, in just a few minutes, they wanted Declan to find something long and thin, feed it through the window, and knock the headlight stalk. To turn the headlights on and immediately off. And repeat. Following that, he'd use a jack to raise the front of the car a few inches, then lower it back into place.

But there was even more. At intervals throughout the night, the security guard would perform the same three tricks. Air pressure – on a different tyre – headlights, jack. Over and over, as often as he could.

And, most important of all, he'd phone the half-brothers regularly, to update them on what the owner and the staff thought of all this weird activity.

5

At 10.10pm, Neil, Sean and the rest of the Allerby Job crew were seated at a couple of large tables in a corner of The Chubby Grub, discussing the final details of the plan, which began with a full run-through. Neil had refused to shut the pub, but he'd roped off a portion of the lounge for his meeting and increased the music volume to enhance privacy.

The team was drinking, but Neil had set a two-pint ceiling to make sure nobody was hungover the next day. Noah sat a little removed from the circle, but he watched everything intently, as was his way. And he was teetotal. Sean, like Neil, had opted for just water.

His men were eager to know the plan. This was the first time they'd ever had a major job whose finer details hadn't been picked and prodded at for weeks. Some already knew more than others, but even collectively they had barely more than a rough overview. It struck many as risky to leave it so late, and they were nervous.

After finally outlining his plan in detail, Neil was inundated with questions about security around the Paix and the buyer. Like Sean, they were highly worried about the immobiliser, tracker and telemetry system. Someone also quizzed Neil on why they couldn't just steal the truck that delivered the hypercar, since their prize would already be on board.

The boss called for quiet. 'Okay, boys, time for the magnificence of my plan to be unveiled.'

He described the fiasco at 7-Star-Car a short while ago, when the Paix's digital brain had registered a loss of tyre pressure.

That event got written off, but the next one, at 8.50, didn't. When the security guard sneaked into the Prime Chamber and jacked up the supercar to raise the front wheels from the ground an inch, it caused panic over in France.

Verninac shut the vehicle down and activated the tracker. The owner also got an alert that his car was being stolen, so he called 7-Star-Car. This time no lowly mechanic could be trusted to appraise the situation, so the general manager made his way to the storage site.

The supercar was still in place, untouched, cover still shrouding it. The security guards were questioned, but they swore that they hadn't been inside the Prime Chamber. Luckily, the GM didn't check the camera recordings and the door didn't register breaches.

The security guard was nearby when the Paix's owner spoke to the manager on speakerphone. The billionaire wasn't happy and blamed the Prime Chamber for irritating his vehicle's electrics. He ordered that the air conditioning be turned off. There were four other supercars in the chamber, but together their worth paled next to the Paix, so fuck them. Off went the blowers.

'You guys asked me why we don't steal the truck with the Paix already on it,' Neil said. 'Well, first of all, once the car is through the gates and into the park, the worry about theft will go down. If they expect a jacking, it'll be in transit. But the major problem is that the truck's got a VFH tracker as well, and we can't shut that off. Mad as it sounds, boys, but it's actually going to be easier to nick an eleven-mill car than it is to take a forty-grand truck.'

His men looked at each other, not comprehending.

'More stuff is going to flag down at Verninac headquarters all night,' Neil continued. 'The owner is going to think something is wrong with his telemetry system. A remote diagnostic check from Verninac's end will reveal nothing and reconfiguring the software won't do anything. Things will still go wrong. They'll want to dispatch a flying doctor to have a gander. Until then, the owner is not going to want his car throwing a panic and hassling him with alerts. He also won't want to risk it claiming theft again and shutting down.'

'Or blasting music,' someone said.

'Or doing some other weird shit,' another guy piped up.

Neil slapped the table. 'Hell no. So he'll have the immobiliser and the telemetry system shut down. And with the telemetry off, bang goes the GPS and the geofence around Allerby Park. No GPS equals no knowledge of what the car is doing. That means no tracker activation.'

The men smiled, and they toasted and high-fived each other. But Sean quickly killed their joy when he said, 'But there's still a major time problem, right?'

Neil didn't miss a beat. 'My brother is right. Verninac has a flying doctor who covers Europe and Russia, so he's going to be a good four hours or so away. He won't be able to fix the problems before the car show. The owner came here specially for the show, and he won't miss it or leave early. His plan will be to take the car to a garage or his UK home or some other place, and have it fixed there.'

To prepare, he continued, the doctor would want the latest telemetry readings, so the system would be turned back on.

That could be anytime, but probably when the specialist was close to the scene. That would give the team perhaps until 3 or 3.30pm.

'Our main worry, though, is the show's runners. They might call the owner, which could raise flags when nobody can contact him. Verninac could kick the system in after that. We have to make sure we get the owner and his bodyguards before they raise the alarm, but we also have to hold them. We will also have to force the owner to call the car show and say he'll be late. 3pm, say.'

Three hours, he stressed. His team of mechanics would have three hours to get inside that car and nullify the tracker and the immobiliser. A jammer placed in the vehicle would take care of the telemetry system's GPS.

'In theory,' Sean said. 'But what if the telemetry system isn't turned off when the car arrives for the show?'

'Then it's game over, and we find a post office to rob.'

6

Around 11pm, the meeting concluded and the boys parted to head home. Another condition of Neil's was: get a good night's sleep. Neil also sent Noah away, which left the brothers alone in their secure portion of the lounge.

'You ever told him to go home before?' Sean asked.

'A few times. I don't think he goes, though. He'll probably hide outside somewhere and keep watch. And it's time you left, too.'

'After I know more about the buyer you've got lined up. You said all in good time. I think it's time since the job is tomorrow morning. It worries me that you're keeping him so secret from everyone.'

Neil pulled his phone and opened it up. Sean saw a Facebook profile of a woman before Neil closed that window.

'Another floozy?'

'What?'

'That woman.'

Neil got the Facebook window up again and showed him. 'No, she's someone in a heart palpitations group I'm in. She's not my friend and I don't know her. And she lives in Canada. She posted some symptoms like mine, back in April of last year.'

'Okay. Why you checking her out?'

Neil looked a little embarrassed. 'To see if she's still alive. Kind of a thing I do.'

Sean laughed. 'You check out people like you to make sure they're not dead?'

Neil shrugged. 'I worry. It helps me to know people with this heart stuff are still around years later. Piss off, okay? Here, the buyer.'

He googled something and handed Sean the phone. He saw a website called Fortune Field, which seemed to be about the world of business. The page featured a man called Christopher Richter, CEO of Forest Energy Solutions, a biofuel company with offices in the UK and USA. Annual revenue of £220 million. Richter was worth £125 million. He was fat, bearded, and fifty-one, but looked older. Except for his left arm, which was a prosthetic to replace the one lost in a farming accident thirty years ago. The arm had AI and had cost him $300,000.

'Jesus, AI in his arm?' Sean said. 'That's risky. Think that would be a good defence if you strangled someone with it? Nowt to do with me! I was looking the other way!'

Neil told him that Richter had been on the shortlist for the Paix when Verninac announced it. But it went to an undisclosed lucky man. Richter tried to put it to the back of his mind and did so for three years, until he got in contact with Neil.

'How did a biofuel magnate and a scumbag criminal get in cahoots?'

Neil punched Sean's arm. 'Who's this scumbag criminal, eh?' Neil said he'd gotten to Richter through the farmer, the one who disposed of bodies and vehicles. The farmer purchased

HVO – hydrotreated vegetable oil – from Forest Energy, and one day he made small talk with a salesman. He learned about the CEO's failed Paix mission.

He made the same small talk with one of Neil's men, who later mentioned the Paix and Richter to Neil one night at the pub. Upon later learning of the car show, Neil had an idea, and out of the blue he sent an email to Richter.

'Just like that? You outright told a rich businessman you'd steal a car for him? Not knowing if he'd go to the police?'

'Not at first. I said I was interested in buying it. We chatted for a few weeks before he mentioned something that gave me the feeling he... wouldn't be averse to owning that car by any means. Then I outright offered. And a few months later, after he knew of my plan, he agreed.'

'He agreed? A successful, legitimate businessman agreed to join a plan to steal a hypercar? I'm not sure he can blame his bionic arm if he gets nabbed for this.'

Neil shrugged. 'Rich bastards find it hard to be denied. He badly wants it.'

Sean still found it outrageous. 'This guy's got a lot to lose if he buys a stolen car that can be easily traced. It's such a risk. This thing will be like the Mona Lisa. A one-off like that can't be sold on, can't be registered, can't be driven around.'

'Adverse Possession, baby. Sometimes it's enough just to know it's yours. "The Storm on the Sea of Galilee." Google it.'

Sean had heard of it, but he knew nothing more than the name of that piece of artwork by Rembrandt. A minute later, he knew a lot more. The painter's 1633 creation had been stolen from a Boston museum in 1990 by a couple of men posing as police officers – a disguise Sean had always wanted to try. They tied up the museum staff and got away with thirteen pieces of art, supposedly worth $500 million. The FBI had apparently identified the culprits, but to this day nobody had been put in handcuffs.

Sean was puzzled. 'You're not saying this guy nicked that painting, are you?'

'No. Or, I don't know. Maybe he did. But he does have stolen art. He's a collector. People like him, they don't need to show off what they have. I guess he'd be happy to put that Paix in a room with a naked woman draped on top and just stare at it. What else are you going to do with your cash? How many houses do you want?'

It was a hard argument to counter if you didn't have a hundred million in the bank. 'And what's he paying you?'

'Two million.'

Sean's jaw dropped. 'Fuck off.'

Neil laughed. 'Nice, eh?'

Sean gave it a moment's thought. 'Actually, no. The car is worth eleven mill. There's no way two mill is a number your ego came up with.'

'Well spotted, you cheeky sod. Richter was a little hesitant to pay anything close to what the car's worth. Stolen and all. I think he was worried about something going wrong. I guess a guy like him can write off two million. And to me it's money for next to nothing, so everybody is happy.'

'Fair enough. How will it go down? Cash payment?'

'Of course it's cash. You think either of us wants to explain away that bank transfer? As for the wheres and whens, Richter's company has nineteen depots across the UK. Richter himself will be at his Barnsley depot all day tomorrow. He'll have a truck to whisk the Paix away to his flash Surrey mansion, and he'll leave behind a suitcase full of cash. Here, look. Proof.'

Neil showed him a text. It was from a number stored under no name, and it simply said GOOD LUCK.

'Hardly proof,' Sean said. 'But I believe you. So what's to stop this Richter stuffing us?'

'That was always my worry. That's why none of the men know anything about him. Someone might think they can cut a better deal. As for Richter himself backstabbing me, well, I have a plan for that.'

Neil showed Sean a map on his phone. Just north of Oldtown, in a wedge between the River Dearne and some train tracks, was an expanse of green fields with the Forest Energy depot in the middle. It was a collection of four buildings on the edges of a car park. The site was accessible via a private road that spiked off Smithie Lane, which ran northeast over the tracks and the water.

'Richter will be here tomorrow. This is where he thinks I'll deliver the car.'

'But you won't?'

Neil indicated a point on the map. Four hundred metres southeast of the depot, past the train tracks, Smithie Lane ran by an Oldtown housing estate with a side street called Carrington Avenue. It was lined with standard semi-detached properties.

'Richter owns a house right here. It's just an overnight place he's got for when he visits the depot. Probably bought it for three hundred grand the same way you'd buy a tent. My plan is to call him just before the delivery time and tell him I'll take the car to his house.'

'He won't like that.'

'So what? If he wants the car, he'll go along with whatever I say. So he'll leave the depot to take the money to his house. But we'll meet him before he gets there.'

Sean understood. 'Another deliberate ambush.'

'I don't want to learn the hard way that Richter has set up a trap at the depot. He's got maybe fifty people working there, and plenty of nice spaces to hide bodies. He's okay with stealing a super expensive car, so maybe he won't think twice about robbing me of my two million.'

Sean checked the map, seeking a prime spot for a deliberate ambush. Between Carrington Avenue and the single-lane bridge over the railway was a portion of Smithie Lane lined with trees on both sides and free of buildings. Just like the area where he and Jimmy had taken down the detective. 'Here? Seems Heaven-sent.'

Neil shook his head and pointed to a pub across the road from the gated entrance to Richter's depot. It had a rear car park not visible from the road. 'We hide the truck carrying the Paix in the car park. As soon as Richter exits the gate onto Smithie Lane, I'll stop him, take the money, and be gone. If he's got a trap planned, it'll be down by his house.'

Sean nodded. 'Sounds good.'

Neil slapped his brother's shoulder. 'Little bro, but this time tomorrow we'll be...'

Neil stopped as his phone rang. He took the call and his jaw dropped. And then he grinned. He told the caller, 'Use a blindfold. Don't let her know she's coming here. Meet you round back. Call Noah and tell him to bring three or four men back here.' He hung up. Sean couldn't breathe.

Neil stood up. 'We got her. The boys are bringing her here.'

Holly. She had been captured somehow.

7

Neil got the barmaid to clear the pub. There was moaning, but nobody wanted to be gassed – a leak from a CO_2 gas bottle in the cellar was the excuse offered. The asphyxiant usually caused danger by displacing oxygen, so in the cellar it might cause danger, but a leak out in the lounge, where there was ample ventilation, wouldn't be a real issue.

Nobody present knew this, so they got out quick and orderly, and maybe thanked their lucky stars. By this time, Noah had returned with four of Neil's goons.

Sean was in a half-panic. He had to do something to save Holly, but didn't know what. He watched the customers file out, and he stood by as Neil sent his staff home. They knew the gas leak was bullshit, but he gave no real reason why he wanted The Chubby emptied. They knew better than to ask. Neil locked the door after them and then headed for the back door, followed by his men. He ordered one to kill the lights in the car park.

Sean was at the rear of this group, numbed and zombie-like. When they got outside, in the car park, they waited for Holly's arrival. It was quite dark, with only the moon to illuminate things.

Neil came up to Sean. 'You okay? Look a bit dazed there.'

'This just came out of the blue,' Sean said. It wasn't a lie. 'How did they catch her?'

Neil said one of his men was in Doncaster, where he visited an Asda petrol station to fill up his car. Lo and behold, who should be in the shop, looking at tampons, but the boss's wife. Small world, eh? The goon skipped outside, got his partner, and they waited for her to exit. The plan had been to trail her car and maybe find the guy she was banging, but instead she walked across the car park and stepped over a barrier, to head down to the river. So they snatched her on the embankment.

It was fate, Neil thought.

Shitty freak luck came as a trio after all, Sean thought.

Holly was now going to give up the truth. When Neil told one of his men to call The Triads, Sean gave a loud and very exaggerated laugh. Neil glared at him. Sean said, 'You forgetting about Zippy?'

'What?'

'I told you, you don't need goons with torture tools. Especially for a bloody woman.'

A couple of Neil's men giggled. Neil said, 'Are you saying you want to question her?'

'I'll get answers, just like I got them from Zippy. Maybe then you'll finally accept that I'm a grand master at the art of interrogation. There are some things not in your repertoire, big bro.'

Neil laughed, but he still looked upset at Sean's insult. 'No ego, though, right? Okay, have at her. But I'm going to stand there and watch. I want to see her squirm. And you squirm when she gives you nothing.'

Neil would be present? That wasn't good news, but Sean couldn't push his luck. 'Whatever you want, boss.'

A car turned up nine minutes later. Sean saw Holly in the

back with a man, and she wore a blindfold. Neil said, 'Bring her to Room X. I want her to walk in and see me there. Don't tell her where she is.'

Neil headed inside his pub. The guy in the back of the car got out, dragging Holly roughly with him. That was when Sean's fear spiked: she still wore his tracksuit. The two men who'd captured her had missed it, but Neil wouldn't. When he saw the name of his local gym on the back of her top, he'd know she'd gotten the outfit from Sean. After she'd escaped from The Chubby.

He rushed over to her, watched by seven men. 'You bitch. You caused so much trouble.'

The shock on her face was real. Sean grabbed her by the arm, ripping her from the other guy's grasp. That bozo was equally surprised. 'You caused embarrassment, so let's see how you like it.'

Right there in the dark car park, he started to strip her. She moaned, but didn't fight him as he roughly tore off her top. He hoped she was playing along and wasn't scared and bewildered by a vicious new change of circumstances.

All but one of Neil's men watched with mixed emotions. The outlier stepped forward and grabbed Sean's shoulder. 'That's enough of this shit, pal,' he said. He seemed like a good man, which made Sean feel a sliver of guilt when he stuck an elbow in the side of his head.

'She nearly killed me, so piss off.'

The guy made no further attempt at heroism, which allowed Sean to continue ripping at Holly's clothing. When the gym top came free, it dragged away Holly's blindfold. From her expression, she wasn't surprised to know she was outside her former home. He dropped the top on the ground and turned on Neil's men. 'Someone, now, a knife, right now.'

Someone held one out. Sean snatched it and sliced away the

gym trousers from Holly's legs. When she was naked but for bra and knickers, he balled up the tracksuit and stuck it under his arm. 'There you go, now you can be the embarrassed one. Someone get this bitch into Room X.'

While one guy grabbed her and everyone headed for the fire exit, Sean threw the clothing onto the roof of the compound containing the wheelie bins.

He pushed past one of Neil's men and grabbed Holly's arm, and pushed away the guy holding her. He stroked her arm with his thumb, hoping it would relay a message that all would be okay.

Neil was waiting in Room X, and not happy that Holly didn't have a blindfold. He ordered Sean to dump her in the seat. Sean guided her there. Neil's men crammed into the room, eager for a show, but he ordered all but two out and told one of them to close the door. He looked her up and down.

'Someone's been a naughty girl,' he said. And then he slapped her hard. She yelped. Her nose started leaking blood. Sean used all his strength and will to keep himself rooted in the spot.

'I don't know what you're talking about,' Holly said, crying now, and not because of pain. 'I didn't go to the police.'

'And how did you know I thought that?'

'I hear rumours. But they're not true.'

She lowered her head. He used her hair to drag it up. 'Keep your damn eyes on me. And tell me what the police know. Right now. Do they know about the job tomorrow?'

'I haven't talked to the police.'

He slapped her again, and pulled back his arm for another. Sean said, 'Wait, Neil.' It paused his brother's arm. 'You said I could deal with this.'

Neil thought, and stepped back. 'Okay, go for it. Slap her.'

'I want to talk to her. Let's get these guys out of here. And you. Let me have a word alone. I'll convince her. I'll get the truth.'

Neil didn't even have to think this time. 'You get five minutes, superstar. Lads, let's go. Five minutes, Sean, and then it's my turn.'

Neil got his people out of there quick. Sean moved to the door once it was shut. He listened with an ear against it, to make sure nobody was lurking right behind. Certain they couldn't be overheard, he rushed to Holly. She stood to take his hug and crushed him right back, crying into his ear.

'I'm sorry,' Sean said, on the verge of tears himself. 'It was the tracksuit, they would have known I gave it you, I had to, I'm sorry, I–'

'It's okay, it's okay, I understand. Don't apologise. I'm sorry I went out. I... am I going to die?'

He pulled back from her and used his sleeve to dab blood away from her nose. 'No, no, no. No fucking way. But I need to think of a way out of this.'

'Please help me. I love you.'

He thought he couldn't want to save her any more than he already did. But her words lit a new fire in him. If necessary, he'd fight his way out of the pub with her, even against a hundred men.

'I love you, too. But I don't know what we can do. I'm sorry. I'm so weak.'

She took his face in her hands. 'I know a way. It's also risky, but it might work. We tell Neil that I was sleeping with that detective.'

'What? No, he'll–'

'Listen to me. Neil thinks I'm talking to the police. But how could I be doing that if I'm sleeping with one of them? They're not allowed to do that. I think Neil will believe it.'

He didn't like it. Neil would punish her for cheating... or

maybe he wouldn't. He had a new girl. He suspected she had betrayed him, and he needed an answer. Infidelity was a damn sight safer than selling him out to law enforcement.

Sean nodded. 'We can try that. I don't know what he'll do, but it should save you.'

She smiled through her tears. 'This should be like when kids want their dad to come home quick and get the punishment over with.'

He still didn't like it, but they were between a rock and a hard place, no alternatives available. He kissed her on the lips and she returned it with interest. Afterwards, she sat on the chair and Sean went to the door. He pounded on it four times and yelled, 'Two minutes. You owe me money, Neil.'

Neil and four of his goons entered the room. Sean said to Holly, 'Tell him what you told me.'

She had her hands fisted in her hair, pain on her face. 'Neil, I was sleeping with that detective. I'm sorry. You were distant. I needed something else. Someone else. Something new. I... NEIL!'

'Bro, what are you doing? Listen to her.'

Neil had pulled a pistol and, just three feet away, aimed it at Holly's head. 'This is the worst kind of betrayal,' he said.

'Worse than selling you out to the cops? Put that gun down, Neil. It's just an affair.'

'But it's who it's with. The ultimate betrayal. I'm going to kill her on three.'

'You can't. You can get past this. She only saw him once.'

'One... two...'

Sean knew his brother's face, every emotion and the thoughts behind it, and he didn't doubt for a second that a bullet would be loosed on three. With no other option within grasp, and no time to think...

'Thr–'

–he kicked at the gun. The blow knocked Neil's arm upwards. The pistol barked and thudded a bullet into the concrete ceiling. Sean didn't know if his strike had caused Neil to pull the trigger, or if his brother had tried to murder his wife.

Three of Neil's goons immediately leaped at Sean and wrestled him to the floor, while number four secured Holly with a knife at her cheek. She yelled for Sean to be released. Sean knew returning the favour was useless.

Neil squatted by his brother and showed him his phone. In that moment, Sean knew it was game over. No more subterfuge, no more tricks, no more hope.

On the phone was a live feed of this very room, from a camera in a high corner. He glanced up there but saw nothing. The camera must be tiny and staring out through a pinprick hole. He knew why it was hidden. If the police raided this room, they'd want that camera, for who knew what crimes it had recorded.

He also knew that Neil, perhaps out of curiosity rather than suspicion, had watched Sean's interaction with Holly. It didn't matter if there was no audio. He and Holly had kissed, and in front of a live audience.

Neil's words – *This is the worst kind of betrayal* – now made absolute sense.

8

Neil stomped around his pool table, injecting too much power into his shots. He had that terrible sinking feeling in his chest again as his heart played up. Stress for sure would down him long before an enemy weapon. His men, scattered around the lounge, waited and fidgeted. Noah sat patiently nearby.

Neil's next stab with the cue hit the white ball too low, too hard, and it skipped off the table. And rolled across the floor. One of his men retrieved it, placed it back on the baize, and said, 'We need an answer, boss.'

Neil grabbed the black and threw it straight at him. It missed, thankfully, and bounced off the back of a chair.

'You fucker,' Neil yelled. 'This is my damn brother. I can't just kill him. Look at all you pieces of shit, just waiting for the order. Fuck off out of here and let me think. Go on, piss off and wait outside.'

They made to leave anyway, but Noah started herding them to the door. After he'd shut it behind them, he located the black ball and dropped it on the pool table. Noah then raised his eyebrows, which was his version of the same question spoken by the goon thirty seconds earlier.

'Get a team to round up the Pest B Gone guys. They're loyal to Sean. Can't have them asking questions or trying something. Oh, and check outside for Sean's car, and get rid of that, too.'

Noah nodded, and waited for more.

It was too risky to kill Holly right now, especially if the police were closing in. He believed that she hadn't spoken to the police, but that didn't matter. She was missing and they were hunting her, and Neil had no idea how much they knew. They might be able to trace the car that whisked her away from an Asda petrol station earlier.

Cops on his payroll had heard nothing about a strike team preparing a raid, but that also was evidence of sweet fuck-all. Sometimes major targets required the formation of a new, secret group of detectives, which lowly uniforms would know nothing about. The Allerby Job was too much to risk.

Besides, the slaps he'd delivered to her face, and the terror in her eyes at being captured, had gone a long way to dampening his anger. 'Take her to the farm. I'll decide what to do with her tomorrow. We'll use tonight to put feelers out to see if the Allerby Job is on cop radar.'

Noah nodded. And waited. There was one more issue, of course.

Neil softly jabbed at the black with his cue and didn't speak until it had rolled into a pocket. 'Take Sean to the farm as well. Make sure they're kept apart. Have The Triad go at him, too. There's no telling what plan they might have cooked up to fuck me over.'

But what then? What if his prisoners hadn't ratted him out and the Allerby Job went smoothly? Could he kill his wife and his brother in cold blood?

Sean had been in cahoots with Holly. Pussy had a way of changing men. It had dissolved Sean's loyalty to his brother.

And vice versa.

9

Sean had his feet bound by cable ties and his hands secured behind his back, and a cloth money bag placed over his head. As a goon dragged the bag on, knuckles raked over Sean's head wound and it hurt like hell. It was all bad news, but at least he was taken out of Room X, just as Holly had been. So he wasn't to face a trial. However, it didn't mean he wasn't due a hell of a time.

He was carried out to the car park and dumped in the back of a vehicle. At least it wasn't the boot. Two big men squashed in next to him. He wasn't sure of which side of the fence these guys sat on. Were they anti-Neil's brother, or would they be sympathetic? Determining this required a test.

'Where are we going?'

'Shut your cakehole,' said the guy on his left. So, that decided things. He had no friends here.

Another test: 'Your mother used to like me putting cake in her hole.'

'Yo momma jokes? How fucking old are you?' the goon said, but that was it. No revenge slap. Maybe the guy was worried about his future if Sean was left alive and possibly even pardoned. Maybe not. It didn't prove a thing.

'I might not forgive you for this,' Sean said. Test number three. The guy on his right said they were only following orders, which was also a good sign that they figured Sean might emerge from this unscathed.

Or he was reading too much into it?

'Holly?' he yelled, hoping she was in the same vehicle – perhaps the boot. But he got no answer from her. The bozo on his left, however, repeated his order to shut up.

They started driving. Sean tried to work out his route mentally, but that failed a couple of minutes in when the driver said, 'Shit, which way is it again? Where the fuck are we?'

'You dick,' Sean said.

'Piss off,' the driver replied.

Sean had to wait for more clues as to where he was destined. The first came when the normal sounds of urban life faded. The next was when the ground beneath the car turned rougher. Soil.

Cowbell Farm. Just great.

The car stopped a couple of minutes later and the trio of goons got out. They shut the doors, so that while Sean heard talking, he couldn't distinguish any words.

Next he heard the obvious scrape of a big door being hauled back on rails. A barn. The goons got back in the car and it drove into the building. Again the trio exited the vehicle, but this time a door was left open. Sean heard the farmer's voice. But before anyone could say something helpful, the door shut.

The barn was good news, though. It meant Neil hadn't yet decided what to do with him. Given that his brother was probably at his angriest right now and likely to mellow as time passed, Sean figured he didn't have an appointment with the Volkan incinerator. Then again, he'd seen things play out the other way in the past.

'Hey, I need a shit,' he yelled.

One of the rear doors opened. The guy who'd sat on his left said, 'Do it in your pants.'

'Really? If I'm going into the incinerator, you'll have to carry me stinking of shit.'

'Seen worse. I'll take your arms anyway.'

'Is your mum here? She used to let me dump in her mouth. She had a thing for–'

A foot blasted him in the left shoulder, knocking him flat on the seat and tweaking his neck. Somehow it also hurt his head wound. 'She's in the ground, dickhead. Right where you're going.'

The door slammed. But by insulting the goon, Sean had kept the door open long enough to hear what one of the other men had said to the farmer: '...on him every hour. And keep the fire ready. Call if there's a problem.'

He would be under observation, which probably meant an overnight stay. Neil wanted him out of the way until after the Allerby Job. Doubtless his brother planned to have him interrogated because he was worried that his big-time mission might be under threat. And afterwards? The 'fire' obviously meant the Volkan. Not a good sign.

Unfortunately, Sean hadn't heard a word about Holly. She was probably also on the farm. It burned him to know she might be facing interrogation or torture right now. And that she was all alone.

And that was that. Everybody left, the big door was slid shut, and there was nothing but silence thereafter.

10

It was impossible to determine the passage of time. Half an hour? Three hours? Was it morning? Had he slept some? Had something woken him?

The latter seemed most appropriate when Sean heard a sound. It was the creak of a door opening, but not the main sliding entrance. He knew the barn had a standard side door. It must be the farmer, here to check on him as instructed. Or maybe to give him grief for what happened two days ago.

He didn't hear another sound until the one of the car's front doors opened. It made him jump, for he hadn't heard anyone enter the barn.

'You after your £20 back?' Sean said. 'It's at home. Cut me loose and I'll go fetch it.'

No response other than the noise of the man opening the glove box and rooting through the contents. So, this wasn't the farmer. 'I want to talk to my brother.' He made sure to use that word, brother, to remind whoever this was of his connection to the firm's big boss.

This time the only response was the shutting of the door.

The rear door on the same side opened. Now a little

worried that a rogue element in the firm had come for vengeance, Sean backed away. He knew he was highly vulnerable with his hands tied behind his back, and his eyes blinded by the money bag.

Which was suddenly ripped from his head.

'Noah?'

There stood Neil's fixer at the opened door, bent over so he could stare inside. Sean glanced out the windows, but saw nobody else. The barn was empty apart from the two cars Sean and Jimmy had driven here the other day and the Seat Ibiza that had already been in place. All three looked like rotting carcasses, having been stripped of at least two-thirds of their weight so far.

Noah held up a multi-tool. 'Use this.'

He dropped it on the seat, then shut the door. He folded his arms and waited, watching through the window.

Sean turned in the seat so he could grab the tool. Blind, he opened the penknife and sawed the cable tie. That done, he snipped the one around his feet and exited the car.

'Why did you free me?' he said.

'I didn't,' the fixer replied. 'You rooted in the glove box and found that tool yourself. I wasn't even here.'

Sean wasn't having any of that. 'Why did you save my sorry arse, Noah?'

The older man looked surprised by the question. 'It should be obvious, even if I was always cold towards you as Neil's right-hand man. I do my job. But I also pay my debts.'

Sean opened his mouth to speak, but Noah shushed him. 'You need to go. Neil isn't yet sure what he wants to do with you, but the fact that you're here means he's leaning towards killing you. I could be wrong, but I don't think you want to stick around and find out. Run and hide. Now.'

'I think you know I'm not about to run away.'

Noah nodded. 'I don't know exactly where Holly is. But I know she's on this farm.'

'Did you already know about me and her?'

'I half-suspected. Try as you might to hide it, there were giveaways every time you were in the same room together. I saw you bump into her once and neither of you apologised. That requires a level of comfort that didn't seem right. I don't think Neil suspected it. But I always believed she was just his trophy wife anyway. Business quickly became his prime love.'

'Believe me, I know it.'

Noah jabbed a finger at the side door. 'Be on your way. You might want to take out the farmer. He's supposed to report any problems to me, and I would have to inform Neil. Incapacitate him and maybe you'll get the rest of the night as a head start. But I can't promise.'

Sean put the multi-tool in his pocket. 'No,' Noah said. 'Leave that on the back seat. This has to look like you escaped by yourself. Dump it and go. Don't tell me your destination, just in case. And don't go for your car, wherever you hid it. Good luck. I hope Holly and you work out.'

Despite ordering Sean to leave, Noah performed that action first. Sean was out the door five seconds later.

CHAPTER 7

1

Neil's new status and wealth convinced him it was time to find his own accommodation and not have his brother under his feet. He rented a luxurious flat in a high-end part of Sheffield. However, he wanted Sean close and helped him find a place nearby. Their old flat would continue to be a whorehouse. Sean was directed to pick one of the girls to take over the day-to-day running.

He chose Sandra, their original worker, but the conversation didn't go as planned. He gathered all the ladies in the living room, after waiting ten minutes for one to dispense with a customer, and laid out the blueprint. Sandra would be the new boss, answerable to Neil. Every day at midnight a representative of his would stop by, to whom Sandra would deliver a cash package. Simple. Her reward for this promotion? Sandra's cut of her own earnings would raise to eighty per cent.

But she didn't seem happy and requested a word alone with Sean. They moved into the kitchen for privacy, and there she surprised him. 'I don't want to do this anymore.'

'Why?'

It wasn't the sex with strangers and she didn't feel debased. She simply wanted to move on. There was no future in this illegitimate work. 'The longer I do this, the longer I have a blank work record. I want to do something with my life. I've waited too long and this is holding me back. I don't want to be old and diseased and regretful.'

Sean felt she was confused and deluded. Sandra hadn't worked a legit job in years and had been selling sex since long before the brothers recruited her. But he understood what she meant because he felt the same way about his criminal work. His heart wasn't fully there and the future was bleak.

Every time he committed a crime, he faced the threat of arrest. Every time his team raided a property or hurt someone, it increased his chances of a revenge attack out of the blue somewhere down the line. Murder, prison, fugitive status – these fates loomed over him constantly.

'Okay,' he said. 'If that's what you want, you can leave.'

She smiled, but nervously. 'Are you sure?'

'Do you need help with it? With getting on your feet?'

She shook her head. 'I have people who can help. I'm not the sad bitch I might have seemed when we first met. Don't worry about me. I'll be fine. This time next year I'll be happy and successful.'

He hoped so. He hoped they both were. His parting line to her was, 'Call on me if you ever need help.'

Neil didn't share this sense of loyalty to those who'd helped him achieve things. Now on the verge of the greatness he so desired, he had no use for the lowlifes he'd surrounded himself with. He had better men in his entourage, tough guys, smart guys, guys with lives, guys whose commitment to him didn't stem from substance addiction.

Many of the lowlifes didn't see far beyond their next hit, so a severance package of drugs made them happy. Others weren't so blinded and begged to be kept on, knowing they would get money nowhere else. Hit hardest was Buzz, the man who made a home out of the bin compound beside the Webbs' old flat. He had to go because while a whorehouse might be a target for thieves, it would no longer magnetise those seeking to hurt the brothers. Buzz was given a bottle of whisky and his marching orders.

But he refused to abandon the brothers. Unaware of where Neil and Sean now lived, he continued to haunt the compound, day after day, hoping one of them would show up. Sean likened him to Hachiko, the Japanese dog made famous by its story of lingering at a railway station in wait for a dead master. For ten years!

The first time Neil visited the whorehouse and was hounded by Buzz, he brushed it off. On the next occasion Buzz was given a stern warning. But when the homeless man found Neil's new flat and rapped on the door, the penalty was a severe beating.

Hearing this story put sympathy in Sean's heart. The next day he went in search of Buzz and found him living in a rotten tent in the woods. Buzz was blind drunk at two in the afternoon and covered in dirt and insects.

'Get up,' Sean said. 'Jesus Christ.'

He got Buzz into his car. The lowlife was scared for his life, but Sean had no plans to hurt him. Instead, he took Buzz to a flat belonging to one his Pest B Gone staff. The owner agreed to vacate the place until further notice. Sean stocked it with food and water, nailed shut the windows, and locked the door behind him when he left. He visited twice a day.

Buzz had no clue why he was there, but assumed the worst. He was a prisoner awaiting execution. For three days he ranted and raved because he had no alcohol and suffered major withdrawal symptoms, but luckily nothing as serious as delirium tremens or seizures. The worst effect, he'd later say, was a feeling that bugs were crawling all over his skin.

On day six, he mellowed a little and finally started sleeping well. By day ten, he was washing and eating better. On day thirteen he wanted to see Sean, claiming he was no longer an addict. Sean brought him a bottle of whisky. Buzz stared at it for a long time as it sat on the coffee table between them.

'Alcohol was my only friend,' he said. 'It made me feel good. We had great nights together. It gave me strength and courage.'

'Doesn't sound like the words of a cured man,' was Sean's response.

'But it wasn't my friend. It was using me. It took my money, my health, my friends, my family, my future.'

Buzz then grabbed the bottle and poured it away.

A week later, Sean felt Buzz could be trusted alone out in the wide world. He convinced Neil to hire him as a dogsbody, although Sean referred to the job as 'assistant'. With some money up front, Buzz got a bedsit of his own. Sean paid a lowlife to keep him under surveillance for a month, and not once did he return to alcohol. Neil even started to respect the man and claimed his dedication to the job would likely propel him through the ranks in the coming years.

This dedication meant Sean's interactions with Buzz dwindled. On the last occasion that the two men chatted like friends, Buzz pulled Sean aside while Neil was in a meeting with a new business partner and thanked him for what he'd done.

'Don't worry about it, Buzz,' Sean said.

'Don't call me that anymore, please. I was always called Buzz because I loved the drink from about the age of seven. I was always chasing that buzz.'

This surprised Sean. 'I always assumed that was your real name.'

Buzz shook his head. 'No. If we go by my birth certificate, then call me Noah.'

2

Cowbell Farm had three barns, a number of silos, a brooder house, stables even though the farmer no longer had horses, and various storage buildings. Too many to quickly search. The farmer was proud of his land and he wouldn't let anyone anywhere without his say-so, so he had probably picked the place where Holly was imprisoned. Since Sean had to do something about the farmer, so the man wouldn't raise the alarm, it was a case of killing two birds with one stone.

So, Sean ran across the dark land, towards the two-floor farmhouse. It was a barn conversion with a cross-gable roof and vertical grey cladding, which gave it a very contemporary appearance. The front door was also modern, made of aluminium and with an intercom and camera. Sean avoided it. He noted an opened roof window. There was a garage attached to the building that would allow easy access to the roof, and a wheelie bin provided a handy boost onto the lower edifice.

From ground to roof: nine seconds. A peek through the window showed him a dark bedroom. He slid through the window, landing softly on the unmade bed. Even in the gloom he saw that the room was a shit tip, so he didn't care about the mud he trod all over the quilt.

The door was ajar. A peek displayed an empty hallway beyond. Four other doors were also open to show no life in any upstairs room. The stairs were carpeted and didn't creak as he went down. He could hear a radio playing the kind of chilled music enjoyed on an Ibiza beach late at night.

The stairs delivered Sean into a foyer with a door on the immediate right, which he peeked through. Living room. Across the way were two more doors, with another behind him to the left. That one led to a sunroom with a swing chair more suited to a garden.

Of the two doors on the far side of foyer, one was shut and one was ajar. The music seemed to be playing from beyond the closed door. Sean scuttled across the tiles and peeked through the door that was cracked open. Kitchen. He swung it wider and noticed, in the lefthand wall, an opened serving hatch into the room the music emanated from. It was probably a dining room. He poked an eye past the edge of the hatch.

What he saw sent him running to the door. On the way, he grabbed a steak knife from a rack.

The dining room had a large oval table in the middle, and on it was Holly, naked and spread-eagled with her hands and feet tied by ropes that ran down and around each of the four thick oak legs. Her mouth was gagged and eyes taped shut. Her skin was covered in glue and gold glitter in curls and whorls and all manner of other decorative shapes. With a brush, the farmer was applying glue to the sides of her nose.

And he continued to do so even when Sean threw open the door. He had his back to Sean and wore headphones that played music so loudly it had been audible from the stairs. Without missing a beat, Sean rushed over and ripped them from the farmer's head.

When the older man turned, shocked, Sean grabbed his hair and drew the blade of the knife across the forehead, hard, fast, deep. The farmer fell backward, screaming, hands to his rent flesh, blood instantly gushing between his fingers.

'I'm sorry, I'm sorry,' he moaned, rolling on the floor in agony, blinded by blood. Sean booted him hard in the guts to keep him down, then tore the bonds off Holly's eyes and mouth. While the farmer worked, she had been numbed by fear into silence and immobility, but seeing her saviour kicked her into life. She burst into tears and yelled her gratitude. Sean stroked her face to calm her. 'It's okay, baby. You're safe. You're safe now. Don't panic.'

He slit the ropes around ankles and wrists and helped her off the table. She saw the farmer and, even though he was down and Sean was here, shied away from him. God knew how long he'd been abusing her, or what else he'd done before Sean's arrival. Sean dampened down fiery rage and led Holly to the door.

'Go shower,' he said when they stepped into the foyer. 'You're safe now. I'll be up in a second after I tie this guy up.'

'I don't want you to leave me. I don't want to be alone in this house.'

'Okay. Wait here. I'll just be a few seconds.'

He re-entered the dining room and shut the door behind him. The farmer seemed to be over his shock now, for he was on his knees and trying to wipe the blood from his eyes. Sean grabbed the bottle of glue and squatted before the man, silent. He waited until the farmer had cleared enough of the blood to flicker open his eyes.

As soon as he saw Sean, he moaned and said, 'I'm sorry, I won't do anything like that again. Please!'

'Promise?'

'Yes, yes, please, yes, just don't hurt me, I promise, I promise–'

There he stopped talking as Sean grabbed the man's chin and jammed the conical cap of the bottle into his mouth, at the same time squeezing hard to unleash a jet of glue deep into the throat. He'd waited until the man had expelled most of his breath.

The farmer didn't react at first, for there was no pain. Then he realised he couldn't breathe. He clutched his throat and bounced around the room. He came for Sean, but was easily pushed away. He also went for a sideboard drawer of cutlery, to stick a fork into his mouth and attempt to clear the drying liquid blockage. It failed. After that, as his lungs no doubt started to burn, he dropped to the floor, writhing in terror. Sean just watched.

A minute later, the farmer's flailing limbs slowed, and thirty seconds after that fell limp.

'I reckon you might just keep that promise,' Sean said, and left the dining room.

3

If the farmer was supposed to check on his prisoners regularly then report in, that could be a problem. As Holly showered, Sean wanted to watch the land from a window, in case people came. But Holly insisted on his presence in the bathroom.

So, he sat on the toilet and watched her scrub glue and glitter away. 'We need to get you somewhere else,' he said. Without saying as much, he wanted to rush her. He was also careful not to use the word 'safe', so as to avoiding broadcasting that the danger was far from over.

It was a wasted effort. 'There's nowhere safe,' she said. 'Neil will find me anywhere. He's going to kill me.'

'He's not. He would have already.' Sean wasn't sure he spoke the truth.

When she was done, he handed her a towel, but she refused it. She didn't want to touch something that might have been around the farmer's body. Sean helped her dry with toilet paper. She returned to their conversation.

'Neil wants me dead. Both of us. There's only one thing we can do.'

'We'll find somewhere to hide. You can't go back to the bridge because Neil's people picked you up around there. I know a place we might be able to use just for tonight. And tomorrow we'll go far south.'

'I don't mean that. I mean Neil has to go away. Maybe the right thing to do is go to the police. Tell them everything.'

Sean didn't respond until after she'd dressed. She couldn't find her own clothing and wouldn't wear any of the unmarried farmer's. Sean instead wore some of the dead man's and gave Holly his own grimy jeans and thick T-shirt.

'It's not a good idea to go to the police,' he said. 'That's an escalation. I think that right now we still have a chance to survive this. Neil will be less angry at us as time goes on. But not if we involve the police. Besides, Neil has police officers in his corner. If one of them finds out, Neil will know exactly where we are.'

Not for the first time, he wasn't sold on his own argument. Neil would be enraged by their escape, and he would probably suspect that Holly would go to the police. An escalation was inevitable.

'I don't know, Sean. It seems the safest bet to me. Protective custody. I think we should.'

'Let's just wait out the night. Please. Let's get somewhere... else. Please?'

She nodded, but reluctantly.

He'd found the farmer's phone and the key to his Toyota Land Cruiser. He used the phone to load the Gov.uk website to check on the vehicle's tax and MOT status. All good.

He searched the house for money and found about £40 in a jar in the kitchen. He put Holly in the vehicle and sat by her, thinking. He considered hiding the farmer's body to give them more escape time, but figured it was a useless endeavour. The dining room was coated in blood and he and Holly were missing. Nobody was going to be fooled into thinking the farmer had moved the prisoners elsewhere.

Instead, he opened up the farmer's phone, which wasn't password protected, and scrolled through the messages, to acclimatise himself to how the man spoke when texting. There were some sexy letters to a woman called Joby, threats to someone listed as Nobhead, and various missives to unknown numbers, which might be burners that had belonged to Neil's men.

The latter included a text from earlier tonight in which a number ending 6634 had said KEEP AN EYE ON THEM TXT ME EVERY 3 HOURS, clearly meaning Neil and Holly.

In two recent messages the farmer had been asked if he or things were okay, and he'd responded with *S'all dandy*. He'd also signed off on other texts with the same line. That would do. Sean sent a text to the 6634 number saying *S'all dandy*. Hopefully that would allay suspicion. Sean doubted that anyone would come here to check the prisoners. Neil and his men had the Allerby House job tomorrow and would need sleep. It would give him all night to get Holly somewhere secure.

He had one more job. He drove to the barn where he'd been imprisoned. The Seat Ibiza's front end bumper had been removed and lay by the car. It retained the grille, but the licence plate had gone. Sean loaded the bumper into the back of the Land Cruiser.

After a stop on a rural lane to drop something off and a visit to a garage to buy two prepaid phones, Sean drove Holly to a suburban address and turned into the driveway, which ran alongside the side of the house and terminated at a garage. He parked as close to the garage door as possible and used a green wheelie bin to hide the Land Cruiser's licence plate from view.

Holly had more enthusiasm by the time they got to the front door. He was glad to see a big slice of her anxiety had eloped. 'Who lives here?' she said.

'A man I hope can help us.'

All the lights were off in the house, but the bedroom lit up when Sean rapped the door. It had a peephole so he made sure he was in full view. He didn't hear a thing until the door opened.

Standing there was Jacob Jansen, proofreader and father to a dead daughter. Despite the hour and the unprompted visit, Jacob was pleased to see Sean. They shook hands. 'Nobody knocks on a door this late unless they need help,' Jacob said.

'I can't explain. But I need a place for the night, for me and my friend.'

There was no pause for thought. 'Anytime. In you come.'

Jacob recognised Holly from some news story back whenever, and he'd heard the rumours about her going missing. But he asked no questions other than to ascertain that she was okay. He gave the couple a quilt and pillows to use on the floor of the empty bedroom at the front of the house. Jacob had split from his wife two years ago, following his daughter's demise, and lived alone. He was happy to have company. That said, he soon left the couple to it.

Sean got in bed while Holly used the bathroom. He remained dressed. Nobody posing a threat knew this address, and certainly not that he was here, but it felt safer to know they could flee at a moment's notice. He typed a text to the number ending 6643 using the farmer's phone. *S'all dandy.*

When Holly got in beside him, also still dressed, Sean said, 'This is nice. Our first time in the same room all night.'

'It seems I've spent the last year worried about Neil. Hiding from him.'

'This beats a quickie in some locker room or hotel.'

'At least back then we knew we'd gotten away with it. Now we know we haven't. We could go back to normal after those meetings. Nothing will ever be normal again.'

His ploy to calm her down hadn't worked, obviously, so he–

The farmer's phone rang. Sean clutched it and stared at it.

'Who is it?' Holly asked.

Ignoring her, Sean got up and paced the room, still staring at the phone. He'd just sent a text, so this call meant something new, something important. If the farmer didn't answer, people might be sent to the farm.

'It is Neil?' Holly said, scared.

Her fear wiped out his. He answered the call, angry. He didn't give a shit if his enemies knew he'd escaped. In his best attempt at an automated voice, he said, 'I'm afraid the person you are trying to call is dead and cannot–'

'Sean? I thought it might be you.'

It was Noah. 'You're the man the farmer was supposed to keep updated?'

'I had to know, hence the call. Neil's sending people to the farm for 2pm. That's how long you've got to get somewhere far away. Is the farmer really dead?'

'Let's just say I hope he didn't owe you ten grand.'

'Speaking of which. There's a safe house in Hackenthorpe. It should be unoccupied. We keep a stash of jewellery there until it's safe to sell. Good luck, Sean. Out. Get rid of that phone or it will be tracked. Write this number down and then memorise it.'

Noah gave a mobile number – not the one he was calling from – and hung up.

When Sean got back into bed, Holly still looked scared, so he told her about Noah's intervention and what he'd said on the phone. It soothed her a little. He had one more trick. He snuggled up close to her. 'I love you.'

She said and did nothing at first. But after a few seconds she kissed his cheek. 'Thank you. Love you too. More so.'

'Probably.'

She kneed him softly in the leg and giggled. That was good enough for him.

4

Sleep, surprisingly, wasn't hard to come by. But it didn't last. Holly woke at 5.50 and Sean stirred when she got up to look out the window. He joined her. It was still dark out.

'You okay?' he asked.

'Yes. New day coming. New life, maybe. What's your plan? I can't think straight. I'll just follow you, whatever you choose.'

That didn't last. When he told her he had something important to do before they left the city, she wasn't happy. 'What do you mean? We need to go. What do you have to do?'

'And go we will. But I have one job to take care of. Don't ask me what–'

'I will damn well ask,' she snapped. 'That man, Noah, even he told us to run. We had a twelve-hour head start on my husband. Now it's less. We need to use what little time we have left to get away.'

She was intently looking out the window, but it wasn't the street that absorbed her. She couldn't look at him, he knew.

'If I tell you what I'm doing, you'll only say no. But we need money, Holly. We've got none. I know how to get some, and please let's leave it at that.'

She didn't like it. She headed out of the room, perhaps to the bathroom. Sean waited. She returned two minutes later and had obviously had a quiet think. 'How long will it take you?'

'Five or six hours. But I need to leave soon. You just wait here. I'll clear it with Jacob.'

She sighed. But she nodded. 'I won't ask. I know it's dangerous. I know you will do your best to come back to me. Don't get hurt.'

He hugged her from behind. 'Not on the agenda.'

She didn't laugh. 'It never is, but that doesn't mean a thing. Please think about the police. I think we need to involve them. And please come back.'

He promised to. Fifteen minutes later, Sean left the house. He backed the Land Cruiser down the driveway, but paused with its back end in the street. He stared up at Holly, still standing at the bedroom window.

She blew him a kiss and he returned it, but neither of them moved. Sean couldn't tear his eyes away from her.

Just in case he never saw her again.

5

At 07.15, a man in a suit turned up on the doorstep of a bungalow in a typical housing estate in Ecclesall. A self-employed breakdown service mechanic lived there with his elderly mother, for whom he was a registered carer. His recovery van, an Iveco with a fourteen-foot flatbed trailer, was in the driveway. There was nothing in the back except for portable ramps and straps for tying cars down.

When the mechanic answered the door, the suited man said, 'My kid kicked his ball over your fence. It's in your backyard. Could you fetch it for me, please?'

'I'll lob it over the fence,' the mechanic said. He was clearly annoyed at the intrusion at such an early hour. He shut the door. The suited man walked to the fence in question, which was six feet high and barred entry to the rear of the property. The wheelie bin helped him leap quickly over. He was at the back door before the mechanic opened it.

When the mechanic opened it, the man in the suit rushed inside and forced the mechanic ahead of him, aided by a sharp knife held at the throat, where it would stay until the intruder fled the property.

'Keys to your truck. Now.'

He escorted the mechanic to a row of hooks just inside the front door. Key taken, they returned to the kitchen, where the mechanic was made to sit on the floor. For about the tenth time, he pleaded for the burglar to not hurt his frail mother, who was asleep upstairs.

'I need your truck until this afternoon,' the burglar said. 'When we're done with it, I'll text you with the location of where I'll leave it. You don't call the police. Understand?'

The mechanic nodded, but of course he did. Figuring he needed more convincing, the burglar got out his phone and showed the mechanic a short video. In it were five mean-looking men with machetes and smiles, posing for the lens. They waved and, as one, said, 'Hello. Maybe we'll see you and your family soon.'

The mechanic's face was a picture. It was clear he understood the message.

'The truck is all we want. So no cops. I've got your business phone number. I'll text the location of the van when we're done with it, and you go get it. If I get a whiff that the cops know it was stolen, my friends will come see you. And what they'll do will have sixty coppers involved. Understand?'

The mechanic nodded.

'Good. So, we're going to go out front like you're lending me your truck. If I get pulled over and the cops contact you, you say I had permission. You go along with this and you'll never hear from us again. Understand?'

Another nod.

6

At 10am, a white van rode down Underhill Lane and tried to turn through the back gate into Allerby Park. Signs for the car show had been laid on the grass, including one that warning that SHOW PERMIT HOLDERS ONLY were allowed. To back it all up, there was a woman in a high-vis jacket with ELEGANT ENGINES on the back. She just about leaped in front of the van.

It stopped and she came to driver's window. 'No vans allowed,' she said. 'I'm sorry, but this entrance is closed today for the show.'

The driver said, 'We're working. Construction on Endro's.'

She had a clipboard, which she checked. If she was looking for something that said the van and its crew were good to go, it wasn't there. 'I'm sorry, I don't know anything about that.'

'We normally don't do weekends. This is a one-off.'

'Let me just call my boss.'

She pulled her phone, but didn't get as far as making a call. The driver hopped out and grabbed her. With a hand over her mouth to prevent yelling, he dragged her through the gate.

Neil exited the van and opened the tailgate. Six men

exited from the cargo area and ran through the gate. One helped the driver with the woman, who would be secured inside Endro's, and another started to work on the height barrier. He broke the lock that held the crossbar in place, allowing him to raise it. Neil drove the van through and parked on the grass outside the construction site. He called a man parked further down Underhill Lane. The guy at the height barrier replaced it.

He turned up thirty seconds later in a flatbed truck, which parked next to the van. The driver got out and the group mingled. Like all but one of the others, he wore beige cargo trousers, T-shirt, high-vis jacket, and a hard hat.

He waved a hand at his vehicle. 'Nice, eh?'

Neil said, 'Any problems with the owner?'

'No. He'll keep his gob shut. Likes his family being alive and all.'

The truck was indeed impressive. It looked old and worn-in, and added to their workmen disguise. The tailgate had been removed and in the back were two loading ramps that could be attached quickly. There was even a bunch of paperwork and empty drinks cartons jammed up where the windscreen met the dashboard. The uniforms similarly had that well-used feel.

'Did you hear good things from that security guard?' the driver asked.

Neil had been very impressed with the guard's work. He'd performed all the tasks required of him and had managed to listen in to four phone calls to his boss from the Paix owner, who had lost sleep due to his car's erratic telemetry system.

Shortly after the last call, some three hours ago, the guard had overheard his general manager tell a mechanic that the billionaire was going to have his – to quote – 'goddamned machine muzzled'. That had to mean the telemetry system would be shut off. Excellent. After leaving work at seven, the guard had been paid £5,000 for his help, and his silence. But he'd remain captive, locked in a car, until the job was over.

'We'll see, I guess,' Neil said. 'Now let's get hidden.'

Someone opened the perimeter fence and the mob entered the building site. Neil carried a large satchel that held machetes, handcuffs, his air rifle, six very real handguns, and a powerful mobile phone signal jammer with a range of 300 metres.

They entered the building for a good nosey around. The windows and doorways were just brick frames, which would help if the team had to beat a sudden exit. The place looked just like the photographs taken by the man he'd sent on a scouting mission. Those were a week old, though, which meant the construction crew hadn't done much work in the time since.

The man who'd taken the woman stepped out of a room that was just a shell. He now wore the steward's high-vis and had her clipboard. Neil gave him a slap.

'Jesus,' the man moaned. 'What gives?'

Neil roughly wiped smudged lipstick off the man's mouth. 'You piece of shit. Touch her again and I'll let her claw your balls off. Get out of my face.'

The guy skulked away.

The mob killed time with card games, talk, and a shot of vodka each for courage. Everyone had a role and knew what to do when the time came. His fuckwit little brother had gotten most of the details right. The only factor Neil didn't have a handle on was enemy firepower. He didn't know if the Paix owner's bodyguards would have weapons, or how likely they were to start blasting. They had a very expensive car to protect.

Neil took the bare concrete stairs to the first floor, where he noticed that the builders had put up a couple of interior walls and done more work on the roof, although the trapdoor was barred only by a slab of wood. He climbed up.

From the top of the building he could look over the

perimeter wall and see everything he needed. The gate, the road, a portion of the lay-by some forty metres away. The parapet was two feet high, ample for him to hide behind when the truck bearing the Paix arrived. He placed the jammer – which was a flat box with fourteen antennae and looked like a giant insect dead on its back – in a corner. Then he lay on his back, and stared into the sky to burn time.

It was 10.30. Ninety minutes to go. He wanted to clear his mind, but how could he? He still hadn't decided what to do with his ex-wife and his brother. He planned to keep them until the Allerby Job was done and dusted, but afterwards? Well, fates might rest on his success or failure. If he got his two million, he might just spare Sean. Otherwise, he might slice that bastard's head off in front of Holly. But either way, the dickhead was due some serious ill-fortune for his betrayal.

The bitch, of course, would die either way.

7

At 10.30, the first of the Elegant Engines stars arrived. Slots had been allocated every five minutes to avoid jams. There would be a steady stream of vehicles until 11.30. Under its own power, a vintage Bentley approached the gateway, followed by a plain car. The guy now posing as a steward stopped the classic car and asked the driver's name, pretended to mark it off the clipboard, and waved both vehicles through. He seemed very pleased with himself for a job well done. The driver of the rear vehicle was an older woman, so clearly not security.

From their positions inside the ring of plastic mesh fencing and atop the restaurant, Neil's men watched it happen. Each of them had read the Elegant Engines programme and knew this vehicle well. It was a three-litre machine from 1929, the last year that the model was produced. This one had been sold at auction for £211,000. It impressed all but one man.

'Why does old shit cost so much?' he said.

At the car park end of the road, Neil had a man lurking in the trees. His job was to look out for staff or police or anyone else who might wander down the road and interrupt things. He watched the Bentley enter the car park and turn through the gap in the trees, to access Allerby House's giant front lawn. The gap had been plugged by a goalpost-shaped gantry, just like at a racetrack. On the crossbar was a rolled-up velvet curtain, which would descend for the Paix alone to give it a special entrance.

A portion of the lawn grass had been roped off and segmented into vehicle bays. The organisers had set up drinks counters, a burger van and snacks stall. The Bentley was met by a man with a clipboard, who guided it into a bay. In that oblong space was a sandwich board with the car's details and specifications, and a table and chair for the owner. The bays were ringed around a much larger central one, obviously the spot reserved for the showpiece.

No patrons were allowed in until 11.30, but curious park visitors were loitering on the outskirts. The space itself heaved with activity as staff continued preparations. To a man they'd remain safe and sound as long as they stayed on that side of the trees. The lookout had orders to subdue anyone who strayed into the no-go zone.

Down at Endro's, Neil's men next watched a blue Ferrari get waved through the gate. The programme said it was worth £180,000. The owner was a black woman and she had a young son in the passenger seat. But no security to keep her safe. Nor did she suspect she might be a target for jacking because she waved at the builders as she drove by.

'That's the 448,' someone said.

'488,' he was corrected.

Five minutes later, a 1955 Ford Popular 103E arrived, but on the back of a truck. Like the vehicle bringing the Paix, it would not fit under the gateway's height barrier. The truck parked in the lay-by so the classic car could be removed. The owner got into his ride. This act gave Neil an illustration of what was to come.

And he couldn't help himself. He quickly got down off the

roof and met the Ford as it turned through the gate. The fake steward watched with puzzlement. Neil waved the car down. In his hand was a screwdriver. The Ford stopped and the driver opened his door slightly. Maybe the window wouldn't roll down.

Neil aimed the screwdriver like a gun, right at the man's head. 'Nice car,' he said, then walked away, leaving the owner puzzled. But still in possession of his pride and joy.

The vehicles continued to stream through the gates roughly every five minutes. Some had security, but some didn't, and that included a Maserati MC20 worth a quarter of a million pounds. A nerdy young man drove it and he was completely alone. One of Neil's men marked each vehicle off using the programme, until, with the passage of a 1981 Ferrari 308 TGS at 11.33, he announced the end.

Not quite, of course. The main event was allowed some fashionable lateness and wasn't due until midday. A compère would introduce it and the Paix would emerge like a sleek black god through the velvet curtain and glide past its weak rivals to take its place centre stage.

Or not.

8

11.20am. Down the road from 7-Star-Car, one of the half-brothers opened a multipack packet of crisps. He lobbed one on the dashboard, one into his kin's lap, and got out of the vehicle with the third. The industrial estate was empty of life, with all but a handful of businesses shut on Sundays. He opened the boot.

Inside, the security guard called Declan Smith stared up, squinting against the bright morning light. He'd been in the boot since the brothers had recaptured him upon leaving work over four hours ago.

'Not be long now,' the half-brother said. He lobbed the bag of crisps in and shut the lid. Back in the passenger seat, he opened his own bag and started munching.

A couple of minutes later, the brothers saw a sleek Mercedes in their mirrors. Behind it were two black Range Rovers.

'That's him,' one said.

'Flash bastard,' said the other. 'I'll call Neil.'

The Merc cruised by as he called the boss. Each Range Rover had two tanned, suited guys inside. The trio pulled up outside 7-Star-Car, about fifty metres away. Neil answered the call.

'Flash bastard's arrived,' the caller told him. 'He's got a Mercedes Maybach as well. That thing's about two hundred grand.'

'And it's probably his school-run car,' said his half-brother, grinning. 'Just a runabout for him.'

'Flash bastard.'

'Shut up,' Neil told both men. 'Call me when the Paix is on the move.'

He hung up. The brothers watched the secure gate of 7-Star-Car rumble open electronically. The Merc slipped through, but the Range Rovers remained outside. They turned around and parked in the middle of the road, a space of about ten metres between them.

Five minutes later another vehicle arrived. It was a white box truck, no doubt the vehicle that would ferry the Paix to the car show. It almost had to mount the kerb to get by the lead Range Rover. It entered the compound and returned ten minutes later. Carefully, it eased into the road, into the gap between the Range Rovers.

A moment later, out walked a man wearing a blue suit under a light brown woollen trench coat. He had matching gloves. It was a look you didn't go for unless you were a big fan of yourself.

'Flash bastard,' the guy with the phone said. 'That's the owner.'

'Billionaire. Owns a film company. Probably has eight girlfriends. Eight more than you.'

The Paix's owner got in the lead Range Rover, and all three vehicles started moving.

'Flash bastard,' the guy with the phone said. He called Neil again and told him the mission was a go.

9

Sometimes, if his paranoia was up, Sean would park his car far from The Chubby in case the cops raided the place. He was glad he'd done so before the meeting, because Neil's men hadn't been able to find it. It was parked on a side street half a mile away from the pub.

The vehicle might be on cop radar, so he didn't collect it. But he did drive by in the farmer's Land Cruiser and stop to collect his stun gloves from the boot and an item from the glove box. Neil's goons had taken his keys off him, but he'd left the vehicle unlocked. He noted that someone had put a note on the windscreen, warning him not to block driveway access. He disengaged the handbrake and rolled the car a few feet to give the author the required space.

Back in the Land Cruiser, he drove to a shop to buy a prepaid phone and lobbed away the farmer's. Then he headed to the Hackenthorpe safe house. It was almost 11.15, but the street seemed to be asleep. He saw no pedestrians, no residents in gardens, nobody driving. It wasn't a bad part of town and he wondered if the comings and goings of people to the house had raised any eyebrows.

He found the front door key under a brick and let himself in. The place was empty, as promised. It was clean, tidy, unlived-in. He didn't know who'd been here last. He stood at the window and called Holly's new burner.

'I was desperate to call you,' she said. 'Are you okay? Are you finished? Are you coming back now?'

'Not yet. Soon. I'm sorry. Just a short while longer. I'm okay.'

She sighed. 'I hate this, Sean. All this worry. This running. I've had enough. I want you to call the police. We need to tell them we're threatened by Neil.'

He knew she'd mention that again. He didn't know what to tell her. Neil had accused him of the ultimate treachery by stealing the man's wife, but there was worse. Selling out his brother to the police was a far bigger betrayal. Could he do it? Would it even save them?

'Let me just think a while,' he said.

'We know where Neil will be at midday, Sean. We send the police there. You've been on the wrong side of the law for too long, and you don't trust them. They're the enemy. I get that, even if I think it's silly. But we need their help. I want you to do it. Call the police.'

'I'm trying to get us money, Holly. If we get enough, we don't need the police and we don't need to worry about Neil.'

She was silent. Was she considering his claim, or saddened by what she perceived to be his naivety? 'Then ignore me and do what you want,' she said.

'Holly, let's not argue. I'm trying to do what's right for us.'

'Whatever, Sean. We might disagree on some things, but there's one thing for sure I know we both want. That's for you to come back to me. So do whatever you're going to do and make that happen. I'll be waiting. I don't know how long for.'

And with that she hung up, leaving him puzzled and a little

scared. What did she mean by her last sentence? Would she call the police if he didn't? Or would she leave without him?

Sean checked the time. Half an hour from now, ownership of the Paix would change hands. As soon as he had that car, Neil's focus would be back on his brother and wife. When he realised they'd escaped, he was going to unleash all his power on a manhunt. Sean had to act now... whatever form that was going to take.

He made his decision. He knew what needed to be done, if he and Holly were to have any chance of a happy, safe life together.

He called the police.

CHAPTER 8

1

When Neil finally told his brother about his new girlfriend, he wrapped it in bad news. She'd come into the country on a study visa and now had a work visa, he said. But it was about to expire and she was due to return to America. He was very sad.

'America? I had no idea. Why did you pick a girl who didn't even live in this country?'

Neil tutted at him, as if this was a silly question. Maybe it was. Sean was hardly an expert in relationships. 'My only chance is to marry her. Which means you have to meet her, I guess. Maybe it was stupid to hide her from everyone for so long.'

Three years, to be precise. Neil was now twenty-four, Sean twenty-one. Neil had taken full advantage of his Niche membership and had enhanced his criminal business profile. He now earned hundreds of thousands of pounds a year and had to do very little legwork, although he still liked to get down and dirty with his boys.

Sean continued to run Pest B Gone, but the firm's shock and awe tactics had become legendary in the criminal underworld and people were less inclined to mess with Keating these days. It meant the workload had lessened and the office was gone. The company now only had a phone number.

Worst of all, Keating now paid the men only when they worked, so a couple of them had had to acquire legitimate jobs part-time. Sean topped up his wages by continuing to buy, fix and sell computers and repair vehicles. He wouldn't ask Neil for money and his brother wouldn't offer it for nothing.

Three years, and not once had Neil named or talked about this girl, other than to admit she existed. Sean had wondered if she even knew her boyfriend was a high-ranking career criminal. Maybe Neil had kept her a secret because she had no idea he wasn't a banker or lawyer or whatever he might have claimed to be. Why else would he segregate these two parts of his life for so long?

Well, now those two worlds would collide. Sean was eager to finally meet the one who had done what so many before had failed to achieve: stolen Neil's heart. 'So bring her to meet me. And now can you finally give me a name other than Jane Doe?'

'Holly.'

Meet they did, but under circumstances that saddened Neil even more. The brothers picked her up for her trip to the airport, where she would get a flight back to the USA. Because it was their last day together, Sean drove and the lovers occupied the back seat, where they cried together and shared promises to be reunited soon.

Sean's only chance to say more than a greeting to Holly came at the airport, after Neil stepped aside to take a call from Keating.

'I've heard nothing about you,' Sean said to her, to kill the awkward silence. He thought she was quite attractive, and he loved her accent. He didn't really know what else to say. He'd never had a girlfriend and interacted only with women who sold their bodies to line Neil's pockets.

'I know quite a bit about you,' Holly replied. 'Neil seems quite... intent on looking after you.'

She probably knew about their mother and father. One in a grave, one in a cell and as good as dead. Sean would not mention them unless she broached the subject. 'I hope some of what he said about me was good.'

She nodded. 'Smart, sharp as a tack. But wayward.'

That sounded like something Neil would say. He liked to remind his younger brother that he wasn't high calibre. 'I'm lazy, that's all.'

'Apparently you don't know what you want to do with your life.'

That was kind of true. He'd become very accustomed to a criminal existence. The evolutionary theorist Carl Jung had once said *You are what you do, not what you say you will do.* Sean had often seriously thought about a future that walked a lawful path, but what had he done to put meat on that desire? And those introspective moments weren't as common as they had once been. 'All I know is I want peace and comfort.'

'Seems hard, given what you do.'

That line startled him. So, this lady did know her boyfriend and his brother were gangsters. And she seemed okay with it. Maybe she liked the bad boys, or the money, or Neil had glossed over the darker parts of such a lifestyle. 'This work... this... stuff... it's all I know,' he said. It was a frank statement to unload on someone he'd just met. He'd never before honestly admitted it even to himself.

She, too, seemed taken aback by his utterance. 'You surprise me. I don't mean to be rude, but... the way Neil spoke. He made you sound like...'

'Like Lenny from *Of Mice and Men*? Or Bertha Rochester? Or the Phantom of the Opera?'

She laughed. 'Not quite. But wow, you're educated. Not like someone I expected to be a...'

She stopped, but he knew what she was going to say. A thuggish criminal. He couldn't blame her for that assumption. Neil was the firm's boss and Sean was only part of a vicious enforcer crew within it. To hazard a guess why, anyone might conclude – and many had – that little bro didn't have big bro's intelligence. Could he really resent Neil for passing along the same opinion to his lover?

'I won't be in this game forever,' Sean said. 'Keep a secret?'

She nodded. His heart beat fast. Was he really about to tell this woman, this partner of his brother's, this stranger, his innermost desires? He didn't believe it until the words slipped out.

'This thing we do, it's like bull riding, or testing experimental planes. You get hurt in the end. I know I can't do this until I'm an old man. I'm like a boxer who knows he can't compete at the top level for too long. I know it's silly to say that. The police know of me because I'm Neil's brother. But I try to keep a low profile. I try to keep my name and face out of the news and off people's lips. Neil thrives on power, but I don't care for it. The last thing I want is the kind of exposure that he has.'

She seemed impressed.

'I want to get married,' he continued, 'but I don't want coppers watching the ceremony through binoculars. I want a nice house with a sunroom that no killer is going to break into at three in the morning. I want kids without worrying if they'll get shot carrying their homework out of school.'

'Wow,' she said. 'Hearing this from you, from the guy I thought you were... it's like hearing a dog meow.'

She glanced left, which prompted him to do the same. Neil was returning. Holly said, ‘Well, Sean, I hope you get what you want. I hope you don’t get institutionalised by this lifestyle. We’ll talk again in a few months, because I also have plans for the future. This country will be my home one day, and I’ll be with the man of my dreams.’

For a second, just one, Sean felt a twinge of jealousy.

2

12.05. Fashionably late. Finally, the white box truck bearing the Paix crested a rise and came into view, partly obscured by the Range Rover before it. Another, of course, brought up the rear.

Neil lowered his binoculars and yelled to his men in the building and construction site below him. 'Get ready. Game time.'

One of his men sliced the plastic mesh fencing from top to bottom and folded the two pieces away to leave a wide exit from the construction site. The others milled about like genuine construction workers. Neil had a stick, which he used like a broom on the roof. It was all show for the security bozos in the Range Rovers. His rifle lay by his feet. He watched out of the corner of his eye as the lead car slowed and turned into the lay-by.

It had to mount the grass at the end to leave room for the truck, which in turn had to allow space for its cargo to be offloaded. The trailing Range Rover couldn't fit, so its driver put the nearside wheels on the grass to avoid blocking the road.

Neil watched as the driver of the truck got out and unfolded some steps at his vehicle's nearside flank, then opened a door that had seemed invisible when shut. Neil's angle gave him sight of only a sliver of gleaming black inside the vehicle. Eleven million pounds of car, right there.

Another man exited the truck's cab on the far side. Neil didn't see what he did, but soon both men had the rear doors open and had unfolded ramps to allow the supercar to reverse off. He wasn't the only one enjoying the show. Looking small next to his quartet of security, the car's owner, in a suit that probably cost thousands, also watched.

One of the delivery men got into the back of the van. Thirty seconds later, the sleek, shiny black car slowly emerged. Inch by sluggish inch, the driver guided it down the ramps, onto the hard mud of the lay-by. Maybe he was terrified of damaging it, or sought to prolong his time with the glorious vehicle.

Neil paused his fake sweeping and just stared. Part of the car was blocked from sight by the truck, but the portion exposed gave him goose bumps. Photographs didn't do the Paix justice. It looked so alien out here instead of on a spotlighted stage. And so gorgeous. Still, eleven million quid? Madness.

The delivery guy got out and the owner took the wheel. He reversed another few feet, so he could clear the truck easily when pulling forward. A second later, the Paix was on the road. In less than another thirty, it would turn through the gate, and into the trap awaiting it.

It was go time.

And that was when Neil felt a chill. Perhaps because of a gut feeling, or a sixth sense developed over a lifetime in crime, he thought of the cops and turned his head to look the other way along the road.

A police car was headed this way, fast.

3

'Hang on, guys, possible problem,' Neil called to his men.

The Paix was halfway between the lay-by and the gate when the police car, still fifty metres distant, flashed its lights. The hypercar's fifty grand carbon-ceramic brakes brought it to a halt and the cop car drew alongside it in the opposite lane, directly across from Neil. It had just one officer inside. He was all in black: shirt, hat, vest, even his face mask and the beard beneath it.

The cop said something to the driver, which Neil didn't catch. The Paix eased forward and into the side of the road, which put all but a slice of the right-hand side of the roof out of sight behind the perimeter wall. The cop car did the same on the other side.

'He's been fucking pulled by a cop,' Neil called out to his men. He stood tall and stared now, no care for if he was spotted.

Below him, out of sight, his men started to murmur. The fake steward poked his head around a gatepost to watch. One guy called up, 'What for?'

The bearded cop got out of his vehicle and walked across the road. The Paix was left-hand drive, so the officer had to come around the vehicle to speak to the driver. Neil saw only the man's head from his elevated position – then not even that as the cop ducked out of sight beyond the wall, presumably to talk through the Paix's side window.

'What's the problem?' the same guy called up.

Neil bolted to the trapdoor and got grounded fast. When he ran from the building and towards the entrance gates, one of his men followed. Neil peeked out from around the gatepost, just like the steward. Just five metres away, the cop squatted at the Paix's driver's window, talking to the owner.

'What's he done?' one of the men said.

'I don't know. I don't see how he could have done anything. Hopefully the cop just wants to fuck with a rich guy.'

'But what if it gets towed?' said the second guy.

Neil cursed loudly. 'The police aren't taking my fucking two million, that's for sure. Just get ready in case we have to snatch it on the way to the pound. In fact, no, better idea. Turn the jammer on now. This bastard cop's calling no one. That's my fucking car and I'm having it.'

4

The Paix was indeed the subject of a traffic stop, and its billionaire owner immediately knew why. As soon as the policeman flashed his lights and pulled alongside him, he wound down his passenger side window and said, 'I never intended to drive on the roads, officer. I'm only going to the next turn. I'm visiting the car show.'

'But you're on the road right now, sir,' the officer said. 'You're aware that cars driven or parked on public roads in the UK must display a number plate at both ends, right? You're missing one on the front.'

'I sure am aware, sir. But I'm not really driving it. I'm just going to Allerby Park. I'm from America. From Florida. That's where it's registered and we don't need a front plate over there. I only shipped it in for the car show. It came on that truck you see back there. Again, it was never my intention to drive on the public roads. Except for this thirty-metre stretch.'

'Just pull to the side and I'll come for a chat,' the officer said. Thirty seconds later, he was squatting by the driver's window. 'You said you weren't driving on the road. This is the road, sir.

Do you think there's a rule that allows journeys of no more than thirty metres?'

'No, of course not. But are you really going to write me up for three seconds of driving?'

The officer adjusted his hat and his face mask. 'Well, sir, it's at my discretion. I could just give you a verbal warning. I could also have this vehicle towed. But it's a fine machine and I don't want to do that. Very exquisite. Beautiful. It's a Paix, right?'

5

The guy who'd accompanied Neil to the gate also stuck his head around the gatepost to watch the scene. That made three heads poking out, at three different heights, like something from a cartoon. They saw the billionaire walk the copper around the Paix, pointing here and there. They chatted like good friends. When one of his men asked what was going on, Neil said, 'I think he's trying to sweet-talk that idiot.'

'Can't be worried about storage charges,' middle head said. 'Only twenty quid a day.'

'But they charge a removal fee,' bottom head replied. 'Hundred-fifty. You believe that? They steal it off you and charge you for it.'

The billionaire and the copper returned to the open driver's door, but it wasn't the owner who got behind the wheel. He let the copper take the helm.

'My sister gave a copper a bag of apples from her shopping once,' bottom head said. 'That's how she avoided a speeding ticket. Or so she said. Maybe she blew him.'

'Let's see if the owner does that.'

The engine revved, and boy did it growl like a bear in a trap.

Behind his damn mask, the copper was probably grinning like a maniac. Neil wanted to gut him.

'Looks like the cop might let him off,' middle head said. Neil prayed he was right.

But that didn't happen. The owner shut the driver's door and walked around the back of the car, to access the far side. Neil knew the man would get in the passenger seat. Of course he would, because the two new best friends were going for a ride. You didn't make a billion by paying out £150 towing fees willy-nilly.

'Get the guns,' he told his boys, yanking them in tandem from their place at the gatepost. 'We're taking it right now.'

Neil continued to watch, and what he saw ruined everything he'd worked for.

The billionaire reached for the door handle – but it was wrenched away as the Paix leaped forward like a greyhound from a trap.

The supercar blitzed by Neil in a fraction of a second, but that was all he needed to catch a glimpse of the face of the driver. The window was still down, and the cop had turned his head to look at the builder lurking by the gatepost. He was bearded, in hat and mask, but his eyes were uncovered and they told him an outlandish, impossible tale.

Yet he believed it.

The copper was his own brother, Sean.

6

The exterior was immaculate, but the Paix's interior was the most beautiful small space Sean had ever seen. It was a world of leather and analogue gauges and switches, yet somehow seemed futuristic. It had a science-fiction aura so potent one might think the vehicle could fly.

But it didn't. It would have to go on the roads, where idiots flung their rusted Fiestas and run-down people carriers around. Sean felt like a man holding dynamite on a bustling tube train. One tiny scratch would probably knock a standard year's wage off this thing. He was terrified to drive it fast.

But speed was essential. His pre-arranged route was half a mile and he needed to reach his destination before the alarm was raised. He turned off the road at the next left, past the perimeter wall of Allerby Park, and soon after took another lane that passed under the Stocksbridge Bypass, which is said to be the UK's most haunted road. He'd encountered no other vehicles during the journey. Just past the bridge was a lay-by.

It was here that he'd parked the Iveco truck he'd stolen – borrowed – earlier.

He'd left the vehicle with its loading ramps already attached and angled slightly so that he had to do little more than turn the Paix's wheels left to line it up for a piggyback. The ground clearance was just enough and he didn't catch the bumper on the ramps.

The front-end bumper of the Seat Ibiza lay beside the van, out of sight from the road. After taking a photo of the Paix, he leaned the bumper against the back end of the hypercar and secured it in place with ropes lashed to the wing mirrors. He covered the vehicle with a red tarpaulin, but left the Ibiza portion exposed. Then he stepped away to check his efforts.

The illusion worked. At a glance, it appeared as if a trashed Seat Ibiza was beneath the tarpaulin, although a knowledgeable person might realise the car was too long, too wide, too low.

Moving fast, Sean removed the ramps then located a hidden bucket planted earlier. From it he took bottles of bleach, which he used to soak the interior of the truck and scrub down exterior places he'd touched. That done, he stripped off the police uniform and his fake beard and tied them up in a carrier bag.

And away he went, jogging through the woods. He made a call on a fresh burner. Direct to Sheffield Road police station, the closest to the Hackenthorpe safe house.

When an operator answered, he said, 'I'm the guy from twenty-eight Yellowstone Street in Hackenthorpe. That mean anything to you?'

'I'm sorry, sir,' said a female voice. 'What's your name?'

She didn't sound panicked. So no alarms had rung yet. He tutted. 'Keep an eye on your patrol officers at all times. They've been out of contact for half an hour. Shame on you lot.'

He hung up and busted the phone into fragments, which he soon after dumped in a stream along with the uniform and fake beard. He hoped the two officers were okay. When they'd attended his bogus burglary at the Hackenthorpe safe house, the last thing they'd expected was to be tased and tied up. But now they had a cool story and might get a commendation. And they'd get their car back undamaged. Officer Renton, however, would need a new uniform.

Half an hour later, Sean was back in the farmer's Land Cruiser, and not long after turned it onto Jacob's street. He backed down the side of the house, stopped before the garage, and again blocked the vehicle's licence plate with the wheelie bin.

He knocked on the door, which was promptly opened by Jacob. Sean entered the house and found Holly standing in the living room. It seemed that she and Jacob had been playing Ludo to pass the time. As soon as she saw him, she beat the Paix for speed as she leaped into his arms. They kissed. Jacob announced that he'd be upstairs and promptly left the lovers alone.

'Did it work?' she said when they parted. 'You got money.'

He took her face in his hands. 'I got something worth money. I might have lied to you a little bit.'

If her eyes were wide with shock at that revelation, they almost fell from their sockets when he unloaded the truth. By the end of it, she was slouched on the sofa, rubbing her cheeks, and crying.

'I don't know... what to say.'

'This is a speechless kind of thing for sure.'

'This... scary.'

He nodded. 'And risky as hell. I must be stupid.'

'Fool... foolish.'

'Mission impossible.'

His flippant attitude did its job. It disorganised her emotions and put puzzlement at the fore. Anxiety was suddenly way down the queue. 'Why are you smiling?'

'Because we're about to make big money, baby. If the next part works.'

Fear was many places behind intrigue, which had just hopped into line. 'What next part?'

Sean pulled his burner and called a number. He'd memorised it from a text message seen on Neil's phone. He put the call on speaker, so Holly could hear. He didn't withhold his ID.

The man who answered did so with caution in his tone. His phone was probably a burner whose identity was known only to one person. But not the one whose number now appeared on his screen. 'Who is this?'

'You speak only to me now, Mr Richter,' Sean said. 'The man you were dealing with before is out of the picture. Don't take his calls.'

'I'm hanging up. I don't know what you're talking about.'

'Fine. I'll list the Paix for parts on eBay. Maybe I'll keep a few bits to see if they fit my Bugatti Chiron.'

Sean hung up. As expected, his phone rang seconds later. Now less perturbed, Richter said, 'How did you get it?'

'I stole it. I know. What's the world coming to?'

Richter paused. In those three seconds he dumped more uneasiness. 'That's my fucking car.'

'It's called Adverse Possession. That means the Paix is now mine. But I'm willing to sell it to you, and cheaper than you expected. I'll knock a tenner off the two million. Everything else remains the same. I'll bring the car to your depot. Make sure the cash is there. I'll call again soon. Be ready to roll with my hard cash in one hour exactly.'

'That vehicle has a sophisticated tracker and–'

'Don't worry about it. One hour, Richter. I'll send you a picture to prove I have it.'

'How do I know you won't trick me?'

'You didn't know if the other guy would, either. On that subject, let me advise you against trying to get one over on me.

The other guy will try to contact you or get word to you somehow. There might be threats, or there might be a new deal offered. Ignore him. If there's a trick when I turn up, I'll burn that car to a shell. And you might be inside when it happens. Oh, one more thing.'

'What?'

'"The Storm on the Sea of Galilee". Didn't steal that, did you?'

'What? No. What are you talking about?'

'One hour,' Sean said, and hung up. He then sent the photo he'd promised.

Holly had waited impatiently by his arm, chewing her nails. Now she said, 'What did he mean by a tracker?'

Sean pulled her into a tight hug. 'Something we won't have to worry about as long as my brother is still a sore loser.'

7

The men left behind in the half-built restaurant had emerged and milled on the grass, agitated by the news imparted by one who'd watched the theft of the Paix. A copper nicked it? They couldn't believe it.

But now they had to make a decision. 'LEG IT!' one guy offered.

A nice idea. The men almost fought each other to get in the van. Neil barged into them, yelling for calm. 'Slow the fuck down. We stole nothing.'

'He's right,' a second guy said. 'Some copper took it. We're in the clear. But what the fuck is going on?'

The other guys quickly got on his page. The Paix was gone, but not by their hands. Had Neil been driving the supercar right now, the van would have blasted out of the grounds, aiming for its fiery final resting place.

Instead, Neil ordered a nice and slow retreat, just like a regular old construction workforce at shift's end. He got someone to fetch his rifle, which was still on the roof of the restaurant, and another man to retrieve the signal jammer. He wanted the device left turned on to delay calls to the cavalry.

They could be a mile away before the Paix owner alerted the cops.

Once they were all aboard and on the move, everyone wanted an explanation from Neil. He couldn't admit that the man most loyal to him had backstabbed him – again. 'I don't know,' he said. 'Some bobby decided he didn't want to wait thirty years for his pension.'

The van exited the park and turned left, away from the Paix owner and his security personnel. Neil looked through the back window and saw them standing in the road, using their phones. Or trying to. They saw the van and started waving. Some of Neil's men laughed... but he didn't. He couldn't. Two million had gone down the toilet.

More infuriating was why. Sean. His damn little brother had used Neil's own tactic against him. He had ambushed the ambush. The bastard. He would pay for that.

The little shit had no idea he was in shit deep over his head. Neil doubted that Sean had a crew in place to help him find and disable the tracker. In about five seconds, the jammer would be out of range of the Paix owner's phone. Two minutes from now, the billionaire would have alerted the cops and informed Verninac that his toy was gone. The telemetry system would be activated, and with it the unblockable tracker.

Hopefully Sean would have his head under the Paix's bonnet when cops swarmed him. Neil could always get to him in prison and–

'Stop!' he yelled. The van ground to a halt in the middle of the road. 'Back up.'

Neil explained his new plan as the van approached the five men standing around in the road. They rushed to meet it.

When the van driver got out, he was told a 'car' had been stolen and was bombarded with pleas for a phone. He said nothing and opened the tailgate. Men cascaded out, with guns.

While his crew grabbed and searched the security quartet for weapons – which they didn't have – Neil stuck his pistol in the billionaire's face. 'Don't worry, I'll get your precious Paix back.'

The shocked fivesome were relieved of their phones and bundled into the van. Unfortunately for a biker who happened along at the exact moment to see it all, he had to go, too. A goon literally kicked at his bike as he tried to blow past, and down he went. He got locked up with strangers and his bike was heaved over the stone wall and into a field.

All but Neil and one man got in the van. The driver had orders to take the six handcuffed prisoners somewhere remote and wait a few hours before releasing them. By then it shouldn't matter what they told the authorities. The chap would also alert the car show's runners about their steward, tied up at Endro's.

Neil and his sole remaining henchman man got in the flatbed truck. While leaving the area, Neil made a call. Highly unlikely, but he got Noah to send some men out to Cowbell Farm, just to make sure that Sean had actually escaped. Maybe the face in the Paix had only resembled his brother's.

He didn't expect good news and wasn't in for a surprise. Noah soon called and said, 'Sean's gone. My man found a multi-tool. Sean must have used it to escape. The farmer's dead in his kitchen. And his Land Cruiser is missing.'

'And my bitch wife?'

'Is that a serious question? You think he might have left her behind?'

Neil's throat burned. He wanted antacids, but he'd swallowed about ten already today. 'Get your people out of there for now, just in case the cops invade it. But have a team ready to go back and erase evidence. Leave one guy there for now so we know if anyone comes.'

He then ordered Noah to dispatch a team to his brother's

house, again just in case. For the second time, Neil got he what he expected. No Sean. No multi-million pound hypercar parked outside. But the invaders had been instructed to look for signs that the occupant might never return, and they had found a wardrobe empty of most of Sean's clothing.

'Trash the place,' he instructed Noah. Then he made another call. One he'd been putting off, for it would set in concrete what he'd feared since the moment the Paix was snatched from him.

It was to Richter.

No answer. But of course. Now there were no more doubts. Sean had always had that damn daft idea of a normal life somewhere quaint. He didn't have a chance at a high-paying legitimate career and wasn't made of the stuff required to succeed on the opposite side of the law.

But now the bastard thought he could buy his dream by selling the Paix to Richter. With two million pounds, he and Holly could disappear and live happily ever after.

Neil could have ruined it all by allowing the billionaire to report his vehicle stolen. But when the roof fell in, he'd also be crushed. No fucking way. This wasn't over yet. He didn't know his brother's whereabouts, but Richter was another matter. And soon the two traitors would meet to swap property.

Neil was owed two million, and he was going to collect it with blood-soaked interest.

CHAPTER 9

1

Two months after Holly got her residency visa, she married Neil. It was a grand event at Falcon Grange, a 17th century mansion in Derbyshire. He paid to have it closed to the public that day and it had a walled perimeter, so his men were able to make sure no plainclothes law enforcement personnel got up close and personal. There was nothing to be done about four big drones that flew over the grounds, stabbing downwards with their powerful cameras.

Sean kept his head down after the indoor ceremony, when everybody moved to the gardens for a party. In part it was to avoid giving his face to the cameras, but a measure of the gesture was also sadness. Before meeting Holly that day on the way to the airport, the vast majority of his female interactions had been with less-than-desirable women, and perhaps that had tainted his opinion of them. Holly had shown him that there were gems out there.

And he wanted one just like her.

He was now twenty-four, but as yet no woman had piqued his interest beyond lust. If he could get out of the crime trade, get himself a house all of his own, then he might think seriously about trying to settle down with a partner.

After the wedding party, Neil and some of his closest people crew returned to Sheffield, where Holly's present from him was unveiled. A public house. He'd wrapped a ribbon around the entire building, placed a giant white bow on the front doors, and scattered roses all over the M-shaped roof. The place had sat unused for half a year, so the exterior needed work and the interior was bare, but Holly was delighted.

Sean was jealous. As soon as he laid eyes on the pub, he vowed to get his own fine residence within the year. Yet again he considered a career outside of crime, but always the doubts immediately crept in. He couldn't forget the word that Holly had applied to him: *institutionalised*. Lawbreaking for gain was all he'd ever known. Could he escape its clutches?

Neil also had a big plan for the future, although he kept it secret until it was all over and too late for anyone to do a damn thing about it. A month after his wedding, just a week shy of the grand opening of his new pub, which he'd named The Chubby Grub, he put his plan into action.

Step one was to get permission from Keating to kill a former employee who'd been talking to the police. That information was as much as he told the boss. However, he shared more with his fellow Niche members.

This wasn't standard procedure. Those in the Niche operated separately, overseeing independent slices of the firm's portfolio. No member got involved in a peer's business and they didn't require any kind of consent from each other. But Neil made a polite gesture to his colleagues by informing them of his plan. He would not go ahead unless they gave their assent, he said. This went down well and he was given the thumbs-up.

The target was a man who enjoyed the company of prostitutes and would be visiting one that very night. Neil didn't mention that the man was a submissive, meaning he liked to be at the whim of a dominatrix.

The dominatrix worked out of a flat in Huddersfield, where she had a room decorated as a desert-like planet, including a black ceiling with stars and a carpet of sand with real rocks. In their role-play, the submissive dressed as an astronaut and got sexually abused by the dominatrix, who was bedecked as an alien creature. Each to their own.

The next night, Neil sent in Pest B Gone, but anonymously. No uniforms, no van with the firm's name on the side. It went down nice and quick. The submissive was stabbed to death in his astronaut suit. The dominatrix, still wearing a bizarre strap-on dildo meant to represent an alien penis, was coached on the benefits of telling no one. The clean-up was also easy because the victim had bled entirely inside his costume, which was a handy bag for carting away the body.

Just days earlier, Neil had come to an arrangement with a local farmer, who would dispose of bodies for a fee. As Neil's men were about to hoist the victim into an agricultural incinerator, the farmer decided he wanted the astronaut's outfit. When it was stripped from the body, Sean got his first look at the dead man's face.

Half an hour later, he arrived at Neil's pub, whose upper floors had already been converted into a residence but required finishing touches before Holly could move in. He found Neil painting a wall.

'Keating!' Sean yelled. 'You just killed Keating.'

Neil didn't even stop painting. He made a mock show of shock. 'Oh no. And my Niche comrades authorised it. That could be harmful to them if news spreads through the ranks.'

Right there Sean realised he hadn't brought terrible news to Neil's door. Just confirmation of a job well done. 'You planned this?'

Still Neil stroked the wall with his brush. 'Keating's gone. Mistake or not, the Niche made it happen. Now they need to hide it. And then they need to vote for one of us to take his place. I already know the other three don't want it. They don't want the exposure Keating had. They don't want a bullseye on their backs.'

'So you planned that, too? All of this was to get Keating's firm?'

Now Neil's hand paused. Paint dripped down the wall. 'Which is now mine. Don't go missing the guy, okay? He turned a blind eye to his dealers recruiting fucking kids to sell drugs on the streets. You should be happy for your brother. Now why don't you grab a brush and do that other wall?'

The next morning Neil met with the Niches to deliver the news. They were unhappy with Neil for this 'terrible case of mistaken identity', but agreed that they needed to keep it quiet in case pro-Keating constituents took offence. They also agreed to vote for a new head honcho. Neil, as he claimed, was the only one who put his or her name forward it. He was in.

Over the next two years, Neil made changes he'd always wanted. Those who didn't conform or complained were ousted. In time he turned the organised crime group into an animal that barely resembled the one thus far known to authorities, forcing his Crown-funded enemies to begin their long-term investigations from scratch.

He also fortified the buffer between the Niche and the guy at helm. Keating had relied on the Niche for information and advice, but Neil cut them off completely with a human barrier. Noah, the former scumbag who had turned his life around and learned at an exponential rate, got the job. Within six months Noah would prove to be so adept that Neil would dissolve the Niche. Two members would gracefully walk away. The third would visit the farm and never walk again.

Using The Chubby Grub as a location, Neil met Keating's suppliers and associates to show them he was a pleasant guy to do business with. He wooed rival gang leaders to convince them he wanted peace, but that he would also vehemently defend what was his. And he socialised with lower-level employees to gain their trust.

It seemed that Neil had everything he wanted and was expert at smoothing out ripples. Until one morning a couple of years later, when Sean visited The Chubby to take Neil for a game of snooker. He parked round back, but before he even got out of his vehicle, the rear fire exit opened and Holly stormed out, shoeless. She yelled something uncouth behind her and he heard Neil's profanity-riddled reply. An argument. Sean decided to wait it out.

That didn't happen. En route to her car, Holly spotted his and changed direction. Before he knew it, she'd pulled open his front passenger door and plonked herself in the seat. 'Take me away from here. That bastard.'

Sean didn't ask for details, but he didn't drive, either. He couldn't just take her away from Neil. His brother came through the fire exit a few seconds later and lobbed a pair of Holly's shoes at her car. Neil then spotted Sean's car and came over.

'Don't wind the window down,' she pleaded as she hit the central locking. Sean was in a fix, unsure what to do. He'd piss someone off either way.

Neil didn't seem to care that his wife was in his brother's car. He didn't try the door or seek to have the window buzzed open. Instead, he jabbed a finger at his wife. 'Good timing, pal. Take miss silly bitch here out of my face for the day.'

And with that he returned to his pub. Sean just sat there, confused, as Holly ran across the car park to collect her shoes.

When she got back in his car, she said, 'Let's go. Take me to my friend's house.'

He had no choice, it seemed. Both partners had given him orders. He drove. Just a minute into the journey, she said, 'I think Neil is having an affair.'

Sean sighed. He'd wondered as much. There had been no real evidence, just a gut feeling based on some curious incidents. The times that his brother had moved aside to take a phone call in private. The occasions when Neil had worn aftershave despite having no reason to. And periods when nobody seemed to know where he was.

'What makes you say that?' Sean asked. He wasn't about to feed the flames without concrete proof.

'I don't know,' Holly admitted. 'I just get the sense of it. Gut feeling. But I've seen things. I found long red hairs in his car.'

She was waiting for his reaction and it was supposed to be awe. He was supposed to leap to her side, but he just didn't feel it. 'Is that proof? I'm not sure that means much. Hairs get transferred around.' He knew this to be true. Last year, someone who worked for Neil had been arrested because his hair was at a crime scene. But it had travelled there on someone else's shoe. That said, the guy in question had masterminded the robbery so still went down for a stretch.

Holly didn't look happy with his response. 'Okay, well what about this. last week I saw an Amazon email on his phone. It was confirmation of a purchase of red hair dye. It wasn't for me. Who was it for?'

Sean shrugged. He knew nothing about dye purchases and didn't feel it was valuable evidence. Neil often bought presents for veteran pub customers and the parents of his employees and local sweet characters. But was he trying too hard to defend his brother? 'I don't know.'

'And he's always more distant from me after he's vanished

for part of the day,' Holly continued. 'As if he's come back to a lesser woman.'

Sean didn't know what to say. He felt he was being pressured into accepting her claim of an affair.

Luckily, Holly spoke again and ended the uncomfortable silence. 'I don't want to face people in this mood. Forget my friend's house. Take me to your place, please. You got a new one last month, didn't you?'

He had. A house, not a flat, and in a nice area. He wanted to keep it separated from his criminal life and had never shown a soul except Neil. It seemed like an unwise move to take Holly there, but nor did he want to say no to her. He made her wear the same baseball cap Neil had worn on his visits. It wasn't much of a disguise, but she could hardly apply the fake beard he also had in the glove box.

She had a quick look into all rooms before they settled in the living room. She sat on the sofa and he remained standing in the middle of the room. He said, 'I should tell Neil you're here. It might look bad if he finds out some other way.'

'Scared he won't know what's going on with his own property?' she replied. Her choice of words puzzled him until she explained what had caused her fight with her husband.

'I was stocking up this morning. We were out of one of the bottled beers, none in the cellar. So I checked that room at the back, in case someone had put some in there...'

Ah. He knew what was coming. The concrete-walled room that Neil had decided would make a nice place for torturing and interrogating enemies. He'd named it Room X.

'What's the problem?' he said, hoping he had this wrong. Room X had been used two days ago and blood had been spilled, but it was always cleaned up afterwards. The space was always left bare, sterile, nothing present but a chair, and surely nobody could get paranoid over a single chair in a bare room?

'There's just the one chair in a room that looks like a cell. I never had cause to go in there before. Now I wish I hadn't. It's obvious that Neil uses the place for hurting people.'

So much for that. He could play dumb... but he didn't want to lie to her. 'Neil hoped to keep that from you. He didn't want you to get upset.'

'Well, upset I am. That's my home, and people get hurt there. I never knew. I mean, I know he's a criminal. That's what drew me to him, I guess. His popular lifestyle. Sometimes girls go for the bad boys. If that was why. I don't even know. But I had no clue how deep he was in this nastiness, not at first. And I was in love with him by the time I got the full picture.'

She wiped away a tear. Sean had left a newly purchased pack of toilet rolls on another chair, so he opened it and handed her one.

She wiped her eyes. 'Only I don't have the full picture, do I? It's much worse than I thought. I hear things all the time. I mean, I always used to, bits here and there, but maybe I blanked it out.'

'That's the game,' he said. It was an old line some gangsters used. He couldn't think of anything else.

But it didn't go down well. She lobbed the toilet roll away. 'A game? Preposterous. Games don't hurt people. There are threats against Neil, against me. I don't like it. I fear for my safety and his at times. I never used to, but it's different now. Now that I know more, know how deep in he is. And this is the game you're in, too. Do you hurt people in that room?'

He had never engaged in the physical side of an interrogation, but he had helped dispose of bodies. He doubted this fact would make her feel better, so he said nothing.

But his silence gave its own message to her. 'You reckoned you wanted out of this,' she said. 'You gave me that line years ago. Yet here you are still.'

'It's all I know,' was his reply, and not the first time it had been used. But it was a weak excuse. 'I'm trying. I'm on the road towards a new life.'

'No, you've stopped dead at the border, Sean. The way ahead is dark and eerie. You don't know if you can survive past that border, in that new land. It's much safer to stay where you are. What efforts have you really put in?'

None, of course. He felt pinned down, under the spotlight, and it wasn't a comfortable position. It made him defensive. 'Hey, you asked, so I told you. What else can I do until I achieve it?'

'Five years from now you'll be saying the same thing. You'll say it all the way into a grave or a prison cell.'

Perhaps her words would have made him angry. He didn't get chance to find out. She grabbed his wrist and pulled him down, so he was by her side on the sofa. Their knees touched. 'Neil can't get out,' she said. 'This game, as you call it, has its hooks in him. It's why he doesn't care about me.'

'That's not true. He married you.'

She shook her head. 'You have to look deeper. This silly game will end up killing him or getting him locked away. What about me? He's not thinking about me. He'd get out and go straight if he cared for a future with me. But he hasn't, so he doesn't care.'

That claim seemed hard to accept, given how often he'd heard Neil profess love for Holly. But, if he was honest, such words hadn't floated in the air for a long time now. And she had a good point. If Neil died or got locked up, Holly would suffer.

'I don't think you're like him,' she said. 'Is that why you've never had a proper girlfriend? Because you're scared of ruining it? Because you know you could lose a girl in a second because of... grudge or judge? That's a term I heard Neil use once.'

Grudge or judge. The end of everything by an enemy blade

or a prison sentence handed down at crown court. Yes, this fate was a worry for him, but she was wrong about its overwhelming reach. He knew exactly why he couldn't commit to a love affair. He would be unable to keep his criminal lifestyle secret from a girl, and she'd reject him upon discovery. His only chance would be to find a partner who already knew his secrets.

A woman like Holly.

'You still have a chance to get those things you wanted,' she said. 'A comfortable life, no police at your wedding, no enemies coming for your kids as they walk to school.'

He opened his mouth to reply, but she cut it off with a kiss on the cheek. It was just a peck, meant only as a sign of trust and pity and a bunch of other sentiments. But the emotion it sparked in both of them was none of those. It was lust. Before they knew it, they were kissing hard and mauling at each other's clothes.

The sex was a really bad idea, but while they couldn't stop it, they could swear never to repeat it. However, that soon proved to also be out of their control.

He called Neil's landline a week after their lovemaking and Holly answered. Instead of asking to speak to Neil, he sought another meeting with her. They collided that evening in a bed in a hotel in Nottingham.

After the sex, Holly snuggled up to him and said, 'I want you. I want to be with you, not Neil. He's not right for me.'

That made no sense. 'We're the same. We're both in this game.'

'But I didn't fully know how deep Neil was in when I met him. I know exactly what I'm getting into with you. Besides, you show a level of care that he doesn't.'

Sean sat up. 'We can't be together. I'd love it, but it's not possible. Neil would eat us alive. I'm happy to continue to see you, though. Is that not enough?'

'Maybe. I don't know. It's fun, but I need more than that. I want the kids, the normal lifestyle. The lack of danger. We could just tell him, tell everyone. He's colder towards me these days, and I'm not even sure he'd be upset if I left him. And then we could be together.'

She was wrong. They could never have a normal relationship because Neil would ruin them. He was often driven by vengeance, and he didn't like to lose what he had, even if he didn't really care for it. A wife running out on him would for sure stoke the fires of revenge.

It went deeper than that, though. They were brothers. Sean couldn't betray Neil just to satisfy himself. Stealing a man's wife was treachery of the highest order, right up there with selling him out to the police.

His pause worried her. 'Don't you want me?'

Badly, more than anything he'd ever wanted. But there was nothing he could do. There was a moral code to follow, especially amongst family. He couldn't have Holly even if Neil divorced her.

Perhaps not even if he tried to kill her.

2

'Nothing,' Holly said. She was on Jacob's sofa with her phone.

Good. Sean relaxed. He stopped pacing and sat by her. The theft of the Paix wasn't yet on the news. The Elegant Engines organisers would have missed their star attraction by now, but either they were still trying to contact the Paix's owner or they were loath to rush him and patiently waited.

One thing was for certain, though. Sean had been right about Neil. His brother could have scarpered, leaving the owner free to call in the theft and have the tracker activated. Instead, Neil probably had the man and his security detail imprisoned somewhere. There was only one reason why: Neil still believed he could acquire the supercar and thus the two million pounds. Sean would have to be very careful.

Holly said, 'That detective is on the news, though.'

It was obvious who she meant. Harper, the sergeant killed by the idiot called Jimmy, now also dead. He took the phone to read about it for himself. The detective's disappearance had been noted. His wife and family were worried. His colleagues in blue were hunting CCTV and witnesses. And they would find some, that much was guaranteed. Sean had to hope it wouldn't wind a trail to his damn doorstep. Wherever that new doorstep may lie.

But he had more pressing worries. It had been twenty minutes since his call to Richter, so he made another. He headed into the kitchen so as not to spook Holly.

'Change of plan,' he said when the biofuels magnate answered. 'I'm not coming to your depot, Richter. Too many chemicals there good for decomposing a corpse.'

'What game is this? Where's my vehicle?'

'Be more concerned about my money. You have a house on Carrington Avenue. I want you to go there and use the direct route along Smithie Lane, but don't leave yet. I'll call you when I want you to leave. It'll be in the next hour or so. Stay right there at your depot until I call. If I see you leave before then, I'll part-exchange the Paix for an old Corsa.'

He hung up. And noticed Holly in the kitchen doorway. She didn't look happy. 'I don't trust the man,' he said.

'So what are you planning?'

'An old trick of Neil's,' Sean replied. 'I know a place that's heaven-sent for a deliberate ambush.'

3

The property next to the Forest Energy Solutions depot was a small airfield, and a five-metre-high grass berm separated them. It was here that Neil got a surprising phone call.

He and another man were lying on the grass, using binoculars to watch the depot for signs of Richter. They had been there only three minutes when the businessman stepped out of an office building to sit on a bench near a small pond and smoke. The man's top shirt button and tie were loose, a sure giveaway that he was under stress. Good. What Neil would have given for his rifle right then.

Richter looked around to make sure he was alone, then pulled out his phone.

That was when Neil's rang. He answered with, 'Why did you ignore my calls? I'll kill you for this betrayal.'

'I wasn't trying to trick you,' Richter moaned. In the binoculars, he got up and started pacing back and forth. 'He called me. He wants to meet me.'

Neil knew who, of course. But he played dumb. 'Who?'

'I don't know. A bastard who threatened me. He wants to sell me the Paix. Is he one of your rogue operatives?'

'You think this man worked for me? No. Like you, he's just a fool who thought he could trick me and ride off into the sunset.'

'Look, I never planned to do that. I wanted the car, and all of a sudden a stranger has it. I still want it. He wanted to bring it to my depot, but now he wants to do the deal at my house. He says I'm not to leave until I get another call. I want to deal with you instead. We had an agreement.'

Bullshit. Neil knew Richter had panicked because of the change of plan. 'So you need my help, in other words. Because you knew I could be trusted, but you chose to deal with this other guy and now you're worried he's going to trick you. I should just let you get on with it.'

Richter stopped pacing. And he had some bravado. 'But you won't do that. Because you want the money. And I've got it for you. So the deal is as it always was. You give me that Paix, I give you a bag full of money. I'm holding it right now.'

Lying little bastard. Neil almost told the businessman he was being watched this very moment. 'I'll sort this problem out, Richter. So do what he says. Do everything he says. I'll be waiting to spring a trap on him. Make sure that you keep that money with you at all times. You won't go behind my back again and live to regret it.'

Neil hung up and laughed. Sean wasn't as smart as he thought. It was obvious why he'd instructed Richter to go to his home on Carrington Avenue, but to await a call before making the journey. Sean didn't trust the businessman and worried that he'd walk into a trap. So he would set up a deliberate ambush somewhere between the depot and the house, which was a road called Smithie Lane. Sean, the fool, had even insisted that Richter use that route. Neil had had the very same idea because of the very same worry.

But where on that road would he take down Richter? Neil pulled up a local map on his phone. Not the pub across the road from the entrance to the depot, a place Neil had originally planned to use. Too obvious. It had to be elsewhere on Smithie Lane.

Then he spotted the perfect place, a tree-lined stretch of the road between the railway bridge and the housing estate. The same location that Sean had indicated when trying to guess where Neil would confront Richter. No buildings. No pavement for pedestrians. Quiet. Neil wondered why he hadn't picked it himself instead of the pub. It was, as his brother had said, *Heaven-sent.*

Now Neil knew where Sean planned to surprise the businessman and do the deal. And Neil would be right there to ruin their day.

This time he would ambush the ambush.

4

The tree-lined, fifty metre section of Smithie Lane was better than Neil had imagined. He got his man to stop the van by a dirt track leading into the trees. It terminated at a free-standing farm gate about five metres into the woods. The gate was probably a remnant of older times because it led nowhere. Beyond it there was no more track, only trees. It was the perfect hiding place. In fact, on this stretch of road, it was the only one.

'Back the van down there,' he said. The driver cut a forward quarter-turn, fast, and just as rapidly reversed onto the track. He slammed on the brakes when just feet from the gate. The sudden halt caused a series of thumps from the cargo area as heavy items hit the rear door. The four men back there cursed the driver, who found his little joke hilarious.

Neil was in no mood to laugh. He made a call. It was answered by the guy he'd station down at the pub across from the entrance into Forest Energy Solutions' land.

'Tell me what you have to do?' Neil said.

The goon went over his task, ending it with: '...and call you before it all happens, so you can call the Nokia.'

'Good man.'

Neil hung up.

Next he called a man parked on Carrington Avenue, near Richter's overnight home. 'Tell me what you have to do?'

The man said, 'Watch for Sean or Richter. Call you if I see either one of them, and follow them.'

Neil hung up. The guy at Richter's home was probably not needed. He was there only in case Sean somehow managed to deliver the Paix. Highly unlikely since it was such an unforgettable vehicle. Richter would probably be given a location for pickup when Sean got the money.

Which would never happen.

Neil phoned Richter and said, 'Has he called?'

'Yes! Just now, just this very second. I was about to phone you. He said I'm to leave my depot in ten minutes and drive straight home. He'll be waiting for me, he said. Do you think he's there already? With my Paix?'

No and no. Richter would never get that car. 'Of course. A deal's a deal. Just make sure you do what he says. Exit your depot and go straight there. Don't even think about the possibility of considering sending a man to go look beforehand. If he's spotted, you lose.'

Neil hung up. Ten minutes. He had to move fast. He opened the back door. His men got out. Neil thumped the van and away it went, to park up somewhere close and await the order to return.

'Nobody shoots unless I order it,' Neil told his men. 'And nobody shoots my brother, full stop. If you do that, turn the gun on yourself afterwards. Now tell me what you have to do?'

Like kids given a question at school, nobody wanted to speak up. Neil pointed one out, who said, 'We find cover and wait for Sean and Richter. We wait until we see the cash, then storm them, take both of them prisoner. We have to make sure we get both men.'

'Good. Get hidden. Go.'

He watched the four men run into the woods and each pick a tree to hide behind. And they were gone. Perfect. Neil walked to the end of the track and raised his binoculars to look northeast along Smithie Lane. He could see about sixty metres, to the single-lane bridge over the railway. It was small and humped, so the road was lost from view beyond it. Traffic lights had stopped the cars on his side and a line of vehicles seemingly emerged from out of the earth at the far end.

This meant he wouldn't see Richter's car coming until it was right upon them. He wasn't sure which direction Sean would appear from. But who would be first?

Sean, surely. His plan was probably to wait right here and pounce into the road to block Richter's path. It would take him just seconds to demand the money, give a location for the Paix, and hop back in his car with a suitcase.

Traffic got busy and too many people driving past from right to left glanced out their windows at him. Neil walked back down the track and past the gate, to hide behind a tree. He saw one of his men at a nearby tree, ramrod straight with his nose virtually touching bark. It looked kind of funny the way he just stood there.

'Ask you a question, boss?' the guy said.

Neil knew he'd been edgy and barking all day. He decided he owed this guy at least some courtesy. 'Go for it.'

'If Richter comes first, you don't want to just take the money?'

That was the other scenario, of course. Sean could call Richter as the businessman drove, and at the last second call and order him to turn onto the track and wait. That bag of lovely cash would be sitting right there, begging to be plucked away. Neil could take it and be gone. Two million pounds was why he'd set the Allerby Job up, after all.

'Fuck no,' Neil answered.

If he just wanted the money, he could ambush Richter right outside his depot, or even storm the place with a squad. It was no longer just about a payday. Richter and Sean had betrayed him. He wanted the traitors, too. He couldn't wait to see the shock on their faces when they were cuffed and bundled into the van.

Richter was destined for a shallow grave. Sean would go into Room X, where vicious bastards would make him give up the car and the bitch he'd stolen from his own blood.

5

Neil's Nokia 3410 was a spy phone version of that device, which allowed him to call and listen in to its surroundings. It didn't ring and automatically opened the line without need for anyone to press a button. He'd given it to the guy he had down at the pub, watching the depot's main gate. He rang it now.

The noise was muffled slightly, so the phone was probably in his man's pocket. He heard the fool moaning. '...fucking shit end of the stick all the time. Like that fucking post office robbery. Who was the only one who didn't get a gun? Fucking me, that's who.'

Keeping the line open, Neil called him from another device. When the man answered, Neil said, 'Nokia's on. Good job you didn't insult me. Five minutes until go time, so what's happening?'

'Nothing yet, so I... hang on. Car coming to the gate.'

'Is it Richter?'

'It's his Merc. Yeah, that looks like him inside.'

'Go do your bit,' Neil said, and hung up.

He listened as it all went down. He heard his man's feet

pounding tarmac as he ran over the road. Heard the slosh of water in the bucket he carried. An electronic gate rumble open. A car horn blare. And wet slapping sounds as his man cleaned the windscreen with a squeegee.

Then Richter's voice. 'Hey, no, I don't want my windows doing.'

'Already done, pal. Sorry.'

'Get out of my way. I'm busy.'

'Three quid, mate. Already done. Should have said sooner. Be cool, cos I normally charge a fiver for big cars.'

'Jesus Christ.' That utterance from the businessman was louder, which probably meant Neil's man was right by the driver's door. He heard more complaining from Richter, but also the clink of coins, perhaps as cash was scooped from the centre console.

'Now please go away.'

'What about that?'

There was no visual, of course, but Neil knew his man was following the script and pointing at the passenger side window. To get Richter to look that way. Afterwards, Neil heard the best part of all: a nice thump.

'No, no more. Just get lost. I'm rich enough to ruin your life. Get away from my property. Get a real job.'

'You can give me a job. You got windows in–'

The last part of that sentence was cut off by the car window buzzing shut. But the Nokia heard Richter just fine as he cursed the squeegee bandit and drove away. Perfect. Neil's man had tossed the Nokia into the back of the Merc unseen. If Sean called Richter, the device would capture their conversation and–

'Have you left yet?'

Neil froze. That was Sean's voice. It was crackly and loud,

suggesting an open phone call via the car's audio system. One traitor had just called the other.

'Just now. I'm a minute from home, or two if the light is red at the bridge. Have you got my car?'

Neil yelled for his men to get ready.

'No,' Sean said.

'What? But you said–'

'I couldn't bring it, could I? Flash car like that? I'd get caught up doing autographs and selfies. I'll give you a What-3-Words address for it once I have the money. Don't argue or it's over. Keep coming.'

Something seemed off. Sean wasn't here. He must have another tactic. But he was surely somewhere close, for he'd told Richer to keep coming. Maybe Sean would drive towards Richter from the other direction and simply stop both cars in the middle of the road. He'd used a similar trick to steal the Paix.

Neil yelled for his men to move. He sent three across the road, to hide behind trees right at the edge. He and the remaining man mirrored their actions this side. Now they were close enough to the traffic to pounce in a flash.

'I just reached the traffic light at the bridge,' Richter said via the Nokia and Neil's phone. *'It's on red. There's a queue.'*

'How many cars between you and the light?'

'Maybe ten. Not sure.'

'Now listen carefully,' Sean said. *'Stay silent, and do everything I say, the moment I say it. No pause, no question, just instantly do it or you'll never get that car. Do you understand?'*

'Yes.'

'Bark like a dog.'

Neil was highly pissed at his brother, but he managed a laugh when Richter obeyed the order.

'Good. I'm going to give you two more orders, and you better

move fast. Get ready. You're almost there. Tell me when you're on the move again.'

Neil's gut didn't like this. He stared down the road. Traffic on this side of the bridge had a green light and was moving swiftly past his position from right to left. But in the next second, the light turned red and everything slowed down. Soon the line of cars was immobile. It stretched from the bridge and way past him, growing longer all the time. Dozens of vehicles. A woman stopped level with him gave him the evil eye.

'Light's green,' Richter said. *'We're moving.'*

'Keep talking. Keep a running commentary about exactly where you are.'

Of course! The bridge was single-lane. Now that Richter's side had a green light, the traffic here couldn't move. Neil suddenly knew the plan. Sean would throw open his door and block Richter's passage.

He was in the queue!

But where? He probably didn't have the farmer's Land Cruiser any longer. 'Check the cars,' he yelled to the man hiding behind a tree on this side of the road. 'Stay in the trees. Go, now. He's in the queue. He's trapped here.'

His man stayed close to the road and moved away from the bridge. Neil headed towards it, keeping deep enough in the woods to remain hidden. He moved fast, blowing by car after car, glancing at every driver. It was just a matter of time – seconds – now.

Richter spoke. *'Just about to cross the bridge now. I'll be at my house in about–'*

'Stop directly in the middle of the bridge,' Sean cut in. Neil's heart leaped.

Richter said, *'What do you mean?'*

'STOP!'

What the hell? Neil ran from the cover of trees and into the road, right beside a Zafira whose central locking he heard engage. Forty metres away, he saw Richter's car crest the humped bridge and halt at the peak. Across the air and through his phone, he heard a horn honk, no doubt from an impatient driver at Richter's rear. He had a really bad feeling.

'Get out,' Sean yelled. *'Right now. With the money. You've got one chance. Drop the bag over the wall. Now!'*

Neil cursed as he saw Richter's driver's door open. Neil unleashed his own line of profanity and started running for the bridge. He saw Richter emerge from the Merc, onto the thin pavement, and heave out a large, heavy sports bag. Neil knew two million in £50 notes, which he'd insisted on, weighed almost fifty kilograms. Cars blocked by the businessman's vehicle began a symphony of honks.

'Richter, you twat,' Neil yelled. 'Drop that bag!'

Neil blitzed past the car stopped right at the red light and mounted the bridge, still yelling for the businessman to stop. He was just four metres from Richter.

Richter was overweight, old, and for sure unfit, but he also had strength. That damn bionic arm, maybe. In mere seconds he had hoisted the bag onto his shoulder and was at the parapet. Neil was right there, feet from his big payday. He yelled *Noooo* and, knowing he wouldn't have the power to grab the heavy bag in mid-air, dove like a goalkeeper at Richter.

His shoulder thudded into the businessman's flank and they both tumbled hard to the pavement. Neil ignored the pain and twisted, throwing his eyes around, praying the bag would be lying on the pavement.

Of course it wasn't.

Richter was moaning beside him, his nose and one hand – the real one – bloodied. Neil ignored the fool, and the sharp pain in his own knee, and scrambled to his feet to stare over the parapet and down onto the train tracks. What he saw made him roar like a wounded *T. rex*.

Straddling the right-hand track was the farmer's Land Cruiser, whose driver's door shut a nanosecond later. Sean. Neil said nothing and just watched as the vehicle raced away, its nearside wheels bouncing wildly over the sleepers.

Amid his rage, he allowed himself a wry smile. Sharp brat, his little brother.

6

The level crossing was four hundred metres away. The barrier was up and traffic crossed the railway track, so he turned right and slipped neatly into the flow. A handful of surprised pedestrians watched Sean drive past. It didn't matter if one decided to call the police.

Just sixty seconds later, he pulled up in the far corner of a Tesco car park, next to another vehicle. It belonged to Jacob and he was in the driver's seat. Sean phoned Richter. He already had a missed call from him.

'Where's my car?' the businessman barked immediately.

'It's not yours because you never got your slimy hands on it. Go ask Verninac to build you a new one.'

'Then I want my fucking money back.'

'But that I did get my slimy hands on. That means it's mine. Adverse possession, my friend. Just call it a contingent loss. I had to use Google for that joke, by the way.'

Sean hung up and broke apart the phone. He'd scatter the pieces when he was on the move again. He hefted the sports bag from the rear seat of the Cruiser and carried it to the back of Jacob's vehicle.

Once it was in the boot, Sean got in the passenger seat. He dumped two wads of cash in Jacob's lap. Each currency strap held a hundred £50 notes, for a total of £5,000 per bundle.

Jacob wasn't surprised. Holly had told him the entire story, knowing he could be trusted. But he did look upset. 'I didn't help you for money, Sean.'

'I know. But the money is for your help. Please take it.'

Jacob reluctantly pocketed the cash. Sean pulled up his hood, kept his head down, and away they went.

Holly was at the living room window, watching as Jacob parked in his driveway. She was sitting on the sofa when the two men walked in, as if fearful of bad news. Even though Sean carried a heavy bag, she asked, 'How did it go?'

Jacob excused himself, to give the couple time alone. Sean dumped the bag and unzipped it. Holly looked mesmerised. 'Is it the whole two million?'

'I don't know. But it's a lot. It's enough.'

'Are we going to get away with this?' she asked.

'Only time will tell.'

'And when do we leave?'

Not until they had a grasp of the scenery out there. He wanted to spend one more day at Jacob's and see if the surging waters calmed. She wasn't happy about this, but agreed. At least this house was a safe haven.

Sean spent the afternoon and evening with a close eye on social media for news updates. The Paix theft was now out there, and trending. The billionaire owner and his security people weren't saying much, possibly to avoid the spotlight, but it was known that the bandit wore a police uniform and drove a stolen marked car. He had help in the form of a bunch of pseudo construction workers, who had imprisoned the billionaire and his security team for over an hour before releasing them.

The female steward who'd manned the gate of Allerby Park had given a description of the driver of the works van, but her memory must have been distorted because it didn't resemble anyone Sean recognised from Neil's crew. He wondered if someone had coerced or paid her off. She was a little pissed that her employers had noted the absence of the hypercar before they'd realised she was missing.

Having had two of their own kidnapped as part of the hypercar theft, the police were seriously eager to solve the case. The bad guys were still in the wind, but the missing car had been found. Once released from captivity, the billionaire howled at Verninac, who abruptly fired up the VHF tracker.

The owners of the hypercar and the stolen truck were men who had seen Sean up close, but so far nothing they'd given the police worried him. The billionaire had seen him in disguise and the mechanic had claimed his truck was stolen while he slept. Sean had been real careful, but it was impossible yet to be certain he hadn't made mistakes that might come back to haunt him. Maybe the police would find DNA somewhere, or his face on CCTV, or the mechanic would decide to talk after all. Or something else. As always, time would tell.

With the construction workers now on cop radar, Neil would surely do what he could to sink the investigation. Evidence of this went out into the world as afternoon turned to evening. Again via social media, Sean learned that the farmer's home and various barns and other buildings on his land had gone up in flames. Neil's work for sure.

Also, his Land Cruiser had been discovered abandoned under a bridge, but Sean didn't worry about that. Like with the truck and the hypercar, he'd used bleach to destroy any biological evidence he'd left behind. The farmer was nowhere to be found and was a wanted man for arson, but he wasn't being linked to the car theft. Nobody had decided there was a connection between three vehicles similarly sterilised on the same day. Yet.

The farmer wasn't the only chap whose name had been scribbled on an arrest warrant, though. Police had released the mugshot of a man called Ally McJames, sought for questioning in the murder of – check this – detective Josh Harper. Intriguing. Sean made a call to the number he'd memorised earlier.

McJames had once been a member of a London-based, rival gang, The Boys' Firm, headed by a man called Eli, who was missing and presumed to be on the run. That gang was now defunct after foolishly trying to whack the head of a much bigger London firm last year. In fear for their lives, various members of The Boys' Firm had fled the city and McJames had relocated to Sheffield, where he tried to start a new criminal enterprise.

When the phone was answered, Noah said, 'Call back in sixty seconds,' then hung up. When Sean redialled a minute later, Noah had obviously moved somewhere private because the background noise had gone. 'I didn't ever expect a call from you. Are you wanting to know Neil's next move? I can't tell you that. But he's–'

'Stop,' Sean cut in. He didn't want to hear anything about his brother's plans or his feelings or his health or anything else. It was all too painful. Everything had turned to shit and he wasn't sure who to blame. Himself? Neil? Holly? His parents, the world itself, God? He'd rather just bury his head in the sand.

But he did need an answer to one query. 'I called about someone else. Ally McJames.'

Noah knew exactly what Sean was asking. 'Yes. It was quite clever. We had Harper's wallet, of course, and also McJames' Voter Authority Certificate, which was his only form of ID. You want all the details?'

No, he didn't. He'd played a very minor role, but still it shamed him. It all did now. Every criminal act he'd ever been part of sat heavy in his gut. Hopefully he'd one day forget everything and be at peace on his deathbed, and with luck that bed wouldn't be in a stone box in HMP Belmarsh. He thanked Noah, wished him a good life, and hung up the phone.

For now, though, memories were fresh, and he recalled Ally McJames well. Within days of moving to Sheffield, McJames had set about bullying locals gangs to build a reputation and begin an empire. He got some cronies and clout and cash and could have survived as a mid-range gangster. But he got greedy and set his sights on bigger fish. He waltzed into the newly opened Chubby Grub and approached the barmaid.

'Get Neil down here. Tell him Ally McJames has a deal for him. One he can't refuse.'

Neil wasn't in but word was passed and he agreed to meet McJames at the pub after hours. Believing he had Neil worried and that they were going to become partners, McJames came alone. Neil had six men present in the lounge, including Sean, but still McJames wasn't scared. He got straight down to business as Neil racked up the balls on the pool table.

'You need security here,' he said. 'I'll provide it for half your takings each week. I hear there's thugs going around starting fights and trashing pubs.'

The threat was understood. The aforementioned thugs would hound The Chubby Grub almost nightly if Neil refused to pay for security. It wasn't exactly a novel or genius strategy. 'That's not nice. Vicious bastards, are they?'

'Sure are. Never know where they'll turn up next. Place like this, they could do ten grand of damage in half a minute.'

'That would cost lots if it was – every night, did you say?'

McJames nodded. 'But I've got some say-so, and I can keep them at bay. Once we do a deal.'

Neil grabbed a cue and handed McJames one. 'Let's play for it?'

'Play for what?'

'You win, I'll buy six months of your security.'

McJames's expression turned to annoyance. Sean knew this was a man unused to his dominion being diluted with caveats. But a subsequent smile said he was willing to play along, even if only out of curiosity. 'And if I lose?'

'You'll meet a colleague of mine. We call him the farmer.'

The farmer? Now McJames's expression was puzzlement: he didn't know who that was. And his ego didn't allow him to hear hint of a threat in Neil's words. Surely with zero intention of taking no for an answer should he lose, McJames agreed to play a frame of pool. Clearly he hadn't learned his lesson after picking a fight with the wrong mobster down in London.

Sean recalled Neil's promise to 'feed the fuzz' a suspect for the Harper killing. He had learned the trick from a peripheral colleague called Fritz, a major gangster plying his trade down south. Fritz, though, liked to pay long-term prisoners to cough to crimes. Neil preferred painting blame on the dead. Now the police were hunting McJames for Harper's murder. They'd never find either man.

It seemed that Sean was in the clear. Nobody was after him.

Except, of course, his own brother.

7

Late that night, Holly and Sean retired to their bedroom. Sean got settled under the quilt, but Holly seemed restless. She sat up, just staring at nothing in the gloom. She hadn't seemed right all day. He'd put it down to stress and the scary prospect of starting over in a new city somewhere. Now he knew it was more than that. He asked what was wrong.

'We should go to the police.'

He also sat up. 'Why?'

'We can't just run. The police will soon know you're missing. They already know I am. It will only get worse.'

He'd tried to pretend this wasn't absolutely correct, which had been stupid on his part. Like burying his head in the sand. Holly had also featured in the news. She had been missing for days and now the general feeling was that she was dead. Neil had been mentioned in every story, with an underlying tone of suspicion against him.

It was time for Sean to get real. 'I agree. We can't run forever. What's your idea?'

'We tell the police what happened, minus a few details. Neil thought I might be talking to the cops, so he kicked me out.

I went into hiding because I was scared. Do you think that story could work?'

'And me? What's my role?'

'You're my boyfriend. We admit the affair. We went into hiding for the same reason. Fear.'

'Neil won't like it if we say that.'

'We won't say he threatened us or anything else the police can use against him. It was just our own paranoia.'

He wasn't sure it would work, but didn't want to say that and upset her.

'Hopefully we can convince the police to leave us alone,' she continued. 'And to keep it quiet where we're going. We might not have to even tell them that. We're adults and we can move freely. As long as they know I'm alive and safe, they'll forget about us.'

Now her idea had more weight. They drive south, enter a police station far from Neil's empire, and tell their tale. Even if South Yorkshire coppers wanted to talk to them, those guys could make a trip. There were problems, though.

'If the police know you've split from Neil, they'll think you're open to dishing dirt on him. And me.'

His words gave her the feeling he was coming round. She got up to turn on the light then knelt before him, more energised now. 'We give them nothing. This is a simple case of showing that I'm alive and well and that we're together. They can't arrest us for anything, can't force us to talk. What do you think? I know you're worried about other things, like the Paix theft, coming back on you. So we can wait a day more or so to see the landscape. But I think this is our best way forward. Our only way. We can't just hide forever. I just want a run-of-the-mill life, Sean.'

As did he, but unlike Holly he couldn't see it clearly defined. There was a great black blot obscuring it, and it was in the shape of Neil. 'My brother will still be after us, Holly. If we go to the police, it will just make him worry more. He'll suspect we've given them information on him.'

'No, he–'

'He will, Holly. Listen to me. Just because the police don't arrest him five minutes after we talk to them, it won't matter. If one of his drug dens is raided six months later, he'll think we gave it up. You know how paranoid he is. And we betrayed him. He won't forgive and forget. If he knows where we are, he'll get his revenge. Even if he has to wait months to make sure the cops don't suspect him. And there's my dad to think about. I can't just abandon him.'

Her shoulders slumped. 'We can't do anything about how my husband feels. Are you saying we can't go to the police? That we just hide like fugitives? Forever? What kind of life is that? That's not going to help with your dad. You wouldn't be able to see him again.'

'Maybe we don't have to hide. If Neil can be stopped somehow.'

She gave him a long, unnerving stare, which he read clearly. Then she got up and turned off the light. She got under the cover with him, not a word spoken. And she lay with her back to him.

He stared up at the black ceiling, thinking. Long ago, Holly had tried to diagnose him. She believed he had never committed to having a girlfriend in case he lost her because of his criminal lifestyle. Grudge or judge: the end of everything by an enemy blade or a prison sentence handed down at crown court.

He had thought along different lines, assuming his lack of commitment stemmed from a fear of rejection once a new partner discovered what he did for a living. Yet Holly knew and hadn't dumped him and the fear was still burning hot in his gut. Why?

Because Holly had been right all along. In this game, you could lose your life or freedom in a flash, or have a loved one snatched away. Danger oozed off him like a smell and he had refused to permit anyone into its range, and it had kept him lonely. Until Holly came along. She was now in serious peril and it was all because of him.

He had to protect her, and there was only one way to do it. Neil was all that stood between them and the 'run-of-the-mill' life Holly desired.

He had to be stopped somehow.

As if reading his mind, Holly said, 'Stay close to me all night, please. Promise?' Like her earlier steely glare, it proved she knew he contemplated unsafe actions.

'I'm right here, babe,' he replied. It was not even close to a promise.

He lay there, trying to sleep, hoping a new day would bring a fresh outlook. But his mind was too wired. He fought the urges clamouring inside him, but uselessly. They had the louder voices.

Quietly, he got up, got his shoes on, and tiptoed to the door. He froze with his hand on the handle when Holly spoke. He'd assumed she was asleep. Her back was still to him.

'Give us our dream. And please come back to me.'

'I promise,' he said, and slipped out the door.

8

Not a single light burned inside The Chubby Grub. Sean parked behind it and got something from the back seat. As before, the rear fire exit opened after a hard press against it for five seconds.

Force of habit from myriad burglaries, or muscle memory sparked by the darkness itself, made him pass through the interior slowly. He found the lounge empty and dark except for a brand of whiskey on an optic with a glow-in-the-dark label.

The same five-second trick opened the door to Neil's upper echelon. He got halfway up the stairs before bright light flashed in his face.

'Who the fuck are you, besides a dead man?'

Sean threw up a hand to block the stinging light. 'It's the brother who didn't fall from the ugly tree and hit every branch on the way down.'

The spotlight died, but on came the overhead bulb to illuminate everything. Sean saw Neil standing in the hallway at the top of the stairs, butt naked and holding his air rifle and a torch. He lobbed aside the latter, but the gun remained in his hands and pointed at the younger brother.

'I nearly blasted your head off,' Neil said. 'How many people have to spray their blood around my fucking house?'

'Not with that toy pop gun. But you still have a chance if you want to grab a pistol. I imagine you're quite pissed at me.'

He looked puzzled. 'Should be. Was as of five minutes ago. All seems a bit different now you're right in front of me. Weird. Besides, finally I foiled one of your ambushes. You cheeky fucker, by the way. I–'

Just then: a noise or a movement from somewhere to Neil's right. Sean didn't catch it, but he saw his brother glance that way and mouth something. Neil continued to stare away until Sean heard a soft click, like that of a door closing.

'Should I apologise for waking your girlfriend?' Sean said. 'And should I consider myself lucky that you didn't come at me with her purple dildo?'

Neil looked at the weapon he wielded, then lowered it. 'Go wait in the lounge and get me a beer.'

'Beer? For real?'

'It's been a funny few days. Go.'

Neil vanished. Sean turned around and walked down the stairs.

He turned on the main lights in the lounge and poured a pint of lager for Neil, and one for himself. He sat at a poseur table to wait. When Neil entered the lounge, he was dressed and no longer had his rifle. He had a pistol instead, although it was in the waistband of his jeans. He took the chair across from Sean and sipped his beer.

'Vile shit,' he said. 'It feels wrong to sell people this crap.'

'Stick to heroin and spice, eh?'

Neil took another sip and didn't grimace – as much – this time. 'I just learned the secret to fixing my heart. Exercise doesn't do it these days. Fright. I was having the palpitations when I heard you come in my house. Gone now.'

'My pleasure.'

Neil leaned to one side to look down at what was on the floor between them. 'You brought my money here.'

Sean also glanced at the loaded sports bag. 'Yours? Ever heard of something called Adverse Possession? The Webb family swears by it.'

Neil lost a portion of his calm demeanour. Obviously he'd expected a blubbering apology and for his money to he handed over without pause. 'I could shoot you and take it. Same rule applies. Besides, deep down we both know that old line was just some silly bullshit from your dad.'

'Didn't you once promise to take care of me forever?'

'You think something I said as a kid will save you? After what's happened?'

Sean sipped his own beer. 'I don't know. I have no idea what lifelong promises another man is willing to break. Maybe what I did to you makes it all null and void. You've got the gun, so I'll just wait here for your decision. It would be nice to finish this beer first.'

'Clever words, but you'd be stupid to think they're enough to wipe out what you did. After all, you brought two million pieces of backup.'

'Then shoot and take the cash. I'm not paying for my life, so it's the only way you'll get it. I had to work hard at stealing a car for that money.'

Neil didn't shoot. He drank. A few seconds passed in silence. Then master Webb said, 'So why is that money in my pub?'

Sean said, 'I want to buy Holly's life.'

Neil's eyes narrowed. He wasn't quite angry, but that destination hovered nearby. 'So she can marry you? And you can both ride off into the sunset? In what world would that happen?'

His direct tone was matched by Sean's. 'This world. The one where I'm in love with her and you're not. The one where you cheated on her because she wasn't good enough. The one where you tried to kill her because of some stupid assumption that she wasn't loyal. And the one where you're going to have to murder me right alongside her.'

'So that's what you want? You want to pay me off and go live that little dream of yours with her?'

'All you have to do is nothing. Nothing except swallow your pride. Just let us go, safe and sound. For a million and a half. I kept enough back to buy a house. But you got what you wanted in the end.'

Neil got up. For a just a moment, Sean thought it was so he could haul his gun and start blasting. But the weapon remained in Neil's waistband as he moved behind the bar to pour whisky into glasses.

Sean was reminded of something a man called Jimmy had said before he got whacked: *I see how the boss decided to come down easy on his bro. You've got a fucking charmed life, haven't you?* Sean had relied upon the thickness of blood to save him here – and a shedload of cash. Back in the bedroom with Holly, he'd had little doubt it would work. Now, he wasn't so sure.

Neil returned with their drinks and sat at the table. He then hooked the handle of the sports bag with a foot and dragged it to his side of the table.

'Get her away from me. Go to the far end of the country and stay there. I don't want to hear from you for a long time. Maybe never again. If and when we do speak again, never mention her. Don't ever tell me about your happy life down there. No matter who we are to each other and how much we've been through, this has driven a stake through it all. My flesh and blood has hooked up with my wife. There's not a man alive that wouldn't burn inside.'

Sean almost groaned in relief. 'I understand. Thank you. And I'm sorry for... everything. Our plan is to just tell the police that Holly went into hiding to cover the affair. It should keep the cops off your back.'

Tension seemed to pour out of Neil. 'That was never a worry for me. But if there is any kind of silver lining to this... well, I know you always wanted the normal, boring life. So go enjoy it. Now get out of here, tosspot. I'll take care of anything that might land the cops at your door.'

Sean didn't move. 'We're not done yet. There's one more thing.'

Neil was flabbergasted. 'You really are in take-the-piss mode. The answer is "fuck no". Get out of here before I change my mind about the whole thing, Sean. Being a brother gets you only so far.'

Sean was well aware that he'd pushed the boat out and was damned lucky it hadn't been sunk by raging waves. He got up and left the table. But he didn't head for the exit. He'd always been one for pushing things beyond expected breaking points.

Instead, he approached the pool table and slapped two £50 notes onto it. 'I need help. I need to visit my dad... but with my brother right by my side.'

Neil said nothing, did nothing, for almost ten seconds. Perhaps anger and pride battled for supremacy within him. Eventually, he stood and pulled his pistol.

And dropped it on the poseur table. 'Rack 'em up.'

THE END

ALSO BY ALEX ROSE

The Boss

The Pact

The Trap

The Threat

ACKNOWLEDGEMENTS

As always, thanks go to every single person at Bloodhound Books and Open Road Media. Notable names are Clare Law, Hannah Baxter-Deuce, and Tara Lyons. Tara is also a novelist, so go check out her psychological thrillers. After you've bought all of mine, that is.

This book is dedicated to my partner, Jen, who says she never reads my work because it would feel *weird*. I owe her this because of that time I stepped on her earbud and blamed the dryer repairman. She still doesn't know it was me.

I guess I'll soon find out if she really doesn't read my books.

A NOTE FROM THE PUBLISHER

Thank you for reading this book. If you enjoyed it please do consider leaving a review on Amazon to help others find it too.

We hate typos. All of our books have been rigorously edited and proofread, but sometimes mistakes do slip through. If you have spotted a typo, please do let us know and we can get it amended within hours.

info@bloodhoundbooks.com

www.ingramcontent.com/pod-product-compliance
Ingram Content Group UK Ltd.
Pitfield, Milton Keynes, MK11 3LW, UK
UKHW040731100326
11172UKWH00027B/1256